Frannie Darling was once a child of London's roughest streets, surrounded by petty thieves, pickpockets, and worse. But though she survived this harsh upbringing to become a woman of incomparable beauty, Frannie wants nothing to do with the men who lust for her, the rogues who frequent the gaming hall where she works. She can take care of herself and feels perfectly safe on her own—safe, that is, until *he* strides into her world, and once again it becomes a very dangerous place indeed.

To bed her but not wed her. That's what Sterling Mabry, the eighth Duke of Greystone, wants. But Frannie abhors arrogant aristocrats interested only in their own pleasure. So why then does the thought of an illicit tryst with the devilish duke leave her trembling with desire? Her willing body begs for release . . . and a wicked, wonderful surrender.

Surrender to the Devil

Lorraine Heath

AVON

An Imprint of HarperCollinsPublishers

This is a work of fiction. Names, characters, places, and incidents are products of the author's imagination or are used fictitiously and are not to be construed as real. Any resemblance to actual events, locales, organizations, or persons, living or dead, is entirely coincidental.

AVON BOOKS
An Imprint of HarperCollins*Publishers*
10 East 53rd Street
New York, New York 10022-5299

Copyright © 2009 by Jan Nowasky
ISBN 978-0-06-173399-4
www.avonromance.com

First Avon Books paperback printing: July 2009

Avon Trademark Reg. U.S. Pat. Off. and in Other Countries, Marca Registrada, Hecho en U.S.A.
HarperCollins® is a registered trademark of HarperCollins Publishers.

Printed in the U.S.A.

10 9 8 7 6 5 4 3 2 1

For Eileen,
one of the classiest ladies I know.

Prologue

From the Journal of Frannie Darling

My earliest memory is of Feagan saying, with his heavy cockney accent, "Frannie darling, come sit on me lap."

To him, I was always "Frannie darling." "Frannie darling, fetch me gin." "Frannie darling, rub me aching feet." "Frannie darling, let me tell you a story."

And so it was that when anyone asked me my name, I would say it was Frannie Darling.

I lived in a single room with Feagan and his notorious band of children who were known for their thieving ways. I cannot remember a time when Feagan was not in my life. Sometimes I imagined he was my true father. His hair was as bright a red and as uncontrollable as mine. But he never claimed me as his daughter. I was always simply one of his kids. The one who sat on his lap and helped him count the handkerchiefs and coins that the others brought in.

I was the one who carefully removed from the silk the thread that formed the monograms. I learned many of my letters from this tedious task because the intricate swirls fascinated me, and I'd always ask Feagan what they meant before I began working to erase all evidence they'd ever existed. Looking back on that time, I am often astonished to realize that a bit of cloth held such value. And yet it did.

I think Feagan may have been a teacher in an earlier life. In a school where he taught letters and numbers and was admired by his students. Or perhaps it was simply that, if he was my father, I wanted him to be more than a criminal.

He never spoke of his past, and I never asked him about mine.

I simply accepted my life in the dreary rookeries as my due. Feagan's lads always treated me as though I were special. Perhaps because instinctively I mothered the lot of them. I mended their clothes. I snuggled against them when I went to sleep at night. As I grew older, I cooked their meals and *tended their hurts. And sometimes I helped them to steal.*

But none of this prepared me for the horror or the fear that gripped me when I was abducted and sold to a brothel at the age of twelve. Luke and Jack—the eldest of Feagan's lads at the time—rescued me from the waking nightmare.

But not soon enough. Luke killed the man who so cruelly stole my innocence.

While awaiting trial, he was visited by the man's father—the Earl of Claybourne. In Luke, Claybourne saw his long lost grandson and our lives took a drastic turn. The Crown forgave Luke his sins and returned him to his grandfather's keeping. The earl made a place for me as well.

He was determined to give us advantages we'd never had. When he hired tutors, I was quick to learn how to read and write and master calculations more intricate than I'd ever encountered. I learned etiquette and proper comportment. But I was never comfortable in the great house in St. James.

And as Luke began to move into the world of an aristocrat, so I began to become awkward around him. I was much more at ease with Jack. When fortune smiled on him and he opened a gentlemen's club, he offered to pay me a very handsome salary to keep his books. I thanked the earl for all he'd done for me. I acknowledged that my life was richer because of his efforts and interest in my welfare, but it was with a measure of relief that I walked away from the residence in St. James.

Deep down, I knew it was far better than I deserved. I was not of the aristocracy and a place among them was rarely gained through effort or accomplishment. It was usually determined by bloodline, and I had no doubt that mine was tainted beyond all imagining. I was glad I no longer had to bear their stares, their gossip, or their whispered speculations.

I convinced myself that my happiness was dependent upon never again associating intimately with the lords and ladies of the aristocracy.

So I banished them from my life. I worked very hard to create a safe haven where I was happy and content. I knew what I possessed was exactly what I wanted, that I desired no more than what I had.

And then he *strode into my safe, little world . . . and once again, it became a very dangerous place indeed.*

Chapter 1

London
1851

Sterling Mabry, the eighth Duke of Greystone, wasn't certain why he took such notice of her.

Later, he would reflect on the moment and wonder if it was the vibrant red of her hair that had first captured his attention. Or perhaps it was the fact that she had stood beside his sister, Catherine, at the altar while she married Lucian Langdon, the Earl of Claybourne. Or maybe it was the way—during the reception held at his newly acquired brother-in-law's residence—that three men migrated toward her, circled around her, each in his own way claiming his territory, much in the same manner as Sterling had witnessed lions in Africa behaving. He was surprised none of them roared.

Standing by the window in the drawing room, holding his flute of champagne, waiting to make the obligatory toast so he could go the hell home, Sterling watched the almost shy smile she gave each of the men, the way she spoke with a slight inclining of her head as though imparting a scandalous secret, and he longed to know what it was. She was much too far away for him to hear her voice, yet he imagined it carried the sweet dulcet tone of an angel—or perhaps she offered the wicked song of a siren, because it was apparent each man stood as mesmerized by her mere presence as he.

Obviously, they shared *something* exceedingly special. Even from this distance, he could see the affection she held for each of the men mirrored on her lovely expressive face. He wondered if at one time or another she had been lover to each of them, for there was a familiarity between them that went far deeper than friendship.

The three men were of little interest to him, except as to how they might view their role in her life. The first he knew well enough. Jack Dodger, owner of the notorious gentlemen's club that Sterling frequently visited since his return to London. The second, taller and broader than the others, wasn't someone Sterling wished to meet alone in an alley at night—or even during the day, for that matter. The third gentleman was William Graves, the physician

Claybourne had sent for when Catherine swooned during their father's recent wake.

Sterling watched with interest as Claybourne now approached the small group and they welcomed him as one might a brother, with broad smiles and claps on the shoulder, handshakes and a bit of ribbing perhaps. No hug from the lady, simply a warm smile that spoke volumes. She admired him, she was overjoyed for him, she wished him well. But most of all, she loved him.

They were together then, the five of them. All products of the street, no doubt. Thieves, pickpockets, murderers, and only God knew what else bound them together. That realization should have quelled Sterling's interest in the lady. Instead it only served to further captivate him.

Hearing the light, familiar footsteps, he mentally marked their approach, turning toward his sister only when she was near and it was obvious he was her destination. Her blond hair was swept up, her cheeks carried a slight flush from the joy of her wedding ceremony, and her blue eyes sparkled like the finest of jewels.

"Fascinated by them, are you?" she chided gently, and he realized his staring may have been not only rude, but also obvious, although he was fairly certain the other guests were taking note of the group as well.

He shouldn't be surprised that so many of the aristocracy had made an appearance. News of the hastily arranged wedding between the "Devil Earl" and Catherine was the talk of London. The curious among the elite had filled the small chapel where the ceremony took place, and now they had been welcomed into Claybourne's home. Even Marcus Langdon—who it was once believed would inherit the Claybourne title—was in attendance. It seemed that he had accepted his fate as the successor who would never be. Without a doubt, everyone was intrigued and scandal was certainly a whispered rumor away.

"I possess a mild curiosity, that's all," Sterling said laconically. "They're not the sort who usually attend our functions. The woman. She stood with you at the altar."

"Frannie. Yes, we've become very close. Had you bothered to attend the celebratory dinner we hosted last night or arrived at the church early enough this morning, I'd have made introductions."

Ignoring her chastisement—he'd have not been comfortable at the dinner and she'd have not been comfortable having him there, when all was said and done—he turned over the name she'd given him. *Frannie*. He'd expected—or perhaps he'd only hoped for—something a bit more exotic, and yet it seemed to suit. "She dresses rather plainly."

The drab blue dress she wore seemed almost as out of place as she did. He envisioned her in violet or scarlet, the silk sliding over her skin to pool at her bare feet.

"I've learned of late not to judge by appearances," Catherine said.

He heard the censure in her voice because she was aware that he did judge by appearances and a person's station in life. He recognized the elite—and then the others with whom he didn't associate unless absolutely necessary. He'd never had a reason or a desire to associate with former criminals.

"Do they provide for her?" he asked.

"Pardon?"

"The gentlemen circling her. Are they related? How does she make her way?"

"Those are hardly appropriate inquiries."

He gave her an intense stare. "Is she someone's mistress, then?"

Although he couldn't imagine Catherine associating with, much less including a woman of questionable morals in her wedding party, but if the woman was a friend of Claybourne's from the streets—

Catherine scoffed. "Whatever gave you that notion? She's a bookkeeper at Dodger's Drawing Room."

A polite name for an impolite place. It made the gentlemen's club almost sound respectable, which Sterling assumed was the whole point. "Unusual."

"I find it admirable. Not every woman is fortunate enough to have a father who provides for her."

"Put away your claws, Catherine. I wasn't insulting her, but you must admit that occupations for women are usually found within households, not within businesses."

She touched his arm. "I'm sorry. I suppose I'm a bit protective of Claybourne's friends. While you were away, they helped me out on occasion."

So Sterling's absence had forced her to turn to known reprobates. That must have pleased their father no end and provided him with yet one more reason to be disappointed in his heir—whom he viewed as a wastrel.

Sterling readily admitted that he'd lived a life of indulgence, seeing to his own pleasures above all else. He and his father had argued about Sterling's choices. But his father had been unable to comprehend what it was like not to be in control. He didn't know how one's flesh prickled when fear took hold. He didn't understand what it was like to gaze into the future and know that it would be nothing more than a dark and lonely place.

"I should introduce you," Catherine said brightly, as though realizing that Sterling's thoughts had begun to travel down bleak paths.

"Not necessary." He didn't think the gents would appreciate his edging into their territory.

"You've changed, Sterling."

"So you've commented before. We all change, Catherine. I could say the same of you."

"Not to the extent you have. You've become quite the cynic."

"I've become a realist. Join your husband so I might make my toast and be done with this affair."

A quick flash of pain passed over her eyes, eyes as blue as his. He grabbed her hand before she could walk away. "I apologize. I do wish you all the happiness you so rightly deserve, you know that. Having been away for a while, most of my time spent outdoors, I'm not quite as comfortable confined in a crowded room." And moving through the maze of people without knocking up against someone had become a tedious chore. If he'd realized Catherine and Claybourne were going to open their doors to so many, he'd have said his good-bye at the church.

"Is that the reason you're hovering near the window as though at any moment you intend to leap through it?"

"Into the storm?" He glanced quickly toward

where the rain pattered against the glass. The clouds were so dark and heavy that although it was morning, it almost appeared to be night, and night had become his enemy. "It's a rather dreary day."

"I don't find it dreary at all. It's the most wonderful day of my life."

Recognizing that he was acting the curmudgeon, he offered a bit of repentance in his tone along with the truth of his words. "I suspect it will be the first of many wonderful days for you."

"I know you don't approve of Claybourne as my choice for a husband, and that, like many, you hold his singular past against him, but I hope that over time you'll come to know him as I do and appreciate his finer qualities."

Not likely, but he had no plans to further dim her joy with the truth of the matter. As though recognizing that he had no intention of commenting, she said, "I suppose you'll be turning your attention toward securing a wife now that you've returned from your world travels."

"Eventually. We're in mourning. I didn't expect this affair to be quite so lavish."

"It's hardly lavish. A few more guests than might be appropriate, but they'll ease Claybourne's way into the thick of Society after years of walking along its edge. Besides, men are never held to the strictures of mourning as diligently as women. You could attend a ball tonight and no one would chastise you."

"Ah, the power that comes with the dukedom."

"Was there anyone you thought about while you were away?" Catherine offered.

"Playing matchmaker already? Surely you're planning to take some sort of wedding trip."

"No, we have some matters to attend to in London."

"Still I suspect your husband will expect to have your undivided attentions for a while. I'm perfectly capable of securing a wife without troubling you."

"It would be no trouble." She squeezed his arm. "I've missed you, Sterling. I'm truly glad you're here. Now, if you'll excuse me, I'm going to join Claybourne, so you may make your toast."

As she walked away, her words sparked his guilt, but he tamped down the uncomfortable emotion. He wanted to be anywhere other than where he was. He drank his champagne, signaled to a footman, and took another glass. Would this affair never come to an end?

Catherine sidled up against her husband, and the man gazed down on her with obvious adoration. Why should he not adore her? She was the daughter of a duke, her lineage the very best British aristocracy had to offer. She understood her place in the world and fit well within it. Sterling could no longer say the same for himself. The need to escape roared through him, and he lost the tether hold on his patience. He began lightly tapping his glass and the murmurings in the room quieted. He raised his flute. "To my sister, Catherine, the new Countess of Claybourne, and her very fortunate husband. May the sun always shine for you, my dear—even during the darkest of days."

He downed the sparkling brew while a round of cheers and clapping echoed through the room. Claybourne and Catherine drank their champagne, then kissed briefly. People laughed, cheered again, and offered them well-wishes.

Sterling reached for another flute of champagne. Maybe if he swallowed enough, he could drown the pain of knowing that he would never possess what the newly married couple obviously did: true love and happiness.

He was the most dangerous man in the room.

Frannie Darling realized she was giving the man standing by the window considerable credit, given that she was surrounded by those who had no qualms about breaking the law when it suited their purpose. But while her friends were dangerous to everyone around them except her, this man was dangerous to *only* her.

She knew it in the way she knew how to judge which pockets were ripe for the picking before she ever slipped her hand inside to take what they held. She knew it in the way she knew a column of numbers had been incorrectly tallied before she ever set about to add the numbers together. She knew it just as she knew that within this room filled with people there were only three with whom she now truly belonged: Jack, Jim, and Bill.

Only recently had she discovered that Luke had always doubted he was the true Earl of Claybourne. But lately, circumstances had arisen that convinced him of the truth, so he no longer questioned his inheritance of the title. He moved confidently about the room, comfortable in his skin, no longer fearing that he was living in someone else's.

She couldn't admit to feeling as at ease. This world was not hers. It was so incredibly large, so incredibly important. Her small world paled in comparison, but she was content there. Perhaps it was her discomfort with the surroundings that made her notice him—the man standing by the window who appeared as though he wanted to escape all this politeness as badly as she did. She knew who he was. Catherine's brother. The newly anointed Duke of Greystone.

A few times she thought she'd noticed him eyeing her. She'd tried to surreptitiously observe him in return. His skin was a golden bronze, as though he was a man who worshipped the outdoors. His hair, a dark blond, had been tamed for the occasion, not a single strand out of place, and yet she could imagine it being whipped by the wind as he galloped over the same roads that Marco Polo may have explored. Greystone was an adventurer, a man who knew no fear. When others had spoken with him earlier, his stance had reflected politeness, perhaps tolerance, but also impatience, as though he dearly wished to be off on another quest for excitement.

"Think they'll be happy?" Jack asked as he offered her another glass of champagne, forcing her to drag her attention away from the man who fascinated her. He was larger than life, and as a general rule she preferred the small and mundane.

Jim and Bill were standing nearby, suffocatingly so, as though they could shield her from her own discomfort with the elegant elite.

"I'm sure of it," she said. "Catherine is good for Luke."

"What do you make of her brother?"

That he was as powerful as the storm raging behind him. That within his arms a woman would discover pleasure beyond anything she'd ever known. Heat swirled low within her as she licked her lips and offered up a small lie. "I'm not sure."

"He's been watching us," Jim said.

"A good many of the guests are watching us," Bill muttered.

"And their pockets," Jack added. "I'm halfway tempted to walk through and lift things."

Frannie scowled at him. Luke's grandfather had taken them out of the rookeries, but he'd not been able to take the rookeries out of them—not completely. "Don't do anything to let our presence embarrass Luke. He's finally being accepted by his peers. It was a bit of rebellion on his part to invite us." The scoundrels of his youth, although she knew he'd never completely leave them behind. Their pasts had forged an unbreakable bond.

"Still watching out for him?" Jack asked.

"The same as I watch out for all of you." She gave him a playful smile. "And you watch out for me."

Although there were times when they watched a little too closely, were just a bit too overprotective. She loved them dearly, but sometimes she craved something more, something that she couldn't quite identify. Perhaps that was the reason she was suddenly feeling the need to stage a rebellion. She glanced back toward the gentleman at the window. "I believe I'm going to introduce myself."

"He's a bloody duke," Jack reminded her.

"Yes, I'm well aware of that," she murmured before handing the flute back to him, taking a deep breath, and walking across the room.

As a rule she avoided those who carried titles because they made her uncomfortably aware of her humble origins, but something about this man demanded her attention, made her desire a moment of recklessness. She'd worked so terribly hard to insulate herself from anything that might bring her harm, and she'd only managed to give herself an incredibly boring existence. Nothing about him struck her as boring.

She felt eyes come to bear on her, other guests making note of her actions. Because she'd never cared much for their perusal, she should have been bothered by their increasing interest in her, but the man chose that moment to settle his gaze on her, and she felt it like a gentle caress that swept the length of her body. Her step almost faltered. Feagan's lads never looked at her with desire smoldering within their eyes. Perhaps that was the reason Greystone was so dangerous to her. Because with only a glance, he made her feel as though she'd suddenly transformed from an awkward girl into an attractive woman with the power to lure a man toward a sinful encounter.

Even more astonishing was the attraction she felt toward him. She'd never met a man who stirred passion within her, who made her yearn for a touch of his lips, a stroke of his fingers.

Fighting off the urge to turn on her heel and

return to her safe haven, she came to a halt before him. His eyes were the blue of a sapphire gemstone that had been embedded in a necklace she'd once lifted from a pompous woman's neck. Feagan had been so delighted with the take that he'd bought her a strawberry. She could never taste one now without thinking of it as a reward for wicked behavior. She thought an evening with Greystone would result in her eating an entire bowl of delicious strawberries.

"I don't believe we've been properly introduced. I'm Frannie Darling."

"The bookkeeper at Dodger's."

She knew her eyes widened at that. She seldom stepped out into the gaming area. Her work was handled in an area accessible only by those who possessed the proper key. "I seem to recall you're a member."

"And I seem to remember your *friends*" —he nodded toward where Jack, Jim, and Bill waited expectantly for her return— "are all thieves."

Disappointment slammed into her with the realization that he was one of *those*, those who didn't believe someone could rise above her station in life, those who had made her life miserable while she lived with Claybourne. She should have left him to his pettiness, but something compelled her to stay. Perhaps she wanted to give him the opportunity to redeem himself.

"As it's customary for the wedding breakfast to be held at the home of the bride's family, am I to assume you disapproved of the guest list?"

"You may assume what you like, but I value my property and prefer not to have light-fingered guests about."

"I see." She was an excellent judge of character, and she didn't have the sense that his was being truly revealed. The most skilled actors in the world were beggars. With a practiced look, they could win over a heart, nab sympathy, cause a person to give away his last coin. Greystone, it seemed, was putting on a performance guaranteed to earn him no kind regard. She wondered at his reasons.

He shifted his gaze to the crowd. "Will he make her happy?"

"Luke?"

"Claybourne."

She gave him credit for recognizing Luke by his title. At least that was something. And it was obvious he cared for his sister. "Immeasurably so."

He gave a brusque nod. "Then that's all that matters. If you'll excuse me—"

He was three steps away when she called after him, "Your Grace?"

He turned back to her, and she smiled mischievously, not certain why she was determined to vex him. He just seemed to be a man who needed to be vexed. Besides, she wasn't about to let his insult to her friends go unanswered, and she had her own statement to make: they weren't the only thieves in attendance. She held up her hand. Dangling from it by its heavy chain was a gold pocket watch. "You left your timepiece behind."

He looked at his waistcoat, patted it as though his eyes might be deceiving him, then slowly lifted his gaze back to her. With a dangerous glimmer in his eyes, he held out his hand. She dropped the watch into his palm, and before she could withdraw her gloved hand, he closed his strong fingers around it and leaned near. "Careful, Miss Darling," he said, his voice a low rasp that sent shivers through her, "I've been away for a while and I'm not quite as civilized as I was when I left."

That aspect of him became so incredibly apparent that her heart thudded against her ribs and her legs weakened. He gazed at her as though he was contemplating devouring her.

With an abrupt bow, he released her, turned on his heel, and strode away. She watched until he disappeared through the doorway, obviously taking his leave. Amazing how quickly the tables had turned and she'd lost the upper hand. She certainly hadn't expected to be left breathless by the encounter, although more than that had her bothered. She'd felt an unfamiliar, powerful pull that had desperately not wanted him to leave.

Sterling wanted nothing more than to storm from the room, but he kept his pace measured, concentrating as he wended his way around people so he didn't bump into anyone. Leaving wasn't nearly as difficult as he'd imagined it would be. Perhaps because whatever his expression communicated caused people to quickly step out of the way rather than try to engage him in conversation.

He knew his behavior toward Miss Darling had been abhorrent, but he'd been unprepared for his reaction to her nearness. She didn't have the voice of an angel. Hers was a voice that stirred passions within bedchambers. Sultry, sensual, and breathless, as though they'd already shared pleasure and she was eager for another round.

Her eyes . . . he almost groaned with the memory. They were a magnificent green, but it was what they hadn't contained that enthralled him. No innocence. None at all. Life had seasoned her. She was unlike any of the young ladies of his acquaintance. She'd seen things—in all likelihood *done things*—that would have caused them to swoon.

He was not a man in the habit of losing control, but he had known that if he didn't take himself out of her presence, he was likely to take her in his arms, and the devil take anyone who objected.

Then blast her, she'd pilfered his watch and he'd not felt her touch. Damn it all, he wanted to know her touch, and as his long strides carried him away from her, he wanted her all the more.

Chapter 2

The encounter with Greystone had left Frannie unsettled. Feagan's lads—although they were men, she would always think of them as his lads—knew better than to hound her with questions, but she needed some time alone to regain her composure. Normally she'd have taken a walk in the garden but the heavy rain made that an unpleasant proposition. So Claybourne's massive residence would have to suffice. Because the servants knew her, they weren't likely to object to her walking through the hallways and rooms where guests were not invited. Since she'd moved out of the grand house, she'd visited on occasion. While she wasn't entirely comfortable here, one room did hold fond memories.

Without hesitating, she opened the door to the immense library and walked inside. Closing her eyes briefly, she inhaled deeply the wondrous fragrance of books. Ledgers never carried quite the same scent. After shutting the door to ensure her privacy, she wended her way among the various chairs and small tables that comprised individual sitting areas and walked along the shelf-lined wall, running her fingers across the spines of the many volumes that the old gent had collected over the years. He'd been a voracious reader. He'd introduced her to the works of Jane Austen and Charles Dickens, among others. Within this room, she'd traveled the world.

That thought brought Greystone to mind. Through Catherine, Frannie knew he'd explored the world and the many wonders it had to offer. She couldn't imagine the boldness of character that particular endeavor would require: to step upon a ship and float out onto the wide expanse of ocean and trust that it would carry him to his destination. What had he done that had caused him to be a bit less civilized? And why, even now, could she not stop thinking about him? His callousness should have effectively ended any interest she might have had in him. Instead she found herself wondering what it was that he feared, because he most certainly was afraid of something.

When he realized she'd taken his watch, fear had hovered for a heartbeat within the depths of his eyes before they'd glinted dangerously. In her world, she'd known too many frightened souls, herself included. She could have understood him reacting with anger, but why had it bothered him to realize that he'd not seen her taking his watch? Or was she misreading the entire situation? It wasn't as though he were a book.

With a mental shake, she chastised herself for lifting his pocket watch. She'd risen above her origins. It irritated her that he'd brought her back down to them. *Why* had she felt the need to prove herself a very skilled thief?

Why had she even cared about his opinion of her friends or her? Rude and arrogant, he represented everything about the aristocracy that she despised. Even Luke's grandfather, for all the good works he'd done for them, had looked down his nose at the urchins his grandson called friends. Still on occasion Frannie couldn't help but think of him fondly.

She crossed over to the desk and sat down. Running her hand over the fine, polished wood grain, she remembered how imposing Luke's grandfather had appeared sitting there. Until the day she discovered his weakness for lemon drops. Then he'd become human in her eyes, especially as on occasion he shared one with her. She opened the drawer where he'd kept his sweets.

"Planning to pilfer something?"

With a small shriek, Frannie pressed her hand to her chest, her heart thudding against her ribs as she spun around in the chair to face her accuser.

Arms crossed over his chest, Greystone was leaning against the wall in the darkened corner, effectively avoiding what little daylight made its way through the window and into the room. Thunder boomed and the rain seemed to increase in intensity. She didn't know why she hadn't noticed him before, because he filled the corner with his presence. "You startled me, Your Grace."

She'd always thought that Luke and Jack possessed a commanding presence, but theirs paled when compared with that of the Duke of Greystone. He was not a man accustomed to being denied, and the attraction she'd felt bubbling up within her while in the drawing room began to make its presence known once again. She refused to give into it. She'd not allow him to mock her tender regard or her friends. Still, she wasn't childish enough to flounce out. She swallowed hard, determined to hold her own against him.

"He used to keep sweets hidden here," she said inanely in response to the thickening silence. Greystone merely stared at her. "The previous earl," she went on to explain. "Luke's grandfather."

Still he held his tongue. She closed the drawer and rose from the chair, refusing to be cowed by him. With her heart thundering almost as loudly as the storm, she strolled over to the window and gazed out on the gray rain. "I used to live here.

The old gent would sit in that chair right there"
—she pointed to a hunter-green upholstered chair
near the window— "and have me read to him each
afternoon. It's strange. In my youth I lived with a
kidsman who I'm quite certain at some point in
his life killed someone, yet I never feared him.
But the old gent terrified me."

"Why?"

Ah, a word at last. She faced him, surprised to
discover that they were standing much nearer to
each other than she'd realized, and she suspected
his inquiry was little more than a ruse to stop her
from leaving. Why did the thought of him wishing her to stay thrill her?

"Because he was so . . . large." She shook her
head, frustrated by her inability to adequately de-
scribe Luke's grandfather. She was much more
skilled with the use of numbers than words. "Not
physically, of course. He was tall, like Luke—but
with more bone than flesh and a bit bent in his old
age—but he had such a fierce presence. Everything about him was incredibly grand. The homes
in which he lived—here and in the country. The
coach in which he traveled. Sometimes he would
take me about London with him when he needed
to visit with someone, and the deference that he
was given assured me that he was a very powerful
man indeed. Much like you, Your Grace."

"And powerful men frighten you?"

"They give me pause, but I am no longer a child to be intimidated by them. I daresay with age comes the inclination not to care much what others think."

A corner of his mouth lifted slightly, and she suddenly had an insane urge to make him smile fully, even as she feared that he'd heard the lie in her words. She couldn't deny that the aristocracy's low opinion of her—and her friends—hurt. Each of them, in their own way, did a good deal for others less fortunate, and all of them were fiercely loyal. They would die for each other. That others overlooked the goodness in them and always expected the worst rubbed raw after a while.

"You say that as though you're ancient," he told her.

"I'm quickly approaching the age of thirty." She didn't know why she felt obligated to reveal her age. Possibly to ensure he was aware that he wasn't dealing with an innocent young miss, but rather a woman who knew her own mind—or at least she had until she'd approached him. At that precise moment she wasn't sure whether she wanted him to stay and entice her nearer or leave before the situation escalated beyond her control. Because with him she wasn't certain she had complete control. She wanted to muss his hair, unveil the uncivilized aspect he'd referred to earlier.

"Quite old not to be married, not to have children tugging at your skirts," he said.

"Oh, I have children." She saw the condemnation flash in his deep blue eyes. It irritated her that he'd think the worst. She almost didn't explain herself, but she felt compelled. On the one hand, she wanted him to think the very worst of her and on the other she wanted him to think her worthy of . . . something she couldn't explain. "I take in orphans. Or I will once my children's home is completed."

"Ah, a reformer."

"You disapprove. Do you not believe in good works, Your Grace?"

"They have their place. But working with orphans seems a waste for a woman as lovely as you."

At his compliment, she felt the heat rush from the soles of her feet to her cheeks. She'd always considered herself a bit plain, or maybe it was simply that she wanted to be plain. She didn't wish to garner men's favor, so she worked very hard not to make herself appealing. Even the dress she wore today for so lovely an occasion as a wedding was designed not to draw a man's eye, and yet somehow it had managed to draw his. "I'm not certain if I've been insulted or complimented."

"Complimented, I assure you. I fear we got off to a rather unfortunate beginning with our introductions—or lack thereof. I'd retired to this room seeking some solace so that I might determine how best to make amends. I'm not typically so . . . unfriendly." He gazed out the window. "The gent you were speaking with earlier, in the brown jacket—who is he?"

She was surprised by the abrupt change in topic and the inquiry. "James Swindler. An inspector with Scotland Yard."

For the briefest of moments, she could have sworn that his mouth twitched as though he were fighting back a smile.

"I wasn't inquiring as to his occupation, but rather what he is to you."

Oh. She found that a rather odd statement. What could he be other than what he was? "A friend. Did you wish an introduction?"

A bit of strangled laughter erupted, before he pressed his mouth into a straight line and shook his head. "No, that's quite all right. He seemed protective of you."

"They all are."

"They?"

"Feagan's lads."

"And Feagan is . . ."

"The kidsman who took us all in."

"The one who taught you how to pilfer pockets?"

"Among other things."

"You were a very deft student, Miss Darling. I didn't even feel your touch. The problem there is that I would very much like to know your touch."

Very slowly, his gaze came back to her. It held an invitation, as well as a promise. How was she to respond to that? To admit that she, too, was wondering what his touch might feel like? From the moment she'd lost her innocence, at the age of twelve, she'd had no sexual interest in men. They didn't frighten her. She'd learned enough from Feagan's lads to know that not all men were brutes. But still she'd never been *attracted* to a man, had never wanted to attract one. She'd never felt this strange fluttering in her stomach whenever she looked at a man, had never had her heart pounding so rapidly when he was near, had never found it so difficult to draw in breath when she gazed into his eyes or studied the intriguing shape of his mouth.

"No retort? No denial that you're not curious about *my* touch?" he asked.

"I have no skills at these flirtatious games men and women play." She didn't know why she'd felt compelled to reveal that little tidbit about herself. She'd always held her own with the boys when it came to stealing or arranging a ruse, taking measures to fleece someone. They often sought out her opinion on their business dealings. But it was all so very distant from what was happening here. She was like a novice explorer, traveling uncharted ground.

"It's not a game, Miss Darling," Greystone said in a low voice that reverberated through her and settled somewhere in the vicinity of her heart.

"And by touch, I suppose you mean—"

"Simply a touch."

She who was always so aware of her surroundings, of the people around her, judging when best to take, when to leave, had somehow missed that he'd leaned nearer to her, his blue eyes smoldering with desire. With the gentlest of touches, he skimmed his fingers along the curve of her face, from her temple, down her cheek, across her chin.

"So soft," he whispered as his thumb stroked her lower lip, his gaze following his movements as though he'd never seen anything quite so fascinating, as though she were some rare creature. "The gentlemen standing near you in the drawing room . . . is any of them your lover?"

"No!" She was insulted by the insinuation, would have moved back if the slow stroking of his thumb just below her mouth wasn't holding her captive as effectively as iron.

"Have you a lover?"

"I'm not certain why it's any of your concern—"

"Have you?" he repeated with an insistence that indicated he'd not let his inquiry go unanswered.

"No."

"Good."

He never took his eyes from her. They never ceased to smolder. If anything, the fire within them intensified and burned through her. She was beginning to feel as though she might melt. She had a ridiculous need to undo some buttons, to let him blow his cool breath over her skin.

"Why is that good?" she asked, barely recognizing her own voice. It was far too sultry.

"Because I would very much like to kiss you, Miss Darling, and unlike you, I'm not in the habit of taking what rightfully belongs to someone else."

His fingers were again on her cheek, his palm cupping her chin. He moved slowly toward her as though giving her time to retreat or an opportunity to object. She did neither. Instead she found herself leaning toward him, her eyes drifting closed. Then his mouth was upon hers.

She'd been forcibly kissed and chastely kissed, but never had a man so gently and so determinedly urged her lips to part in order that he might gain entry. Never had she wanted to so willingly comply. He tasted of champagne, rich and flavorful. He tasted of desire.

One of his arms came around her and drew her up against him. As a woman she'd never been this close to a man. She'd never had her breasts flattened against a man's solid chest. She'd never inhaled a masculine scent so deeply that it became part of her. She'd never had a man's talented tongue playing with hers, and she'd certainly never slipped hers into a man's mouth wanting to taste him fully. Everything she'd never envisioned experiencing she suddenly wanted with a desperation that should have been frightening.

But he didn't frighten her. He enticed her into winding her arms around his neck and rising up on her toes for easier access to that which she so desperately desired. With a low groan, he shifted the angle of the kiss and delved more deeply, more thoroughly, exploring every aspect of her mouth. The heat intensified, and her body took on a languid quality as though she could melt into him. Was this passion, this all-encompassing sensation that the two of them could very easily become one?

He drew back slightly and she gazed into the deep blue of his eyes.

"As you don't have a lover, Miss Darling, I'd like to offer my services. As I believe we've just proven, we're quite compatible."

Chapter 3

"**A**re you all right?"

Traveling in the coach Luke had lent them for the journey back to Dodger's, Frannie turned her attention away from the window where she could see little, save the rain, to look at Jack. "Of course. Why would you ask?"

"You seem particularly preoccupied."

She was. With thoughts of Greystone's scandalous proposal, and her even more scandalous reply. "I'll consider your offer."

Which meant what, exactly? Was she seriously considering it or had she simply not known what else to say? With a no, would he ever ask again? Would she ever see him again? With a yes, would she later change her mind? Would she have regrets?

After tugging free a glove, she laid her bare fingers against the cheek Greystone had stroked. The sensation was nothing compared to the sensuality he had brought to the fore. Her touch failed to elicit the incredible heat that coiled in her belly and flowed outward until she felt like molten wax. She slid her fingers over to her lips and toyed with them a moment. Again the sensation was nothing like the sweet pressure of his mouth against hers, urging her lips to willingly part . . .

Once Luke had kissed her and it had been as light as a butterfly landing on a rose petal. Nothing about Greystone's kiss had been gentle, but neither had it been rough. It had been . . . hungry, as though he were a starving man and she alone could provide his sustenance. Where were these insane thoughts coming from? Were they a reflection of her own desires, her own cravings to once more be sampling all he had to offer?

Gazing out the window again, she asked, "Jack, have you ever taken a lover?"

"I should think it depends."

She snapped her gaze back to him. It had seemed a simple enough question. Either he had or he hadn't. Was there more to this lover business than she realized? "On what precisely?"

"On whether or not you consider a bought woman to be a lover." He crossed his arms over his chest and looked up at the ceiling of the coach as though the answer to a riddle rested there. "I suppose you can't. A lover, it seems to me should be with you willingly, with no expectations of earning a coin. So with that in mind, I've never taken a lover." He lowered his gaze to her. "Seems a strange question coming from you."

For the first time in her life, she wasn't comfortable with him, couldn't tell him that her heated encounter with Greystone had prompted her inquiry. Where did a woman go for answers, because she knew if she listened to her own yearnings, she'd be knocking on Greystone's door this evening. "I'm simply curious. I'm not exactly certain what the expectations are for a lover, what the situation actually entails. Would a lover . . . love her lover? Would he love her?"

"Good God, Frannie, love is hardly involved at all. It's simply a polite way of saying a gent wants what's beneath a lady's skirts."

With a nod, she looked back out the window. Certainly that was all that the gentleman truly wanted. She was good enough to bed, but not to wed. He saw her as no better than a prostitute. His currency was a wicked mouth rather than coins, but dear Lord help her, she'd been almost willing to accept the terms.

"Ah, dammit, Frannie, I shouldn't have been so crude." Jack leaned forward, his elbows on his thighs. "Why the sudden curiosity?"

The heat of embarrassment—or was it shame?—

warmed her cheeks, and she was grateful that the gloomy weather might prevent him from noticing her blush. Their childhood had forged a bond that allowed them to share the most intimate of thoughts and know they were safe from scrutiny or judgment. She darted her gaze to his, then dropped it to her hands. "I've had an offer."

"An offer?"

Gathering up her resolve, she returned her gaze to his. "Someone wants to be my lover."

He narrowed his eyes for a heartbeat. She'd seen the look before. It often preceded his giving someone a sound thrashing. "Who's the blackguard?"

Ah, God, she wished she hadn't said anything, but Jack was one of her best friends. Unfortunately she suddenly realized some things shouldn't be shared, but who else was there for her to ask? She certainly couldn't ask Catherine, when her brother was the one causing Frannie's dilemma. "I don't want to say. Forget I even brought it up."

He flung himself back against the seat. "Greystone, the bastard."

"What? No! Why would you think him?"

Leaning forward again, he took her hands. "Frannie darling, I'm a man. I saw the way he eyed you, as though you were a delectable morsel that would satisfy a man's hunger. He disappeared for a bit. You were gone for a while. I'm thinking he took advantage of the opportunity and during a clandestine moment he made his indecent proposal."

It hadn't felt indecent. As a matter of fact, she'd been quite flattered, but then she'd also been lightheaded and lost in a passionate fog, following his heat-searing kiss. But what really astounded her was Jack's description of the way Greystone had been looking at her with hunger that she could satisfy. She'd had men leer at her, had them look at her as though she were fine crystal that could easily crack, but never with hunger. It was quite exhilarating. She squeezed Jack's fingers. "Would it be so wrong, do you think—to entertain the notion of being someone's lover? I've been a thief, a whore—"

"It was not your choosing to be a whore," he ground out.

"A man paid for me, Jack. Call it what you will, I've never freely given myself to a gentleman. I'm nearly thirty, years past the age when most ladies marry. Until Luke asked for my hand in marriage, I'd never given any thought to being a wife. I can't see myself married."

"Why ever not? Jim would marry you in a heartbeat. So would I, for that matter, if I didn't think you deserved far better than me."

She gave him a wry smile. "Jack Dodger getting married? I don't quite see that happening."

As though to further his argument, he reminded her, "He's a duke."

Jack knew the discomfort she experienced around the aristocracy. They all did. It was the reason they'd circled around her at Luke's. "That would be a problem if I had plans to *marry* him— which I do not. Lovers are private, a secret sin, aren't they? I wouldn't have to move about in his world."

"The answer to your earlier question is no. No love exists between lovers. You're likely to get very badly hurt, Frannie, and I'd feel responsible because you have a skewed view of the world from working at Dodger's. I provide men with a safe place to engage in sin, but I don't want them sinning with you. Besides, any decent man would be fortunate to have you for a wife. You shouldn't settle for less."

With a nod, she worked her hands free of his and sat back against the seat. "I suppose it wasn't truly a compliment he was paying me."

"No, it wasn't," he said tartly.

"I daresay I probably should have slapped him."

"Absolutely."

She sighed and gazed back out the window. The problem was that all she'd really wanted to do was to kiss him again. To want to be so close to a man was a new and exhilarating experience. Pity was she couldn't stop thinking about it, and the more she thought about it, unfortunately, the more she wanted it.

Sterling knew the hour was fast approaching when everything that had been within his grasp would be beyond his reach.

Sitting in his library, drinking his brandy, listening as the incessantly loud clock on the mantel marked the passage of his life, he tamped down the raw fury that threatened to erupt. Anger required energy he could ill afford to squander. Not now. Later perhaps, when he had nothing better to do except reflect on how much better life might have been if only . . .

He'd been determined not to have regrets, and yet they hovered near, waiting to make their presence known. He would reflect on them later as well.

Meanwhile, he was obsessed with filling up his reservoir of memories. He had one more he desperately wanted to add to his treasure trove. A night with *her* might very well be his crowning glory, his last indulgence, his final bit of wickedness before he turned his attention to duty. He had little doubt she would be worth delaying the inevitable course of his life.

Frannie Darling.

She was slender, but something about her made her appear larger than she was—as though she'd battled life's disappointments and known the taste of victory. Being a commoner, she was not the sort a man such as himself considered taking to wife. But as a lover, he had a feeling she would excel.

Closing his eyes, he brought forth images from their encounter in the library. Her fingers had run up into his hair. Her mouth had played skillfully over his. Her delicate rose scent had wafted around him, and even now he could still smell her fragrance lingering in his clothes. He wanted her fragrance lingering in his bed. It had been so very long since he'd actually anticipated holding a woman in his arms, and she hadn't disappointed.

He could hardly fathom now that he'd actually propositioned her, had suggested they become lovers. Her bold answer, before she'd turned on her heel and waltzed out, had stunned him.

"I'll consider your offer."

Did she mean it? Or was she teasing him? It was a strange game they were playing. She was the devil masquerading as a seductress. Or at the very least she was a witch, because she'd cast a spell over him that he was unable to escape. He was obsessed with the softness of her skin, the green of her eyes, the vibrant red of her hair. He wanted to kiss her again, wanted to slowly peel off her clothes and reveal all the hidden treasures. He'd seen much during his travels, but nothing had ever held his interest as she did. Would she come around? Would her answer be yes? How could she refuse a duke?

But a time would come when even his title would gain him nothing. She would have no interest in him, then. No woman would want him. Hadn't his father shouted the truth of that loudly enough?

It was the reason his father had opposed Sterling traveling the world, had insisted that Sterling see to the matter of taking a wife first. But he couldn't explore the world—and women—as he wanted with a wife in hand. He had every intention of remaining faithful to his wife, although he doubted she would grant him the same consideration when she learned the truth of his circumstance. And he had learned the hard way that it was best to keep his failings a secret as long as possible. Lady Angelina had scorned him, had taught him that love was an illusion easily shattered by the truth.

He'd not make that mistake again. He'd hold his secrets until after he had a wife. But before he began to seriously pursue marriage, he wanted one last night of unbridled passion. And for that, only one woman would do.

Frannie Darling.

He could still taste her on his lips. He longed to release every button that denied him a view of her skin. Based on the smooth complexion of her face, he had little doubt that she was exquisite perfection beneath her clothes. Her breasts would fit nicely in the palm of his hand; her nipples would harden beneath the slow stroke of his tongue. He wanted to trail his mouth along—

"More brandy, sir?"

The unexpected voice should have startled him, but lost in thoughts of Miss Darling along with the abundance of brandy he'd swallowed had made him lethargic. He was almost floating, knew he should refuse, because he hadn't even heard his servant enter the room, but that wasn't unusual. His servants always exhibited the utmost in decorum and glided along without a sound, as though their feet never touched the floor.

In answer to the question, Sterling held the glass up slightly, in the mood to get completely foxed. Maybe then he would be able to shut Miss Darling out of his mind so that he could sleep. Or maybe it would be better to entice her into his dreams, where she would desire him as much as he—

The brandy spilled over the rim of his glass, onto his thigh, and splashed onto his shirt. "Dammit, man!"

Unsteadily, he lurched out of the chair and spun around—

To discover a servant hadn't entered his sanctuary. No indeed. It had been violated by Jack Dodger and James Swindler. He supposed he should count his blessings that only two and not four of the ruffians had sneaked in on him.

Swindler set the decanter back on the table with incredible delicacy for a man so large.

"How did you get in here?" Sterling asked, wishing his words didn't sound quite so slurred. He was having more difficulty than usual bringing his shadowed world into focus. Damnation, why hadn't he lit more lamps or poured himself fewer snifters of brandy?

"Not important," Jack Dodger said. "What is important is for you to realize that you can do nothing to keep us out if we decide we want in."

"I would threaten to call around for a constable, but I suppose that would do me little good considering an inspector has broken into my residence."

"It'll do you no good at all, Your Grace." Swindler's sneer left no doubt as to where he stood regarding Sterling's title. He apparently considered it as worthless as he did Sterling.

"Could I offer you gentlemen a drink?"

"You're to stay away from Frannie," Swindler stated succinctly.

No, then, to the drink.

"Or what?" Sterling asked.

"I can make you disappear."

Ah, nothing like an unveiled threat to make matters perfectly clear. Unfortunately, Sterling didn't appreciate threats. If anything, they only served to make him more stubborn and determined to have his way. "Indeed? And are your superiors aware of this unusual skill you've apparently honed?"

"Frannie is special to us, Greystone," Jack Dodger said. "We have no intention of seeing her hurt."

"Well, that makes three of us, as I have no intentions of harming her."

"You may not intend it, but if you make her your mistress, that'll be the result."

As a muscle in his jaw tightened, Sterling narrowed his eyes. Had he been that obvious?

"She told us," Dodger said, as though a question had been asked. "She's that innocent."

"She doesn't kiss as though she's innocent."

His meaty hands balled into fists, Swindler took a step toward him. Dodger grabbed him by the back of his jacket. "Hold up, Swindler."

The delivery of the words carried enough authority to halt Swindler, but it was obvious he didn't appreciate the interference. Sterling, on the

other hand, did appreciate it. If it came to fisti-
cuffs, Sterling knew he would give it his best, but
he wouldn't stand a chance. Not that he was in the
habit of fighting, but Swindler looked as though
he was. It also appeared he was in the habit of
winning.

Dodger stepped in front of him, putting himself
between Swindler and Sterling, but Swindler was
tall enough that Sterling could still see the fury
in his green eyes. Of the two, he was undoubtedly the more dangerous, although Sterling wasn't
stupid enough to underestimate Jack Dodger.

"The thing of it is, Greystone," Dodger began,
"Swindler, Graves, Claybourne, and I consider
ourselves to be her brothers. Each of us would
willingly go to the gallows for her."

"I've heard you're protective of what's yours."

"I am. I fear I've had to terminate your membership at Dodger's. You'll need to seek your
pleasures elsewhere."

"Gentlemen, if I truly want something, you do
not have it within your power to stop me from ob-
taining it."

The pain that ricocheted through his face was
almost as fierce as the pain bouncing through his
skull when he hit the floor. He hadn't seen Swindler move, and he certainly hadn't seen his fist
coming at him from the side—his Achilles' heel.

Swindler was suddenly kneeling beside him. With his mammoth hand latched on to Sterling's shirt, he jerked him upright until he was almost sitting.

"If you hurt her, I'll kill you."

"I appreciate a man who doesn't mince words."

Swindler released his hold, and Sterling once again made painful contact with the floor. Swindler stood up and stormed from the room, the tread of his heavy footsteps reverberating through the floor.

Dodger knelt beside Sterling. "Greystone, you have to understand we come from the streets. When Frannie was a young girl, we weren't able to stop someone from hurting her very badly. The four of us swore an oath that we'd die before we let anyone harm her again. It's a vow we *will* keep."

Sterling lay where he was long after Dodger left. He had been correct about one thing: they did love her.

Unfortunately, he found little consolation in being correct, but he was more determined than ever to have her.

Chapter 4

After making the last needed notation in the ledger, Frannie blew softly on the ink to hasten its drying. The numbers were astonishing. Having been in Jack Dodger's employ for ten years now—and his partner for five—she should be accustomed to how much money men frittered away on games of chance.

"The house always wins in the end, Frannie," Jack had told her when she'd initially questioned his wisdom in opening a gambling establishment. "And the end is all that matters."

With a sigh, she set aside her gold-nibbed pen—a gift from Jack, who enjoyed fine things and knew she'd never spend so senselessly on herself—and carefully closed the book so as not to smear the ink. Jack liked everything neat and tidy. But then, so did she. She was fairly certain it was because they'd grown up in squalor.

Her office was sparsely decorated. The desk,

a couple of chairs, a couch where she sometimes took a quick rest, and shelves that housed the ledgers that provided a history of the establishment.

It was almost two in the morning. Although she was tired, the late hours worked well for her. Working on the accounts at night left her free to see after the children's home she planned to open soon. The furniture was scheduled to arrive early the next week. Now all she needed was to hire employees. But that was a task for tomorrow. For tonight she had a few more matters to attend to before she could retire.

Opening the ledger with member accounts, she began making notations regarding whose memberships were coming due. When her lower back began to ache, she straightened, yawned, and stretched—

A large figure loomed in the doorway.

With a self-conscious laugh, she assumed a more decorous position.

"Don't let me stop you from relaxing," Jim said as he took a step into the room. His brown jacket wasn't fancy, but it suited his unassuming demeanor. His dark brown hair was thick, his eyes green. From appearances, he seemed non-threatening and in many ways simple. In truth, she considered him far cleverer and more dangerous than any of them.

"I was simply taking a moment before I studied the customer accounts," she said.

"You do keep odd hours."

"No more odd than you. Are you working now?"

"Jack had asked me to check on some personal matters for him regarding this inheritance he's come into. I was just reporting what I found. Thought while I was here that I'd stop by to see how you were doing."

"I'm doing well, Jim."

Nodding, he stuck his hands in his coat pockets, then took them out. "Has anyone been bothering you?"

That's an odd question.

"Were you thinking of someone in particular?" she asked.

"No, simply curious." He took a step forward, and then as though concerned that he might frighten her, he took a step back. "I just wanted you to know that I'm available if you need anything."

"I may need some help rounding up orphans when the time comes."

"That goes without saying. I've been keeping a list of boys going into prison, when they'll be getting out. The younger ones, the ones who can be turned around, I'll be picking up. I'll bring them to you."

She gave him a soft smile. "That means everything to me, Jim. The furniture should arrive next week. Will you be free to help?"

"Absolutely."

"Thank you. I'm feeling a tad guilty that on the streets are children who need a home, and I have the means to provide one, but am still arranging matters."

"It's a lot you're taking on, Frannie."

"But it's something I want to do—terribly. I've thought about it for so long, planned it, and now it's about to happen at last. I'll send a missive 'round to your flat when I have the day and time."

"Splendid." He smiled brightly—which was something Jim rarely did. "I look forward to helping you." He made a motion to tip his hat, must have realized he wasn't wearing one, and gave an awkward sort of slight bow. "See you soon, then."

He exited with a quickness that astonished her. She didn't know why he was sometimes awkward around her when he wasn't with the others. Perhaps because he was two years younger, and she'd mothered him more than most. She remembered the day Luke and Jack had brought him to Feagan's. It was immediately following the hanging of Jim's father. He'd been so quiet that she'd feared he'd never again speak. The shock of it all, she supposed. That night, after they'd all gone to bed, she'd heard his quiet whimpers and she'd left the comfort of Luke's embrace and gone to hold Jim while he wept. Even then she understood the pain of loss.

And among Feagan's brood, they'd all lost something valuable. Some, she suspected, were still searching for it. Not Luke. She gave a slight smile. She'd never known him to be quite so happy since he'd taken a wife. And thinking of Catherine led Frannie to thinking about her brother.

It had been a little over a week since the wedding, and to her everlasting irritation, Greystone often occupied her thoughts. Through a back stairway, not accessible to customers, she and Jack had access to a few shadowy balconies that allowed them, without being seen, to look out over various areas where their customers were entertained. Twice she'd searched for Greystone and not seen him. Not that she was certain what she'd do if she *did* see him, but she couldn't deny the disappointment that she'd not caught a glimpse of him. Was he as handsome as she remembered? Was he as darkly dangerous?

Was he anxiously waiting for her to respond to his proposal? Would he know that the answer was no if he never heard from her? Should she tell him when he was here one night? Should she send him a letter? Should she simply remain silent?

She debated the methods as often as she debated her answer. She knew Jack was correct, knew the answer she should give was a resounding no, but Greystone intrigued her. She had no logical explanation for that. They couldn't be more opposite. But why, with everyone else in Luke's drawing room, was he the one who had drawn her attention, and more important—in spite of her best efforts not to be noticed—why had she drawn his?

And why was it acceptable for men to seek the pleasures of numerous women, while women were to know only one? Certainly in the area of London where they'd grown up, girls attached themselves to one boy for a while and then moved on to another. Her friend Nancy had done just that and no one ostracized her for it. But Frannie supposed the price for being accepted by polite society was to embrace their rules for proper behavior, and ladies were supposed to value their chastity. A bit difficult for her to accomplish when she no longer possessed it.

It had been nearly eighteen years. Over the years, the nightmares regarding that night had faded, although she knew they would never leave her completely. But she didn't fear men. She knew the passion and the tenderness that could pass between a man and a woman.

Several years ago, Jim had shown her. Dodger's had a viewing room where the lords who wished to demonstrate their prowess would perform with a lady of their choice while the patrons observed from darkened corners and through discreet peepholes. Jim had invited her to watch while he made love to one of the girls. *Made love.* The precise words he'd used. He wanted her to know what it *could* be like. That night he'd given her an amazing gift. The encounter had been sensual, erotic.

Frannie had always known that what she'd experienced at the age of twelve was not the way it should have been—and that night, watching Jim with Prudence, she'd lost some of her hesitancy at the thought of being with a man. But still, she'd never known a man she wanted to be with in that way . . . not until she'd crossed paths with Greystone, a duke, the very last man she should want.

Perhaps it was a touch of the forbidden that drew her to him. Or was it something more?

She might very well drive herself insane thinking about all of this. She had records to verify, memberships coming due—

Her gaze fell on a notation scribbled in Jack's almost indecipherable handwriting. Blast him!

Snatching up the ledger, she charged out of her office and into his. He, too, kept late hours. He was sitting behind his desk, studying a ledger.

"What's the meaning of this?" she asked tartly, holding up her own ledger.

With brow furrowed, his dark eyes serious, he looked up. "Of what?"

She slapped the book down on top of his. "It

says here that Greystone's membership has been terminated."

Reaching back, Jack grabbed one of several bottles he kept within easy reach and refilled the glass on his desk. "I decided I didn't like him."

"Jack—"

"Frannie." He downed his whiskey and started to pour again. She snatched the glass away.

"Dammit, Frannie!" He scooted back, grabbed a piece of paper, and tried to blot up the spill. "That's my best liquor. Why waste it?"

"All your spirits are your best. I'm going to re-establish his membership."

He stopped his frantic movements, looked up at her, and glared. "I'll just undo it."

"You can't cancel the membership of every man who expresses an interest in me." Not that anyone had ever expressed an interest in her before, but she was striving to make a point.

"He did more than express an interest."

"I know you're trying to protect me—and I love you for it. But this isn't right. I can handle myself."

He studied her for a moment, and she knew he wanted to argue further. Instead, he snapped his fingers. "Give me back my glass."

She handed it over. She knew he'd never admit to being wrong on this matter, but as he'd shifted

the conversation, she was going to mark it as a win
in her favor. Besides, she knew he now had more
important matters on his mind. One of Jack's customers, the Duke of Lovingdon, had left Jack all
his non-entailed properties. And Jack, in typical
Jack fashion, didn't trust his good fortune, so he
was scrutinizing every aspect of the arrangement.

"Will you send a missive to Greystone or shall
I?" she asked.

He gave her a pointed glare.

"I suppose I should do it," she said. "He'd never
be able to read what you wrote. You didn't do anything else to him, did you?"

"No, I did not."

"Swear to me."

"God, Frannie, I said I didn't, and I didn't."
He studied her for a moment. "You still carry the
dagger I gave you?"

She patted her hip. She kept it in a scabbard
hidden inside her skirt. "Always."

"It's been a while since we've practiced. Maybe
we should, tomorrow. Make sure you still know
how to use it."

"I know how to use it."

"Remember, the object is not to wound, but to
kill. And don't worry about him being a blasted
lord. Jim will handle any inquiries."

So now he was suggesting she should kill Greystone? Lovely. "I think if he was going to take advantage, he would have done it in the library when he . . ." She realized just in time that she was traveling down a path she shouldn't go with him.

"Luke's library? What did he do?"

"Talked."

"What did he say?"

"That I was interesting." She took back her ledger and cradled it against her chest. "Shall I interrogate you regarding your encounter with the young Duchess of Lovingdon?"

"It's very different. The widow is not looking to take advantage of me."

She nodded. Strange thing was, she hadn't been under the impression that Greystone wanted to take *advantage* either. Rather he wanted to give and receive something that might have been very pleasant for them both.

"Good night, Jack." She turned on her heel—

"My heart was in the right place, Frannie," he called after her.

It was so difficult to stay angry at the lads. "I know."

She returned to her office and wrote eight letters to Greystone until she finally wrote one that didn't say too much or too little, that gave nothing away regarding her own feelings on the situation. It reflected nothing except business. It would do.

She rose from her desk and strolled across the room. She snatched the cloak hanging near the door and draped it around her shoulders before walking out of her office and into the hallway that never was quiet enough. The exuberant activities that took place beyond the closed door at the end of the hall leading into the gaming area always echoed through the building. She'd grown accustomed to it and barely heard it any longer. On the other side of the hall was the door that led outside.

She unlocked it and stepped out onto the stoop, where a lantern cast a ghostly glow around the dark alley. Quickly she locked the door. She didn't take the lantern because she knew this area as well as she knew the back of her hand and was comfortable in the shadows. Her room was up the stairs to the left. At her door, she inserted another key. Jack's apartment was next to hers, but he seldom stayed there anymore, not since he'd inherited a fancy residence in St. James.

Closing and locking her door behind her, she walked over to a nearby table and lit the lamp. With a sigh, she hung up her cloak and began to undress as she made her way across the apartment to the area where she slept. Her small rooms were as sparsely furnished as her office. A sofa, a bed, a vanity, a few odd chairs, a couple of small tables.

She didn't require much in the way of possessions for her happiness.

After she'd washed up and slipped into her nightgown, she sat at her vanity and began to brush her hair. She detested its shade and the abundant curls that made it so difficult to manage. She wondered if Greystone had found it unattractive. She leaned toward the mirror. Her green eyes were her best feature. She remembered how often he'd gazed directly into them. Could he become lost in them? Was there something she could do to ensure that he did?

But she wanted him to become lost in more than her eyes. She wanted him to become lost in her. What a dangerous, dangerous desire.

With a moan, she got up and carried the lamp to the table beside her bed. After crawling beneath the sheets, she extinguished the flame in the lamp and stared into the darkness above her. With very little effort, she imagined Greystone rising over her. He would come to her unclothed and every bit of skin that she could reach would be sun bronzed.

Releasing a groan, she rolled over to her side. When she finally drifted off to sleep, she dreamed that she'd sent him a very different sort of letter than the one she'd written earlier. One that had contained a single word.

Yes.

Chapter 5

As Catherine sat in what had been her father's—and was now her brother's—library, she noted the changes in Sterling one by one as he stood at the window, his profile to her as he gazed out, slowly sipping his brandy while the late afternoon sunlight cast a faint glow around him. His once golden hair had darkened considerably, which made him appear older than his twenty-eight years. His shoulders had broadened as though *he*—rather than servants—had handled a good deal of the difficult labors of traveling the continents. He'd acquired a thin scar on his left cheek, just below his eye. He'd lost his smile.

Of all the changes he'd undoubtedly undergone during the years he'd been away, the last one tore painfully at her heart.

"So will you see to it?" she asked her brother.

He'd risen from his chair behind his desk,

poured himself a spot of brandy, and walked to the window as soon as she'd made her request. His reaction had seemed disturbingly odd.

He turned slightly, his sapphire eyes homing in on her, as though he now wished to study *her* because he suspected she was not completely sane. "Let me make certain that I have the right of it. You want me to arrange for the two hundred pounds Father stipulated in his will that I pay you each month to be handed over instead to Miss Frannie Darling."

"Precisely."

"Is she blackmailing you?"

"Don't be silly. It's for her orphanage. I realize that I could simply give her the money myself, but this seems more efficient, and she'll be assured that she can always depend on it arriving at the first of the month." And her request served as an excuse to visit with Sterling, and perhaps to lure him back into Society. The fact that Catherine needed an excuse said more about the strained state of their relationship than anything else. He was her brother, for God's sake, yet in the two weeks since her marriage, she'd seen him not once. But then, as far as she knew, neither had anyone else.

"Father wanted you to have the funds so you'd have a measure of independence," Sterling told her.

"I'm married to one of the wealthiest lords in England—"

"That does not guarantee your independence."

She knew the truth of that well enough. Her desire to help the Duchess of Avendale escape from her horrendous marriage had first led Catherine to Claybourne's door.

"I'm sorry, Catherine, but I don't feel that I can alter Father's terms, even at your request. A time may arrive when you wish you had your own means of support. Until then, send Miss Darling the money yourself if you have no need of it."

"Why are you being so stubborn about this request?" she asked. "It's my money to do with as I please."

"I don't consider this a wise move. As your brother, I'm charged with looking after your welfare and preventing you from making ghastly misjudgments."

"Not any longer. I'm married. And what about loving me, Sterling? Loving anyone? It has come to my attention that you've been in London for at least four months. Why did you not visit Father? You must have known he'd taken ill. It was no secret."

"Checking up on me, are you?"

Not intentionally. But since her friends had recently become those who occasionally flirted with the darker side of London, she sometimes picked up little tidbits of information. "I'm trying to understand what happened to the brother who gave me a magical rock to protect me from nightmares when I woke up crying as a child after Mother passed. I'm not certain I know you any longer."

"Be grateful."

"What the devil does that mean?"

He walked over to a table of decanters and re-filled his snifter. "Are we done here?"

Not by half.

Rising gracefully from the chair, she decided to take a different tack. While he was her brother, his title was one of the most powerful in England. It carried weight and influence. Her father would be vastly disappointed if Sterling didn't live up to his potential. "Perhaps you should consider joining us tomorrow. Claybourne and I are going to the orphanage to assist Frannie with the arrival of the furniture. We could use an extra pair of hands."

"Surely you're not suggesting I lower myself to engaging in manual labor."

"I'm suggesting that you might want to be involved in something that touches so many. Frannie intends to provide a home for a hundred children."

"I still fail to see why I should care."

"If you don't understand, then I certainly can't explain it to you." Refusing to allow his bored tone to dissuade her, she walked around the desk, opened a drawer, and removed a sheaf of stationery.

"What are you doing?" he asked.

Ah, a bit of interest at last. Perhaps all was not lost.

"Writing down the address in the hope you'll change your mind and join us. I've discovered, Sterling, that being involved in something like this tends to change one's perspective on life."

"I don't need my perspective on life changed."

But he needed *something*, of that she was certain. She set the pen aside and walked over to him. "I do wish you would tell me what you and Father argued about."

She couldn't help but believe his present attitude related in some way to what had happened before he left. He and their father had engaged in a heated row one night. She heard the anger reverberating through the walls, but not the words. The next morning she received a missive from Sterling begging her not to worry, but he had decided to travel the world. She'd not seen him again until after their father died.

Sterling averted his gaze. "As I've told you before, Catherine, it didn't concern you."

"What did it concern?" She watched the muscle in his jaw flex. She touched his arm and felt him stiffen. "I love you, Sterling. If there is anything I can do—"

"Leave me in peace."

"Are you not at peace, then?"

He heaved a sigh. "You've become quite the annoying young woman."

She smiled, hoping to touch that place inside him where she knew a heart had once resided. "Oh, you have no idea."

"More reason for me not to honor your request and designate that your money be diverted elsewhere. Claybourne will no doubt grow weary of you in short order."

She laughed lightly at that. "He appreciates that I'm headstrong and determined. I would like for you to get to know him better."

"The Devil Earl? He's a murderer, Catherine."

"Yes, he killed a man—"

"His uncle."

"—for good reason. There is nothing about my husband that I do not admire. I think the two of you would get along splendidly if you'd give him half a chance."

"On the contrary, I suspect he'd dislike me as much as his friends do."

She furrowed her brow in confusion. "When did you gather that impression from his friends?"

With no comment, Sterling walked back to the window, his snifter once again full.

"If you need me for anything, please send word," Catherine said as she retrieved her reticule from the table beside the chair in which she'd been sitting.

"Get on with your life, Catherine. I shan't need you."

"We all need someone, Sterling."

"I bloody well hope not."

Yes, her brother definitely needed something—or someone.

Frannie Darling.
The moment Catherine had mentioned the woman's name, Sterling wanted her to leave. He relished the images that came to his mind with thoughts of Miss Darling, and in spite of the dire threats he'd received, he wasn't quite ready to give up the notion of being intimate with her.

After Catherine left—thank goodness she'd not taken it upon herself to visit him before all evidence of his nasty encounter with Swindler had disappeared—Sterling traded his refined brandy for a bottle of whiskey, his study for the garden.

Frannie Darling. He gave the name leave to roll through his mind and stir the few memories of her he'd hoarded away.

Sterling wanted one night with her, damn it all. What was this madness that had possessed him ever since he'd met her? Her hair was as wild as he imagined she would be in bed. Her eyes were the green of spring. Her lips were plump and ripe. The taste of her was fading from his mind, replaced with all the brandy he'd been drinking in an effort to tamp down his impatience while she considered his proposition.

A missive from her had arrived recently, and the anticipation that had burst through him was unlike anything he'd ever experienced. Until he opened it.

My Lord Duke,

Your membership at Dodger's has been restored.

Yours faithfully,
Frannie Darling

So damned formal. Not even a hint as to her leanings regarding his proposal. And he'd been unable to stop thinking about her since.

He dropped onto the bench at the far end of the garden and brought the bottle to his lips. Hardly a civilized way to drink spirits, but of late, he wasn't feeling very civilized.

He'd spent the past two weeks in residence, waiting for the bruising around his eye and over his cheek to fade completely. With his position, he had no desire to raise questions or start rumors that he'd been involved in some sort of brawl— especially as he'd looked as though he came out the loser. Good Lord, he'd nearly been attacked by a gorilla in Africa and had been attacked by a tiger in India—but neither of those creatures had seemed as deadly dangerous as Swindler.

If only he'd seen the blow coming, he could have deflected it or countered it with one of his own. But devil take it! Late in his adolescence his sight had taken a dreadful turn. It had seemed innocent at first. He'd had difficulty seeing at night. Spectacles hadn't offered any help. Then his peripheral vision had begun slowly eroding until now it was as though he wore permanent blinders. He'd tested his limits during his travels in ways that he couldn't in London or at his estates. Now, he had a difficult time admitting that he could no longer control some aspects of his life.

Perhaps that was the reason he was opposed to arranging for Catherine's money to find its way to Miss Darling each month. Sterling didn't want the lovely lady to gain financial independence at this juncture because it might lessen her likelihood of accepting his offer. He needed to provide her with a reason to want to be with him as desperately as he wanted to be with her. Money was an incredible motivator. Perhaps he would go around to the orphanage tomorrow, take the opportunity to remind her of his proposal. Perhaps even suggest that he'd provide for her orphans . . .

Or would she likely take insult at that tack? Would she see it as beneath her to accept a gift from him in exchange for providing a night of pleasure in her arms? He might have to take a little more time than he'd planned with this seduction, but seduce her he would. A time would come when things he wanted would be denied him, but the time had not yet arrived.

Immensely satisfied with the direction of his plan, he drained the last few drops from the bottle and sat back. A moment of panic surged through him when he realized darkness had fallen. Damnation. He had been foolish to come out here so near to dusk and to be so absorbed with thoughts of Miss Darling that he hadn't noticed the dimming light.

Standing, he focused on the lights spilling out from the windows of his residence. They were muted, difficult to see. It was always more difficult at night to make out his surroundings—but if he just went slowly . . .

Of late, it seemed he was forever going more slowly. It wasn't a luxury he had when it came to the lovely Miss Darling. He needed to take a wife while he could still give the impression that his vision was not a problem—which meant in turn that he needed to satisfy this craving he had to taste and relish every sensual aspect of Frannie Darling.

Chapter 6

Sterling had not expected the long line of wagons that his driver had recklessly swerved around in order to gain entrance through the gate of the orphanage. He'd not expected this home for children on the outskirts of London to be so monstrously large, reflecting such exquisite architecture. He'd not expected all the people scurrying around, hauling furniture inside.

As his driver brought the coach to a halt, suddenly Sterling very much did not want to be here. Crowds, blast it all, when he could not easily see those who surrounded him, had become the bane of his existence.

The footman promptly opened the door. Sterling was about to tell him to instruct the driver to return home when he spotted Catherine, and—damnation—she spotted him. The joy on her face at the sight of him only served to add to his unease.

"Sterling, you came!"

As she hurried over, Sterling realized he had no choice now except to endure a few moments with all these people and this activity. As he agilely leaped out, he turned his head to see that his footmen had already disembarked from their carriage and were standing at attention waiting for their orders. He'd thought Miss Darling would be so grateful for his generosity in offering his own servants—

Stupid. Why did he feel this insane need to impress a woman of the streets? It should be enough that he wanted her. Most women whom he desired were flattered by his attention. They required no more of him than that.

Catherine came to a stop in front of him. While she was appropriately wearing black, still mourning the loss of their father, her dress looked as though it might have once been worn by a washerwoman. Dirt smudged her nose and one cheek, and her hair was in danger of toppling from its pins at any moment. He didn't know if he'd ever seen her look happier.

"I brought servants to assist," he said gruffly.

"I can see that. Frannie will be absolutely delighted. Come inside, so I can let her know you're here."

"You told her to expect me?" What if he'd

changed his mind? Would she have been disappointed?

"No, of course not. But she is a bookkeeper and she keeps tally of everything, so she'll want to know you've come to help."

Catherine was babbling about all the work that needed to be done as she guided him toward the entrance. He could see now why Catherine wanted her money to go to this endeavor. The upkeep would be monstrous. Miss Darling would certainly be in need of financing for her enterprise. Bookkeepers didn't receive an exorbitant salary.

As they walked through the door into the building, Claybourne was striding out. He came to an abrupt halt. "Your Grace, what an unexpected surprise."

"By its very nature a surprise is unexpected," Sterling said, annoyed that Claybourne appeared so comfortable in these surroundings, while he felt decidedly out of his element.

"You have me there. You can put your jacket in the corner office, roll up your sleeves—"

"I brought servants."

"Frannie will be pleased with the extra hands."

"Where is she?" Catherine asked.

"Last I saw her was upstairs. She should be down momentarily."

"I want to let her know Sterling is here."

Claybourne narrowed his eyes. "She's very precious to us, you know."

Another warning? Did he not know that one had already been delivered? "As my sister is to me," he replied.

Catherine sighed. "I don't know why the two of you must always act distrustful of each other."

Perhaps because they knew how men thought. Sterling was growing weary of the encounter. He should simply leave. He lifted his gaze to the stairs and suddenly, nothing else mattered. She was there, standing halfway down, Swindler halting and glancing back up as though they'd been walking down together and she'd come to an unexpected stop.

His memory of her didn't do her justice. What he had considered vibrant had been nothing more than washed-out images. In person, her hair was a deeper red, and he knew her eyes would be a more alluring green. Her dress, buttoned clear to her chin, left everything to a man's imagination, fueling it, making him wonder if what he envisioned could truly exist in the flesh. He thought nothing would be more satisfying than undoing each of those buttons at his leisure and discovering the treasures they kept hidden.

Swindler said something to her—but not before giving Sterling a condescending once-over—and she jerked her attention to Swindler and smiled. The slow movement of her lips was enough to almost bring Sterling to his knees. What in God's name was wrong with him? She wasn't even bestowing her charms on him, but he was enchanted all the same.

Miss Darling began to walk down the stairs. Swindler joined her, his gaze shifting between Miss Darling and Sterling as though he could see the strange bond that joined them. Sterling already knew he didn't approve of it. He was simply grateful that no evidence of his bruised eye remained.

"Your Grace," Miss Darling said with a slight curtsy as she came to stand in front of him.

Like Catherine, she had a smudge of dirt on her cheek, and he clamped his hands behind his back to stop himself from reaching out to rub it away. It didn't detract from her perfection. In some ways, it enhanced it.

He bowed. "Miss Darling. I've brought six footmen to assist you in your endeavors."

"How very kind of you." She turned slightly. "Have you been introduced to Inspector Swindler from Scotland Yard?"

"We've met," he said curtly.

Her brow furrowed slightly as she glanced suspiciously between the two men. "I see. Would you care for a tour, Your Grace?"

"I would be most interested, thank you." And perhaps they could dispense with some of the damned formality.

"Jim, will you see to giving his footmen instructions?" she asked.

"Maybe I should stay with you." While his words were to her, he was still scrutinizing Sterling as though he considered him some reprobate.

"We'll be fine. The more quickly people are put to work, the sooner we'll be done and I can start moving in orphans." She touched Swindler's arm, and Sterling had an irrational urge to snatch her hand away. He didn't want her touching others, he wanted her touching him. "Please."

Swindler nodded. "I can never refuse you, you know that." Then he walked off, his shoulder clipping Sterling's as he walked by. Sterling should have anticipated that bit of bravado was coming. Instead he'd been watching Miss Darling, so he continued to give the impression he'd chosen to ignore the unspoken warning.

"We should get back to work," Catherine said, slipping her arm through Claybourne's and leading him away.

Sterling hadn't seen enough of Catherine with her husband to judge their relationship, but it seemed she wasn't averse to giving a few orders—and Claybourne had no qualms about following them. Once they were beyond hearing, Miss Darling said, "The upstairs is rather boring. It's only bedchambers."

"I've never found bedchambers to be boring."

She blushed and glanced down at the floor, and he wished he'd bitten his tongue before speaking. He'd obviously embarrassed her. Working in Dodger's where women often provided men with companionship, she had to possess a keen understanding of what transpired between a man and woman. He wondered if she was remembering his proposition.

"But I suppose they are very much all alike," he said, and her gaze shot up to his, her brow furrowed as though she was trying to determine if he was referring to her familiarity with bedchambers or his. "Where would you suggest we start?"

"If you'll follow me," she said and led him down a hallway.

She opened the door to a room with shelves lining the wall.

"The library, I presume," he said quietly. "I've a fondness for libraries."

Blushing becomingly, she strolled to a large window that overlooked a garden. He could see several gardeners toiling. Miss Darling was apparently determined to make this orphan asylum resemble a home as much as possible. He considered closing the door, but he supposed considering the looks Claybourne and the inspector had given him that he needed to take care not to offend or give the wrong impression. Besides, if he did close it, he might find himself deciding that gentlemanly behavior was no longer warranted. Now that he was back in her presence, he wanted her all the more.

"I'm quite surprised you're here," she said softly. She faced him. "I suppose you came for an answer."

"Truthfully, I'm not certain why I came." He ambled over to the window and allowed his gaze to fall on her. "That's a lie. I know exactly why I'm here. I wanted to see you again."

"I'm at Dodger's every night. I see to his books, as you know."

"But I imagine if I were to go into the hallways barred from customers that I might meet resistance. Tell me, Miss Darling, where do you live?"

"I have an apartment at the back of Dodger's."

He'd heard Dodger provided rooms for some of his employees. She had to be spending every farthing she'd ever earned on this enterprise. He looked at the gardeners hard at work, digging and arranging. "I'd not expected something so . . . elaborate. The land, the building . . . they cannot have come cheap. How will you maintain them?"

"We have benefactors. Luke in particular is

very generous. Perhaps you'd care to make a donation, Your Grace."

The devil was in her bright green eyes as she gave him an impish grin. Sunlight, which had been absent the last time they stood together in front of a window, poured over her. She had a faint sprinkling of freckles across her delicate upturned nose. He wanted to loosen the top two buttons of her blouse, just to catch a glimpse of the column of her throat. He wanted one night with her, but he wanted no moment rushed. "How much would please you, Miss Darling?"

She licked the lips that he had tasted and desperately wished to taste again. "We're talking about a contribution to the orphanage, aren't we?"

"Yes."

"It would come with no strings, no expectations of receiving anything in return?"

"It seems it should come with something. A smile, perhaps. What is a smile worth to you?"

Disappointment washed over her features, and he wondered how she could have possibly taken offense.

"It's wrong to place a price on things that should never carry a price," she said.

"Everything carries a price, Miss Darling. I would think that being raised as you were that you'd be aware of that."

"That's very presumptuous of you, Your Grace, to believe you know exactly how I was raised."

He swore beneath his breath. She was correct. He knew nothing about the reality of her life. "I've somehow managed to insult you."

"We come from very different worlds. Have you never given anything away simply for the joy of giving it away?"

"Ah, but you see, there is still the trade. You give away something and in return you gain joy."

"By that notion, seeing the smile should be its own reward and should require no payment."

"I can see you're too clever by half. All right then, I shall donate five hundred pounds to your cause."

"Thank you, Your Grace, and for that I shall most definitely smile."

And she did, a beautiful smile that lit up her entire face. He would have paid ten times that amount to keep it there, but he suspected money was not the key to her heart. His thoughts stumbled. It was not her heart he wanted. He wanted her curves, her flesh, her heat . . .

Before he could convince himself it would be unwise, he settled his mouth over hers, not at all surprised to discover that it fit exactly as he remembered. He'd dreamed about it often enough during the past two weeks. She tasted of lemon and sugar. He was willing to bet the previous Earl of Claybourne wasn't the only one with a penchant for keeping sweets handy. Moaning low, she opened her mouth fully to him and he suddenly wasn't thinking about anything except how wonderful it felt to once again have her in his arms.

She fit against him as no other woman ever had, as though she belonged. He cursed himself for not closing the door earlier.

As her arms wound around his neck and her fingernails scraped along his skull, need ripped through him with a blinding fierceness. He wanted to know the full measure of her passion.

Panting and breathless, she tore away from him. He wanted to yank her back, take her in his arms, and carry her to his coach. He wanted her in his bed. He wanted her slowly. The fire of passion burning in her eyes ignited the flames of desire within him. He'd sampled women in every country he'd visited, but he couldn't recall wanting one more than he yearned for her.

"Come with me." He barely recognized the low raspy voice as his own.

She shook her head quickly. "I can't. I have responsibilities here." She touched his chin as though she'd return for another kiss and just as abruptly dropped her hand to her side.

He cradled her cheek. "Apparently I unintentionally lied earlier. It appears I came for your answer, and it seems that I have it."

Her lips parted—

"Frannie?"

She jerked away at Swindler's voice. The inspector was standing in the doorway, flexing his hands. "We've got some chairs here, but we're not sure where they're supposed to go."

"I'll be there directly." They were words of dismissal, but Swindler stayed where he was. She turned her attention back to Sterling. "If you'll excuse me, I need to see to some things."

He didn't want to excuse her, but the polite words were leaving his mouth before he could stop them. "Yes, of course."

"Please feel free to look about at your leisure." How could she suddenly sound so damned calm? She took a step away, then glanced back. "Meet me in the garden in ten minutes. I'll have your answer then."

Sterling watched as she strolled out of the room in her plain dress, which for some reason didn't appear plain at all. She touched Swindler's arm. He looked down on her and something warm passed between them. Sterling flexed his fingers. At that moment, he thought he could bring the inspector down with a single punch. By God, he was feeling possessive in a way he never had before.

Then Swindler glared at Sterling, before following Frannie into the hallway. Sterling turned his attention to the garden and pressed his hand to the cool window, but it failed to ease the boiling in his blood. Only one thing would accomplish that: a night with Frannie Darling.

Ever since she'd ordered the furniture, Frannie had been envisioning where each piece would go, and now she looked at the plush bright yellow chair and couldn't remember if it was for the sitting area in the library or the offices for one of the staff. She simply couldn't think.

She'd seen in his eyes that he intended to kiss her, and rather than discourage him or move beyond his reach, she'd stayed exactly where she was and welcomed his mouth playing havoc with hers. Even now, she could still taste him, smell him, feel him . . .

She wanted to be with him in the garden, wanted things she could never have.

A throat cleared and she jerked her gaze over to Jim, who was waiting for her answer, and studying her as though he was searching for something else.

"The library," she said smartly, deciding she could always move it later if it wasn't where it belonged. "If you'll excuse me—"

He moved in front of her before she'd taken more than a couple of steps. She could see the worry and concern in his green eyes, but then he always looked at her as though he expected her to shatter at any moment. "He's not one of us," he said quietly.

"Neither is Catherine, yet she and Luke get along well enough."

"Because he's one of them."

She couldn't chastise him for saying exactly what she'd been thinking at the wedding. She knew he worried over her, they all did—but sometimes she wanted absolute freedom, although the one time she'd sought freedom had ended in disaster. In all likelihood, this situation with Greystone would end the same way: with regrets.

"Is it so obvious what Greystone wants, or did Jack give you a hint?" she asked.

The muscle in his jaw jerked and his cheeks flamed red. She thought of the animosity that she'd sensed between the two men.

"Have you spoken to Greystone?" she prodded again.

"I delivered a message."

"From Jack?"

"From both of us."

She loved them, she truly did, but they had to understand that she was a woman fully capable of making her own decisions. "And what, pray tell, was the message?"

"To stay away from you."

And he had stayed away until today. A suspicion niggled at the back of her mind. "What did you do to him?"

His jaw tightening, he slid his gaze over her head.

Dread mixed with anger and disappointment roiled through her stomach. "How badly did you hurt him?"

He brought his gaze back to her. She knew he'd never lie to her. "Not as badly as I could have, not as badly as I wanted to."

They came from such rough beginnings, but sometimes she grew weary of them.

"Do you trust me?" she asked.

"With my life."

"Then trust me to know how best to handle this matter."

"I just don't want you to get hurt."

She gave him a soft smile. "I don't want that either."

"He won't appreciate what you're doing here. One of the lads I'll be bringing you is serving three months in prison for stealing a crown. Hell of it is, he doesn't know the difference between a shilling and a crown. Those I work with think they're putting an end to crime when they arrest these children for petty offenses like stealing an apple. You should ask your duke how many apples he's stolen."

"He's not my duke, and why would you think he'd stolen?"

"Just ask him."

She pointed back toward the chair. "The library."

He nodded when she knew it was the very last thing he wanted to do. "Thank you. And thank you for caring, Jim."

She found Greystone in the garden, intently watching the gardeners working. She had the distinct impression that he wanted to offer them advice. Could men never leave well enough alone?

She came to stand beside him, but he was so engrossed in studying the gardeners digging up the soil that he didn't notice her, giving her an opportunity to observe him. His profile was sharp edges, dominated by an aquiline nose and a strong jaw, a sturdy chin. He had a tiny scar on his cheek. Strange. She hadn't remembered that from their first encounter, but then the glaring sunlight had been absent. Or was it a remnant of Jim's visit?

His eyelashes were dark, darker than his hair, and she wondered if his hair would eventually match their shade as he grew older. Or would it simply fade to silver, gray, or white? Silver, she decided. More distinguished. After all, he'd traveled the world. He would take his place in the House of Lords. He was a man who could make a difference if he put his mind to it. His determination was evident by the intensity with which he scrutinized so simple a task as digging dirt—to the exclusion of everything else.

"I don't believe those flowers will smell nearly as enticing as you," he said quietly.

Her heart hammered. How was it that he had such power over her without even touching her? "And here I didn't think you were aware of my presence."

Turning toward her slightly, he smiled. "I'm always aware of your nearness."

She wished she had more experience with flirtatious games. She needed to get them back on even ground. "Our little garden must pale when compared with all the exotic plants you saw during your travels."

"I find nothing more beautiful than an English garden . . . unless it is the woman standing within it."

The heat of pleasure warmed her cheeks, but she'd grown up in a world where every word, action, and deed was a ruse to gain something to which one wasn't entitled. "I fear I'm never impressed with false flattery, Your Grace."

"I'm saddened that you would think it false, that you're unaware of your own attractiveness. Let me assure you, Miss Darling, that I find you incredibly lovely." He leaned forward conspiratorially. "I'm not in the habit of kissing hags."

She bit back her laughter, fought not to be charmed, and knew that she blushed ever more deeply.

As though suddenly aware of the gardeners' proximity and ability to hear what they said, Greystone glanced around and brought them back to safer ground. "You have quite a bit of land here."

"I have need of it and plans for it," she said, much more comfortable discussing her good works than herself. "Shall we take a turn about the area?"

She wanted to get away from the gardeners, from anyone who might overhear what was certain to become a very personal conversation. He offered his arm. She wasn't at all surprised by the firmness and strength she felt in it when she placed her hand on his. His arms had drawn her up against him, and she had the fleeting thought she'd like for him to do so again.

As they began walking she said, "You're quite fit, Your Grace."

"I have scaled a mountain, Miss Darling."

"Truly?"

He grinned. "At the very least an extremely tall hill."

"I can't imagine the things you've seen."

"They were all quite remarkable. But again, not as remarkable as you."

The heat swarmed her face again and raced down her neck.

"You'll have to forgive me, Miss Darling, but I enjoy bringing that flush to your cheeks. I'd have not thought someone raised on the streets would blush so easily."

"It's been a good many years since I've been on the streets, and I was quite young when I left."

"But the street never leaves you completely, does it? That's what all this is about, isn't it?" He swept his arm in a wide circle to encompass all the land that now belonged to her.

She was impressed that he'd accurately read how terribly important her plans were. "You're quite right. The home for boys is only the beginning." She pointed to the west. "Over there I plan to build a dormitory for girls. As we acquire more orphans, we'll build an infirmary and a school. We'll be using rooms in the present building for those services now, but eventually we'll outgrow everything, which in a way is not how I wish it was. I wish there were no orphans. I wish there were no lost children."

"Why have you made them your cause?"

She wasn't certain if he was truly interested or simply striving to prolong their walk about the grounds. But if she'd learned anything it was to embrace opportunity when it presented itself, and if she could make one duke see things her way, she'd be one step closer to victory. After all, he would sit in the House of Lords, as would Luke. Her orphans would have at least two voices.

"I suppose it's because my most trusted friends are orphans. If not for Feagan, they'd have no doubt lived—and in all likelihood died—on the streets."

"Are you not an orphan then?"

How was she to answer that? Was it better to have been abandoned or to have a disreputable father? Why did she care what he thought of her or who her family might be? Perhaps because he could trace his ancestors back for generations. He'd known who his parents were and who their parents had been. Just as Luke had within his home portraits of those who had come before him, so she suspected Greystone did as well.

"Quite honestly I don't know if I was an orphan or stolen—that does happen, you know? Kidsmen stealing children because they think they'll suit whatever nefarious purpose they have in mind. Even Feagan, as good as he was at providing food and shelter, kept us because of what we could do for him.

"If you're not part of the streets, you can't comprehend how many lost children there are. Even some who aren't orphans have the most horrid parents. It's a world of filth and fear, and a child might do anything to escape it. They'll believe promises that are made never intending to be filled. They go to gaol, prison. They're transported to penal colonies. With my endeavors I can help change a child's path, and I can't help but believe that in many ways Britain will be better for it."

As usual, she'd become so impassioned with her vision that she was nearly breathless. They ceased walking, and he eased in front of her. She noticed that he'd done that before, faced her so he could look at her directly. She liked that, interpreted it as a sign that he had no qualms about looking a person in the eye when talking.

"It's quite admirable what you're doing."

"I'm not doing it for personal praise. I don't give a bloody damn if credit for my work goes to someone else. I care about only the children."

"And here I feared I was competing with some other man for your attention. Inspector Swindler perhaps."

"Jim and I are merely friends."

"I'm not certain he realizes that."

Of course he did. Didn't he? But Jim wasn't the reason she'd finally come to terms with the answer she had to give the duke.

"My answer is no . . . to your question. The one—"

"I can easily determine which question as it's the only one I've asked and you're the only one of whom I've asked it." He didn't seem angry, but she did detect deep disappointment in his voice. "You'll have to forgive me, Miss Darling, but I'm not certain how a night in my arms will steal away from you anything you wish to accomplish."

"A girl on the streets thinks nothing of lying with a man. I'm from the streets, but I like to think I'm no longer *on* them."

He bowed his head. "I insulted you with my offer."

"Strangely, no. I was quite flattered, but when I lie with a man, I want it to be because he wants me for more than one night."

"That could be arranged."

She couldn't explain why he charmed her or why she took such delight in his wicked banter. Even Luke, who had once proposed marriage to her, had never indicated that he actually desired her. Greystone desired her. He didn't love her.

Quite possibly he held no affection whatsoever for her. But he wanted her. To be wanted was something she'd never before experienced.

"You're quite charming, Your Grace, but in the end, I don't think we'd suit."

"If Claybourne wasn't striding toward us, I might try to convince you otherwise with another kiss—but as I insisted he marry Catherine after seeing them kiss, I suspect he might not be completely understanding regarding any passion that I couldn't keep tethered."

Whether he'd intended it or not, he'd confirmed that marriage would never be an option for them. He wanted her body but not her heart, and while she thought that she should have been insulted, she wasn't. She was a realist, not a dreamer, and she understood they came from disparate worlds.

He lifted her hand and placed a kiss on her fingers. "If you ever change your mind . . ."

His voice trailed off, the darkening of his blue eyes invitation enough, and she had the answer to something she'd once wondered. If she said no, he *would* ask again.

Chapter 7

Since Frannie had disappointed him with her answer, Sterling had decided to move on with his life and more important matters. It was the very reason that he was at tonight's ball, even though the Season was drawing to a close. He needed to look the selections over. He had to give the aristocracy credit. They had the right of it when it came to the marriage market. These little soirees were designed to display the latest crop of marriageable ladies.

Considering what he had to offer, he thought it only fair that he not aim too high. On the other hand, this woman would be the mother of his heir and his spare. And he might throw in another son for good measure. He despised the cousin who would inherit if Sterling didn't provide legitimate issue, so he needed a woman of good stock.

Standing near some fronds and watching the couples circling on the dance floor, he decided that choosing a homely girl would be a mistake.

They always looked so damned grateful. He needed someone who was secure in herself, perhaps even a bit in love with herself. It was imperative that she not be the sort who required love or who might fall in love with him. Loving him was a sure path to disaster.

Although he couldn't see her, Sterling was aware of the lady approaching him because her overwhelmingly tart fragrance arrived long before she did.

"Your Grace?"

Turning toward her voice, he smiled at his hostess. "Lady Chesney."

She smiled brightly. She was as round as her husband. No surprise there. Her household boasted the best cook in all of London. "I would be honored to introduce you to some ladies who are in need of dance partners."

"I appreciate the offer, but my feet are a bit rusty. I believe I'll just watch this evening."

"Oh, come, Your Grace. I remember how dashing you looked upon the dance floor. You can't have forgotten what seemed to have come so naturally to you."

"Lady Chesney, this is my first ball since returning to London. I prefer to ease back into the social life."

"But it is a *ball*, Your Grace. Lady Charlotte is

quite the accomplished dancer. I'm sure you'd be most comfortable swirling her—"

"I don't wish to dance," he ground out through clenched teeth, especially as he was unable to do so with any sort of grace these days.

Lady Chesney jerked her head back and widened her eyes considerably. *Damnation.* He bowed slightly. "My apologies, but I'm still mourning the loss of my father. It would be inappropriate for me to take pleasure in dancing."

"Of course, I am sorry. That was thoughtless of me."

"I'm sure some are even questioning my being here at all as it has been a little over a month since his passing, but" —he glanced around as though about to impart a secret and she leaned nearer in anticipation— "I am in want of a wife and I do not wish to wait until next Season to make my selection."

Her eyes sparkled with merriment. "Oh, you need not worry there. Men are forgiven for not taking mourning as seriously as women."

"I take it very seriously, but I have a duty to my title that my father would want me to honor."

"No one would dare question your dedication to duty. I'm certain once word gets around that you're seriously pursuing matrimony that you will have no trouble at all finding the perfect wife.

Now if you'll excuse me, I need to see to my other guests."

And begin spreading the rumor that he was looking for a wife, no doubt. Good. Since Catherine was honoring the mourning period, she'd be of little help to him, so he was going to have to rely on others. He needed a wife now.

His father, blast him, had been right. Seeing to his own pleasures and touring the continents had placed him in an awkward spot, but he couldn't regret one single moment.

He turned his attention back to the dance floor. He decided he would go with beautiful. After all, he would have to bed her. Confident. She would need strength for the future. Self-absorbed. Yes. Someone who would tell him to go to hell once the truth came to light and then get on with her life.

No guilt, then. He'd set her up in London and he'd retire to the country. He and his father had fought about that as well. "Your place will be in the House of Lords."

His place was in hell.

He caught sight of Lords Canton and Milner ambling toward him. He gave a brusque nod. He liked them both well enough, had gone to school with them, often played cards with them at Dodger's.

"Greystone, old boy," Canton drawled. "What's this I hear that you're actually *looking* for a wife?"

That didn't take Lady Chesney long to accomplish.

"You'll give the mamas cause to expect the same for the rest of us. You don't announce it, man," Milner said.

"The Season is almost over. I don't have much time. I thought being forthright would speed the process."

"But good God, Greystone, you're only eight and twenty. Far too young to be tied down with the same woman every night," Canton pointed out.

"If I learned anything at all during my travels, gentlemen, it was that life is precarious. I do not intend to let the dukedom fall to my blasted cousin."

"Hardly blame you there," Canton muttered. "Wilson Mabry is a cad."

"You're too generous by half with that assessment." Wilson Mabry personified the seven deadly sins.

The two gentlemen who had joined him turned their attention toward the dance area.

"My sister's not yet spoken for," Canton said quietly. "I'm sure my father wouldn't oppose your suit."

"I like your sister, Canton. Therefore, she's not on my list of considerations."

Canton jerked his head around and gave Sterling an odd, questioning look. Sterling shrugged. "I know myself better than any man and I have no doubt that I'm poor husband material. I suspect your sister will want at least affection—if not love—in her marriage. I'm unable to accommodate such whimsy. I'm in search of a wife who is content to see to her duty without complaining and will expect no more of me than I can give."

"Lady Annabelle Lawrence might suit you then," Milner offered. "From what I've heard she hasn't an affectionate bone in her body." He visibly shuddered. "Cold as ice, from what I understand. Wants a husband who won't interfere with her life."

"Which one is she?"

"There," Milner nodded toward the dance floor. "Dancing with Deerfield."

Sterling spotted the couple right off. Lady Annabelle had an air of entitlement about her. It might work in his favor after he had his heirs, but until then, life could very well be miserable. She was certainly beautiful, with her black hair—

A flash of red passed before his vision, and the attractive Annabelle was forgotten as he desperately searched the crowd . . .

He gave himself a mental shake. *She* wouldn't be here. Frannie Darling didn't move about in his circles—although on occasion he wandered through hers.

"Want an introduction?" Canton asked.

"Not at the moment, thank you. I'm going to step out for some fresh air."

As soon as he walked onto the terrace, he realized the foolishness of coming out here. It was always more difficult to make out things clearly in the dark. Carefully, he made his way over to the edge of the terrace. Closing his fingers around the railing, he took a deep breath.

Red hair. It hadn't even been as vibrant as hers. No one's was as vibrant as Frannie Darling's.

He could have any woman in London, yet she was the only one he wanted. She haunted not only his dreams, but every waking moment as well.

He'd come here tonight hoping to distract himself from this fierce need he had to see her, but with just one glimpse of red, she was again taking possession of every thought in his head. Strangely, when he thought of Miss Darling, it wasn't so much the pleasure he would derive from her but that he might give to her that occupied his thoughts. How he would use his hands and mouth to stir her passions, how he would cause desire to burn through her, how her voice would sound when she cried out his name.

This was insanity. If he could but see her one more time, kiss her once more, then perhaps he could move on with his life.

*   *   *

" 'ere! 'e's over 'ere!"

Frannie quickened her step, striving to keep up with the boy who'd grabbed her hand on the street and pulled her into the alleyway. She'd been almost finished making her nightly rounds at the rookeries, searching for children in need of what she had to offer when the lad had approached her.

"You the red angel what takes boys to a better place?" he'd asked, no doubt referring to the shade of her hair. She wore it loose and wild when she came to this area of London because she knew it distinguished her from others.

She'd been gratified to know that she was developing a reputation for helping the children. Thus far, she'd managed to take in only eight, but word was apparently spreading that she provided a safe haven. "I am. Do you want to come with me?"

"Nah, but Mick . . . I think 'e's dyin'."

As Frannie now knelt beside the child curled on his side, she feared his friend might be correct. He was battered and bruised, fevered and trembling.

"Can ye 'elp 'im?" his friend asked.

"Yes." Or at least William Graves could. How would the poor and indigent feel to know that the man who treated their ills and never asked for payment also served as a physician to the queen? Twisting around, Frannie grabbed the older boy's arm. "But I won't help him unless you come with me as well."

"Can't do that. Sykes'll kill me."

She wasn't surprised to discover that Sykes was his kidsman. Both lads fit his requirements: small and wiry. She also recognized his handiwork as exhibited on the hurt boy. "What did your friend do wrong?" she asked.

The lad shifted uncomfortably. "Didn't steal enough naps."

Handkerchiefs. The boy hadn't met his daily quota. Sykes had probably charged him with being lazy and had decided that nearly killing him would motivate the others. He placed no value on the lives of children. She suspected he placed no value on anyone's life save his own.

"I won't let Sykes harm you. I swear it."

Shaking his head, the boy wiggled out of her grip and was racing into the darkness before she could stop him. With extreme tenderness, she lifted the hurt boy into her arms. With Bill's help, she'd save him.

Then she'd return to the rookeries to search for more boys—in particular those who worked for Sykes. If she couldn't stop his brutality, she'd seek to move beyond his reach as many boys as possible.

*   *   *

During the week following the ball, Sterling had lost an unconscionable amount of money at the gaming tables, hoping to catch a glimpse of Miss Darling—with absolutely no luck at either spying her or winning back his stakes.

Tonight was no exception. Sterling had purchased his chips on credit. Dodger's was civilized in that regard. At the end of the month a statement of accounts owed would be sent out. Considering Jack Dodger's reputation, Sterling doubted anyone ever reneged on settling accounts, but if he did, Sterling wondered if Miss Darling would attempt to collect. As bookkeeper, perhaps she'd come around herself. It would provide him an opportunity to see her which sitting here attempting to make sense of his cards wasn't. His mind wasn't focused on playing as his dwindling stack of chips testified.

With his limited vision, he knew that she might well walk right past him and he'd not notice her until it was too late. Numerous times he'd considered attempting to access the offices, but he'd seen Dodger use a key often enough to know the door leading to them was always locked. He knew the apartment she had was accessible through stairs on the outside and had considered waiting for her in the alleyway, but she'd given him her answer. He should respect it and get on with his own matters.

But the fervor with which she'd spoken about

her orphans haunted him. Was there anything in life that he cared about so passionately? He cared for his title, to be sure. The estates were a source of pride. But nothing consumed him, not in the manner in which Frannie Darling was consumed with aiding orphans.

Sterling was accustomed to ladies discussing light-hearted matters such as dressmakers and hats. Miss Darling, he suspected, had no time or patience for such frivolity. She was passionate about everything that mattered to her.

He wanted to matter to her.

He'd continued to make his servants available to her each day until they reported that all the furniture had been arranged to her satisfaction. She'd sent him a polite note thanking him for lending her such fine workers.

He'd sent her five hundred pounds. She'd written him promising to put it to good use.

Each letter was precise, unemotional, indicating she'd moved on with her life—as should he.

He became aware of an unsettling sensation that he'd felt on more than one occasion. Glancing at his cards, he asked, "Are there peepholes at this place?"

"Good Lord," the Earl of Chesney muttered as he gave his cards another glance. "They're all over the place."

"Do they overlook this area?"

"Mmm. The curtained balconies above. From what I hear, only accessible from the back rooms, which are only accessible to Dodger."

And his bookkeeper.

Sterling lifted his gaze to a shadowed balcony in the far corner. How could he have not noticed it before? It was too far away, too shadowy to make out clearly, but somehow, he knew—

Frannie jerked back from the small opening she'd been peering through. Damnation, she was fairly certain he'd spotted her spying on him, because she'd felt his gaze as though he were standing in the balcony with her, trailing his finger along her throat.

Tonight he certainly looked sharp in his dark green jacket, black waistcoat, and soft gray trousers. Had he spent his evening in the company of a lady before coming here? She didn't like thinking of him being with someone other than her, which was rather silly on her part. He was a duke. Eventually he would *marry* someone other than her. All he wanted from her was one night. She had little doubt it would be a night filled with charming words and sensual touches and blistering kisses. It would be a night that might leave her longing for more. Was it better to have one night and forever wish for another or to always wonder what that one night might have been like?

She'd known so many of Feagan's lads, but not one had ever caused desire to curl within her. She'd thought when she gave Greystone her answer that she could walk away and never think about him again. Instead, she found herself wondering if she'd made a mistake.

If she had, would she find the courage to admit it not only to herself, but to him?

The gin palace was raucous, but as Feagan sat in a dark corner sipping his gin, he appreciated the rowdy and boisterous activities. He grew lonely in his quiet dwelling now that his children had left him, but he wasn't of a mind to try to replace them. Too much work involved in training them to be effective thieves. He managed quite well on his own to obtain what he needed to get by. His requirements for a good life were few: a bit of gin—rum when fortune smiled on him—good tobacco for his pipe, enough clothes to shelter his aching bones from the cold, warm stew on occasion, and a roof to keep out the rain. Yes, indeed, he considered himself a most fortunate man.

A huge hulking shadow blocked his view. He lifted his gaze. The only thing Feagan feared now stood before him. "Mr. Sykes, to what do I owe the pleasure?"

Sykes pulled out a chair, dropped into it, and

leaned forward. "You need to have a word with your gel. She's messing with my business."

"Frannie?"

"Aye. She's coming into the rookeries and taking my apprentices. You, yourself, know how much work is involved in training one."

Feagan sipped his gin. His Frannie had always had a kind heart. He suspected she'd been the reason that most of his lads had stayed with him, and the reason many had left after she did.

"I don't see 'ow I can 'elp ye. I ain't seen her since she left with that damned lord."

Sykes scoffed. "You know everything about everybody. You know where she be or how to get word to her. Tell her to leave my boys be. She can take as many of the others as she wants, but not mine."

Feagan wiped his roughened hand over his cracked lips. "I'll tell 'er."

"See that you do. I'd hate for anything unpleasant to happen to her."

Before Feagan could issue his own dire warning, the man was gone. Feagan peered into his glass. "Ah, Frannie, Frannie, Frannie. What kind of trouble are ye getting into now?"

Bringing the hood of her cloak up over her head, Frannie walked through the streets of her youth. It was early enough that revelers were still about, late enough that the prowlers and prostitutes were beginning to poke around. She wondered what Greystone would think of her if she brought him here, if she showed him exactly from whence she'd come.

"How about a quick bump in the alley?" a gentleman asked, blocking her way.

"No, thank you." Touching the hidden dagger for comfort, she shouldered her way by him.

"You're not from here," he said, moving to once again stop her.

"Actually I am."

"You sound like a lady of quality."

"I'm meeting a rather large fellow with big hands that are very good at squeezing things, such as your neck, so you might want to let me pass."

"Haven't seen him, but I'd be happy—"

"Ah, there he is. Excuse me." She hurried on, but the man didn't follow, nor was there any large fellow waiting to meet with her. The largest fellow she knew was Bob Sykes, and she certainly had no desire to cross paths with him.

Wending her way through the crowd, she stayed alert, always conscious of nimble fingers. She carried nothing of any value when she came to this part of London.

She felt bony—yet surprisingly strong—fingers

tug her into the alleyway. She had her knife half-way out of its scabbard when she recognized her abductor. "Feagan."

" 'ello, Frannie darling."

"You startled me. What are you doing here?"

"I got something fer ye." He dragged a small, spindly lad forward. "Master Charley Byerly."

She hadn't seen Feagan in years. Seventeen, to be precise. His hair was no longer the vibrant red of hers. His face was more wrinkled. Somehow she'd expected him to always remain the same. She darted her gaze between the two. She despised that she didn't trust Feagan. His looks may have changed, but she was fairly certain that his character was carved in stone, never to be altered. "How did you know I was in search of orphan boys?"

"I 'ear things."

Frannie crouched in front of the lad. "Hello, Charley. I'm Frannie. I'm going to give you a home."

"Don't need no home."

Feagan slapped the boy's head. "Wot I'd tell ye, boy? Mind yer manners."

The boy gave Feagan a mulish look.

"Have you a mother or a father?" she asked.

"I wouldn't 'ave brought 'im to ye if 'e did," Feagan protested.

"Charley?" Frannie prodded.

"Got nobody. Don't need nobody."

Frannie took the lad's hand. She didn't want to stay in this area any longer than necessary. "What do I owe you, Feagan?"

"Awe, Frannie darling, why would ye go and spoil our reunion like that. Why think I'd expect anything at all?"

"Because with you there is always an expected payment in some form. You are not charitable by nature."

"Blimey, but ye've turned into a hard lass."

She reached into a hidden pocket. "I have only a crown."

"Ew, that'll do just fine, thank ye very much."

She dropped the coin into his outstretched hand.

"Spend it wisely, Feagan."

"I always do."

As she turned to go, he grabbed her arm and whispered, "Sykes come to see me. Ye gotta leave his boys alone."

"I take boys where I find them. I don't ask who they answer to."

"Frannie darling, ye'd be a fool to mess with Sykes. He's done nuthin' but grow meaner over the years. Leave his boys be."

Even in the darkness of the alley, she could see

the worry in his eyes, eyes as green as hers. Leaning over, she pressed a kiss to his forehead. "I'll not provoke him on purpose."

He gave her a crooked grin. "Good gel."

But as she walked away, Charley Byerly in tow, she also swore to herself that she wouldn't *not* take a boy in simply because he was unfortunate enough to have an association with Sykes.

Chapter 8

Sterling had mistakenly believed—since the last ball of the Season had been held and many of his peers had already escaped to the country—that the Great Exhibition would be far less crowded. Throughout the summer he'd heard all about the astonishing number of people who'd visited the wondrous exhibits. But with his diminishing vision, he didn't do well in crowds, so he'd waited until he'd determined a more favorable environ would be awaiting him. He'd judged dreadfully wrong.

But he possessed a stubborn streak, and once he'd arrived and seen the crowds lined up to enter the Crystal Palace, he wasn't about to tell his driver to return him home. It was one thing not to confront the enemy and another entirely to retreat once the confrontation was made. His vision was not yet to the point that he would give in, turn tail, and run.

Therefore, face the crowds he did. So far, all had gone amazingly well as long as he strolled slowly through the corridors, which fortunately were immense. If he did bump into anyone, he apologized with the excuse of being enthralled by the marvels before him.

Even he, who had seen the Taj Mahal, was fascinated by the glass and metal structure that contained exhibits representing cultures from all over the world. For him, it was far grander than anything it housed. British ingenuity at its finest.

As Sterling glanced around, trying to determine in which direction he should go, he decided it was an absolutely marvelous time to be alive. Within this massive building, even the common man was given a glimpse of the world beyond England's shores. As he strolled casually along, he enjoyed watching the people's amazement as much as he enjoyed viewing the exhibits.

He felt the ruffling of his jacket, wondered who he'd run into now, and turned. No one was in close enough proximity to have brushed against him, although he did spy an urchin running away. Sterling slipped his hand in his pocket and discovered it empty. "You there! Thief! Hold!"

But the boy kept running. Sterling dashed after him. It was only a handkerchief, for God's sake. It wasn't as though he didn't have a dozen or so—but it was the principle of the thing. "Stop him! You there! Thief!"

Most people glanced around as though confused. Those who caught the gist of it found themselves grabbing at air as the boy effectively evaded capture.

Ah, he was fast, the little bugger, like a little monkey. If Sterling hadn't been traipsing over continents, often lugging a heavy rifle or from time to time some crucial supply, he might have found himself winded as he tore after the irritating thief. Unfortunately, the boy could do what Sterling couldn't—dart in and around people effectively, while often Sterling misjudged their nearness and clipped them or heard startled gasps as he got too close and they jerked back. In the back of his mind, he realized the pursuit was probably futile, but he was determined not to let the crafty criminal escape. The boy needed to be taught a lesson.

Remarkably, Sterling somehow managed to gain ground and catch up with the thief just as he was taking a sharp turn around a dark skirt. Anger spurring him on, Sterling reached down and grabbed the boy by the scruff of his collar, closing his hand effectively around his jacket and hauling him up.

"Lemme go! Lemme go!"

"You little thief. I'm going to haul your bony hide to gaol." Turning abruptly, Sterling found himself staring into the gorgeous green eyes that frequented his dreams.

"Your Grace," Miss Darling said, smiling softly, obviously as pleased by his appearance as he was by hers.

"Miss Darling." The boy was struggling against Sterling's hold, but he couldn't twist around to inflict any damage to his captor. Sterling was tempted to release the little devil, simply so he could take Miss Darling's hand to kiss it and give her a proper gentlemanly greeting. How ironic that he'd spent so many nights at Dodger's hoping for a glimpse of her and he'd crossed paths with her here.

"What's Charley done now?" she asked.

Sterling looked at the boy, took a careful glance around, and realized three other lads similar in size to the squawking one he held were gathered near her skirts. "He's yours?"

She nodded, frustration and perhaps a sense of embarrassment evident in her expression. "What did you do, Charley Byerly?"

"Nuffin'."

But he stopped fighting and hung his head as though all strength had been drained from him.

"What did you do, Charley?" Miss Darling repeated. "If His Grace has to tell me, then you shall spend the rest of the afternoon in the carriage with Mr. Donner."

"Caw. Blimey. Not 'im."

"Charley."

Her voice was so stern, so filled with disappointment, that Sterling was on the verge of confessing something himself, anything to see her smile return.

"Snatched a wipe," Charley grumbled.

She held out her hand.

"Everything all right over here?" a deep voice asked.

Quick to turn his head around, Sterling caught sight of the constable standing there. With so many other people walking about it was easy to miss his footsteps. Just the person he'd been searching for a few minutes ago. But he would suffice just as well now to take this troublemaker off Sterling's hands, haul him to gaol, and see that he was punished for his transgressions.

"Yes, Constable, everything is fine," Sterling said. "Just one of the lads getting a bit more rambunctious than he should with all these exhibits around. But I have him well in hand now."

Not what he'd planned to say, but he'd decided at the last second it was what he needed to say in order to stay in Miss Darling's good graces, which was where he dearly wanted to belong.

"Very good then." With authority, the constable strode away.

Sterling turned his attention back to Miss Darling. Gratitude shone in her eyes, but he didn't want gratitude. He wanted passion, fire, desire.

"Your arm must be getting tired. I'm certain you can put him down now," she said.

"I'm much stronger than I look, Miss Darling."

" 'n' quick, too," Charley muttered.

"Is he likely to run off if I release him?" Sterling asked.

"No. You won't will you, Charley? I should be terribly disappointed if you did."

Charley shook his head. To Sterling's surprise, he didn't take off when his feet landed on the floor. Miss Darling held out her hand again. "Give it over, Charley."

He brought out what had once been a crisply ironed handkerchief and was now a wrinkled, balled bit of cloth. Sterling hoped he'd have no reason to need it before he returned home.

Miss Darling seemed to recognize his disgust with the object because she said, "I shall wash and press it before having it returned to you."

"I believe that's acceptable." He studied the boys brushing up against her skirts. One towheaded lad, two with hair as black as coal, and the brown-haired imp who'd picked his pocket. "Are these your children, then?"

"Yes, from my orphanage. I've been bringing a few when I have time in hopes of giving them all a chance to at least see some of the exhibits. We were about to have our lunch, before I lost sight of Charley. I'm grateful to you for herding him back toward me." She glanced around as though about to ask him to steal the Koh-i-noor diamond, which was on exhibit. "We're going to enjoy a small picnic. I feel I owe you because of the trouble with Charley. Would you care to join us?"

He gave a low bow. "Miss Darling, I would be truly delighted."

Sitting on the blanket she'd placed over the grass, Frannie could hardly believe that Greystone had accepted her invitation and was lounging beside her, stretched out on his side. He'd loosened the buttons on his beige jacket to reveal his pale yellow waistcoat. His green cravat went so perfectly with his weathered complexion.

Mr. Donner, the driver of Luke's carriage, and the footman were keeping an eye on the boys as they ran around the park, working off some excess energy. She knew it was difficult for them to be on such good behavior within the confines of the Exhibition. They were only newly off the street and accustomed to scampering about London with no adult supervision, far too old for their years.

"I must apologize again. I'm terribly sorry that Charley took your handkerchief."

Greystone nibbled on a bit of cheese. "I'm not. Do you have any idea how much money I've gambled away at Dodger's, hoping to catch a glimpse of you?"

"Five thousand pounds."

His eyes widened and she gave him a teasing smile. "I am, after all, the bookkeeper."

His deep laughter echoed between them, circling around her, and capturing her as effectively as if he'd used his arms.

He grew serious, his blue gaze holding hers of green. "So, now I'm intrigued, Miss Darling. You must have some interest in me; otherwise why remember how much money I've handed over?"

"I've never claimed not to have interest in you, Your Grace. As a matter of fact, considering our encounters, I believe it fair to state that I've undoubtedly expressed an interest in you."

He rose up on his elbow and leaned nearer to her. "Tell me, Miss Darling, have you been spying on me while I've been at Dodger's?"

She wanted to cradle his face between her hands and kiss him. Was it proper for a lady to initiate such an action? Would he think her wanton or would he welcome her as she had welcomed him? She swallowed hard. "Why ever would you think that?"

He trailed his bare finger along the palm of her hand as a fortune teller might and then up to the pulse at her wrist. She wondered if he could feel her heart picking up its tempo.

"Sometimes, it's as though I can feel you watching me," he said quietly.

Dragging in a breath was suddenly very difficult, as though she'd laced her corset too tightly. "I was simply curious, wondering whether you'd returned to Dodger's after the unfortunate incident of your membership being terminated. Nothing more."

Lifting her hand, he pressed a kiss to the center of her palm. "I would have thought a child of the streets would have been an excellent liar."

Normally, she was when she could concentrate. The man was decidedly skilled at distracting her. "It's not very gentlemanly to call a woman a liar to her face."

He ran his tongue over her skin, as though she were part of the meal. "You strike me as someone who wouldn't care to be talked about behind her back, would prefer the slight come from the front."

She thought she might burst into flames. To get herself back on an even keel, she worked her hand free of his hold, heard his dark laughter, and watched as the boys ran past, chortling with wild abandon. She'd done that. Brought back their joy. She had the means to do so because of things she'd suffered.

"You're not being a gentleman," she chided.

"Did you truly want me to be?" He sat up until his shoulder was almost touching hers. "Was that what you wanted when you watched me through the peephole?"

"It wasn't a peephole. It was through curtains."

"From a hidden balcony?"

"Not so very hidden if you know about it. We use it to watch cheaters and troublemakers."

"Which category do I fall into?"

As hard as it was, she met his gaze, surprised to find that he appeared amused. "Are you teasing me?"

Leaning across her, he plucked a small yellow flower and brushed the petals along her chin. "I'm flattered that you would think me worth watching. I now have hope that perhaps you're reconsidering my proposition."

She took the flower before he drove her mad with wanting, as she imagined his fingers creating the gentle stroking. "I'm not reconsidering your proposition."

"Pity."

But he didn't sound disappointed. Rather he sounded as though he didn't believe her. She remembered a time when she could lie with the best of them. Were her skills suddenly lacking, or was he simply very good at reading her? He draped a wrist over an upturned knee. "So, the carriage? Yours?"

A change in topic was most welcomed. "Claybourne's. He loans it to me whenever I have a need. I don't use it enough to invest in one . . . and then of course there's the matter of the horses."

"Do you not like horses?"

"I don't like paying for their care. I'd rather put the money toward children."

"You should have some of your own."

She laughed, working to ignore the disappointment she'd felt for years now. It was silly, because she knew one of Feagan's lads would be happy to provide her with children. But she desired more. She wanted a family built on love, surrounded by it. "I believe I'm well past the age when a man would consider me for marriage." The boys loped by again, playing some game that seemed to involve one of them trying to tag the others. "Besides, London has enough children. I mentioned the school to you before, but I want to do more than teach them to read and write. I want to give them the skills to find good employment. Poverty brings us all down." She shook her head. "My apologies. I vehemently believe social reform is needed. I fear I get a bit impassioned and carry on about my plans, which can't possibly interest you."

"Everything about you interests me, Miss Darling."

"I should warn you that I'm not a woman easily enticed by words. I prefer action."

His eyes darkened, and she realized she'd used a poor choice of expression when he said in a low sensual voice, "I'm in total agreement. Perhaps later—"

"You are a lord, Your Grace, and I am a commoner. I'm not even certain friendship between us is allowed."

"You're friends with Claybourne."

"That's different. He was once one of us. You don't turn away those to whom you owe so very much."

"It seems then that I must find a way for you to owe me . . . *so very much.*"

Frannie had expected them to part ways after their luncheon, but he stayed with her, helping her corral the boys when they became impatient with the pace of things. He had patience with the lads that she'd not expected.

When they got to the exhibit of a stuffed elephant, Greystone crouched in front of the boys and told them that he'd ridden a real one. Their eyes popped and their mouths dropped.

"Were you scared?" Charley asked.

"Not in the least. He's a large beast, but you see in the jungle, it's not always the largest beast that's the most dangerous. It's the one who is the craftiest, the most intelligent. The one most cunning."

"Which 'un would that be?"

Greystone grinned. "Why, me of course."

The boys guffawed, and Frannie laughed. When he unfolded his body and extended his arm, she didn't hesitate to entwine her arm around his. "So you were the most dangerous beast in the jungle?"

"Indeed. Didn't hurt that I also carried a rifle."

As they strolled along, she asked, "Were you really not frightened?"

"Sometimes I was terrified, but that was the whole point."

"You wanted to be afraid?" She couldn't imagine deliberately putting herself in a position of fear.

"I wanted to test my courage, my determination. It was a journey of discovery, but it was more about what I discovered within myself. What I discovered about the world was simply a bonus."

"And *what* did you discover—about yourself, I mean?"

"That I'm not nearly as weak as I thought, nor nearly as strong as I'd hoped. I rode the elephant but shied away from facing the tiger."

He sounded disappointed in himself.

"Which proved you were indeed the most intelligent, and thus, the most dangerous beast in the jungle."

He grinned. "I don't suppose I ever thought of it exactly in those terms. I suppose it would have been silly to end up as his dinner."

She smiled at him. "I'm glad you didn't."

"As am I, Miss Darling. Otherwise I'd have missed out on these moments with you."

When they strolled through the exhibits from Egypt, he told them about the pyramids and the sphinxes. His voice held excitement as he recounted his memories of his travels. She was fascinated with all he'd seen, all he'd done.

"You've had quite an intriguing life, Your Grace," she said as they left the Great Exhibition and she ushered the boys to where Mr. Donner waited with the carriage.

"Is there any point in having any other kind?" he asked.

"I'd always heard you were a man who saw to his own pleasures first."

"It's good to know the gossips are sometimes accurate. And speaking of my own pleasures . . . while the picnic was terribly lovely, I fear it doesn't quite make amends for the little scoundrel stealing my handkerchief."

They'd arrived at the carriage. While the boys scrambled inside, Frannie faced Greystone, surprised to discover that she was anticipating what she was certain would be another inappropriate proposal. "And what, pray tell, Your Grace, would make amends for the taking of a bit of silk?"

"The opera."

"Pardon?"

"Attend the opera with me this evening. We'll have dinner afterward. Otherwise, I might have to send a constable around to your orphanage to arrest Mr. Charley Byerly."

"You wouldn't."

He shrugged. "Are you willing to risk that you've properly ascertained the nature of my character?"

"And here I was beginning to like you." She spun on her heel—

"I'll send my coach 'round to Dodger's at seven."

Oh, the unheralded arrogance of the man. With her hand in the footman's and her foot on the step, she glanced over her shoulder. "Half past seven."

He gave her a victorious smile that left her almost giddy with anticipation. As she settled back against the plush seat, she couldn't remember the last time she'd felt so joyous.

"Why ye grinnin' loike a fool, Miss Frannie?" Charley asked.

Because she was discovering that she enjoyed having a man's attentions. Especially when they came from the Duke of Greystone.

Chapter 9

Her clothing was simple enough that she didn't normally require the services of a maid. But for tonight Frannie had sought the help of one of Jack's girls.

Sitting in a chair holding the silver-backed looking glass—a gift from Luke—she watched as Prudence worked to tame Frannie's wild red hair. Pulling it back into a tight bun simply wasn't what she wanted tonight.

Frannie had no misconceptions regarding where this encounter would lead: to absolutely nowhere. He was after all a duke, while she was quite simply . . . Frannie Darling. But she couldn't deny an attraction existed between them that she'd never before experienced with any other man. And the way he looked at her—as though he'd gobble her up if he could—had once frightened her, but now she rather liked it. She enjoyed listening to his stories, was fascinated with his kind regard toward the boys, was charmed by the devil that danced in his eyes whenever he touched her in ways they both knew he shouldn't. The picnic had been one of the most sensual experiences of her life, and all he'd done was give attention to her palm. She wanted it everywhere.

It was liberating to find herself craving a man's attentions. Even if things between them went no further than a kiss, for the first time she wanted a man sharing the intimacies of her life. How odd that she'd grown up surrounded by Feagan's lads yet never felt this deep, womanly stirring. Their laughter, their teasing, their gazes incited none of the riotous emotions that Greystone's did. Even when he wasn't touching her, it felt as though he were. She didn't understand why he was so different from every other man in her life, why she yearned for his attention.

Every dress Frannie had ever purchased was done with one goal in mind: to make her appear common. She was comfortable in those clothes. But blast her soul to perdition, tonight she didn't want to appear common.

A year earlier, Jack—who loved bright, bold colors—had purchased her an emerald-green gown. Once, in the privacy of her room, she'd even put it on and waltzed around, pretending that she was what she had no hope of ever being: a lady of true quality. So she knew it followed every curve perfectly. She grew warm imagining Greystone's large hands and slender fingers following every line.

"So who is the gent who's caught your fancy?" Prudence asked.

Startled from her fantasy—when had Frannie ever fantasized about men?—she hesitated to answer because she didn't want to hear Prudence say, "Oh, I know 'im. 'e's ever so good in bed. 'ad 'im just last week, as a matter of fact."

"Come on, gel, yer secret's safe with me."

Frannie lowered the mirror to her lap and traced her fingers over the intricate design along its back. "Greystone."

"Dunno him."

Relief swamped her. Prudence oversaw all the girls. If she didn't know him it was unlikely that he'd availed himself of any of the other girls either.

"'e a customer?"

"He's a customer, yes." Frannie spun around in the chair and looked up at Prudence. "Don't say anything to Jack."

Prudence pouted with full lips that had probably kissed several hundred gents. "Already told ye I wouldn't."

With a nod, Frannie turned back around. "I know you did. It's just that it needed emphasizing. Jack wouldn't approve."

"'e must be titled then. Jack don't loike the titled gents."

Frannie didn't know why she felt compelled to confess, "He's a duke."

"Blimey."

Shooting out of the chair, Frannie began to pace agitatedly. She felt as though she was on the verge of coming out of her skin. "God, Pru, am I making a dreadful mistake here?"

"Depends what yer expecting. It's like I tell my girls. 'e won't marry ye, ye know."

She took a deep breath, trying to calm the erratic beating of her heart. "I know."

Leaning against the vanity, she studied Prudence. She was two years younger than Frannie, but her face revealed the harshness of the life she'd lived before she came to Dodger's. Her blond hair trailed down her back, and she always wore silk that flowed around her and could easily slide down her body with a shrug of her shoulders. "Have you ever been with a man who didn't pay you?"

"Yeah."

"Did you feel dirty afterward?"

Prudence threw her head back and released the deep, throaty laughter for which she was so well known. "Caw, no. It was bloody marvelous. 'e got transported, ye know? To Australia. Sometimes I dream 'e'll come back fer me. A gel's gotta 'ave 'er dreams." Scrutinizing Frannie, she patted the brush against her palm. "Need some hints on how not to get knapped?"

Releasing a self-conscious laugh at the notion of taking this . . . whatever it was . . . to a point where she might get with child, Frannie shook her head before giving a quick nod. Feagan had often taught them things that he'd told them they probably would never use, but knowledge gave them advantages if they got in a tight spot. "I probably won't need any preventives, but I spend an awful lot of time thinking about him and wondering what it might be like if he did more than kiss me."

Prudence grinned. "Kissed ye, 'as 'e?"

Feeling as though she were suddenly ten years younger, carefree with never a worry, Frannie had an insane urge to giggle as she'd once seen a young girl with a beau behave as they'd walked down a street arm in arm, lost in each other. Silly, really, to experience this giddiness at her age. "Don't you dare tell Jack."

"Wouldn't dream of it." Prudence slapped the back of the chair. "Sit down, let me finish with yer hair and I'll tell ye wot I know."

What she knew, unfortunately, usually involved the cooperation of the man. Frannie couldn't imagine discussing such intimate matters with

Greystone, and if she couldn't discuss them, she probably shouldn't be *doing* them with him.

So why, then, had she gone to so much bother? Her hair looked quite lovely pinned up with green ribbons woven through it. Where Prudence had obtained the ribbons, Frannie had no idea, but they matched the emerald green of the gown Jack had purchased for her. It left a good bit of her shoulders exposed. She was torn. Would it entice Greystone into trailing his fine mouth over her skin? Did she want him to? Cursing herself as a coward, she drew on a silk shawl. She tugged on the white kidskin gloves Luke's grandfather had given her years ago. She felt as though she needed something else, but what?

Then she remembered a gift Feagan had given her the day she and the others had said their good-byes, when they'd moved into Claybourne's London residence, leaving Feagan behind. She'd not wanted to go, but he'd insisted. "Ye'll 'ave a better life, Frannie darling, and 'ave I not taught ye that ye always go for the big purse, not the small one?"

Opening a small carved wooden box, she carefully removed a strand of pearls. "A little gift to remember me by."

Other than the clothes on her back, it was the only thing she'd brought with her from the rookeries. Her clothes had been burned later that night after the filth of the rookeries had been scrubbed from her body. She'd never worn the pearls before, because she was afraid they'd been stolen and someone might recognize them, but as far as she could tell, they possessed no identifying marks to distinguish them from any other strands she'd ever seen. Tonight she was quivering with nervousness and needed a bit of Feagan with her.

"Yer as good as anyone," he'd once told her.

With a deep breath, she tucked the sentiment away into the corner of her mind where she kept precious memories.

It had grown dark by the time she grabbed a small reticule, left her apartment, and locked the door.

Frannie had not been this terrified or this excited since the day that she, Luke, and Jack sneaked out of Feagan's at dawn to go to a fair. He'd have not minded if they'd told him what they'd planned. He'd have assumed they were going to pilfer pockets. But the night before, when counting the coins, she'd pocketed a crown for them so they could take pleasure in the day without worry of getting arrested. Rather than stealing, they'd purchased food to eat. As much as she'd enjoyed the day, it had been tainted with worry, because she'd been afraid Feagan would discover that a coin was missing and be sorely disappointed in her. It was one thing to steal from strangers, another entirely to steal from him.

It was how she felt now. Excited to be going, terrified that she would disappoint the lads if they discovered her plans, for surely they wouldn't approve when they knew as well as she that nothing lasting would come of this encounter. She was a bit of sport for a lord of the realm, and while he might treat her as though she were a lady in the beginning, at the end she'd be nothing more than a memory, if that.

She was halfway down the stairs when she spied Greystone, limned by the gas lamp that hung outside the back door of Dodger's. The alleyway wasn't brightly lit in this area, but it provided enough light that she could recognize his silhouette. The breadth of his shoulders, the narrowness of his hips gave him away. His outline alone was elegant.

What was she doing going anywhere with this man?

"Miss Darling." He gave her a low bow before extending his hand upward to assist her in descending the last few steps. Slipping her hand into his, she felt his long, strong fingers wrap around hers and her heart gave a little patter. Thank goodness, they both wore gloves. She was still on the steps, her eyes level with his, when he said in a low, sensuous voice, "You look beautiful."

"Anyone can appear beautiful in the shadows."

Why did she sound breathless, as though she'd raced down the stairs?

His grin flashed white in the dim light of the alley, as though he understood she was so nervous she might expire on the spot. "My coach awaits."

She took the last step and would have walked on but his hold on her hand stayed her. She lifted her gaze to his.

"Relax, Miss Darling. Tonight it is merely the opera and dinner."

"I'm well aware of that. I had no plans for anything more."

This time his grin seemed to be calling her a liar, but she didn't challenge him. Although she had mixed feelings about the condom Prudence had given her, the one she'd tucked in her reticule . . . just in case.

She didn't know whether to be relieved or disappointed that it would not be used.

Once they were in the coach, sitting opposite each other as they traveled through the London streets, his gaze never wavered from hers, and to her disappointment, she was the first to look away. Whenever he watched her, she grew uncomfortably warm. She'd never experienced this inexplicable change in her body around any of Feagan's lads, even when they were all younger and slept on the same pallet. This awareness of the male allure had never visited her as it did now whenever she was in Greystone's presence.

It was intriguing and terrifying. To distract them both from where this journey might lead, she said, "Did you know that Luke asked me to marry him? It was how he and Catherine came to know each other. She was supposed to teach me how to be an aristocratic lady."

"I wasn't aware of that. So how is it that you didn't marry Claybourne?"

"I'm well aware that I do not belong with the aristocracy."

"Yet here you are with an aristocrat."

"You and I both know, Your Grace, that marriage is not what you have in mind."

His eyes darkened as his gaze traveled from her upswept hair to the toes of her recently polished shoes. "No. Marriage is not what I have in mind."

Of its own accord, her head gave a little bob. She wasn't exactly sure what she was acknowledging. She knew only that she wasn't offended by his candor. Rather she was quite relieved by it. She preferred knowing exactly what she was getting herself into.

Yet even with his acknowledgement she feared she truly had no clue.

Chapter 10

That Sterling had been able to walk straight to the coach, without stumbling, after having the breath knocked out of him at the sight of Frannie descending the stairs was a miracle. Only on his way home, after he'd issued his invitation, had it occurred to him that she might not possess anything appropriate to wear to the theater. He'd been debating having Catherine send a gown over to her—they were near the same size—but that carried with it the danger of Claybourne discovering their little tryst, which might then result in Sterling acquiring another black eye. He'd decided that no matter what she wore, he would be delighted to have her on his arm.

Instead, he'd arrived to discover that she was stunningly beautiful. Fortunately, he had an oil lamp in the coach so he could feast his eyes on her as they journeyed through the London streets. She'd grown quiet after he'd confirmed that marriage was not in the offering, and although he wanted her in his bed, he wanted her there as honestly as possible. He'd never used false promises to lure a lady into his arms, and he wasn't about to start with Frannie. She deserved that much consideration at least. In truth, she deserved a great deal more.

"The way you're staring, I'd think you've never seen a woman dressed in an evening gown," she finally said.

"I'm not staring. I'm admiring. I've never seen you dressed so provocatively. Why didn't you wear that gown to my sister's wedding?"

"It was her day, nothing should detract from her. Besides, it's a bit bold for such an occasion."

"I like bold in a woman."

She laughed lightly, an amazing sound that was far lovelier than the most skilled orchestra he'd ever heard perform. "You should watch your words, Your Grace. I shall take them to heart."

"I should like that, Miss Darling."

"You seem to be flirting with me, Your Grace, but I don't think you should lose sight of the fact that I'm with you tonight only because of your threat to have one of my orphans arrested."

"I only *seem* to be flirting? Then I must put forth greater effort so I leave no doubt."

"I'd rather you didn't. Put forth more effort, I mean."

"You do realize that a good many women would be flattered to have a duke escort them to the opera."

"Perhaps you should have invited one of them."

"None of them intrigue me as you do, Miss Darling."

"We both know the infatuation will be short-lived."

"On the contrary, I know men who have had the same lover for years."

She gazed out the window, giving him the opportunity to study her profile and the elegant sweep of her neck. He wanted to cross over and sit beside her, kiss his way from her shoulder to the sensitive spot just behind her ear, feel the rapid flutter of her heart against his lips as he neared his destination, but he feared if he went too fast, took too much too soon, that he'd be in danger of losing his ultimate reward, that she would seek to evade him as quickly as Charley Byerly had.

Besides, strangely, he wanted to sit through the opera with her, wanted to enjoy dinner. He yearned to have her in his bed, without question, but he longed for a good deal more. He wanted, with her, memories he'd never sought with any other woman.

"Why do you suppose women do that?" she

asked quietly. "Settle for being a lover instead of a wife?"

"Because sometimes it's the only way to have someone in your life, when circumstances dictate marriage be based on something other than love."

Slowly, she brought her gaze back to bear on him. "Have you ever loved a woman?"

"I suppose you're referring to something other than the brotherly love I feel for Catherine." It was now his turn to gaze out the window. "Once. I thought I did. But my affection for her turned so swiftly to dislike that I'm no longer certain."

"What happened?"

"I told her the truth."

"About what?"

He gave his attention back to her. "About me, Miss Darling. In spite of my rank and wealth, I shall make an unsatisfactory husband. So consider yourself fortunate that there is no hope for a marriage between us."

Her brow pleated. "What is your failing?"

"Miss Darling, I have every intention of seducing you, and I have enough skill at seduction to know that revealing my failings is not the way to go."

"I suppose I should be forthright and reveal that I have no intention of being seduced."

"I so enjoy a challenge, Miss Darling."

"I shall keep that in mind, Your Grace."

"Are you nervous about coming to my residence later for dinner?" he asked.

She shook her head, met his gaze. "No."

"I'm not sure I've ever met a woman who meets my gaze as often as you do."

"A man's eyes can tell you a great deal. If he is quick to anger, if he's the vengeful sort. If he's proud. The proud ones are the best for fleecing."

"I'd have thought they'd be the worst."

"They don't usually report that they've had their pockets picked. They fear it will make them appear the fool. So they simply replace whatever it is you took."

"You say that with a certain amount of pride, as though you believe stealing is honorable."

"I can't deny that I've always taken a certain satisfaction in being so very skilled at what I did. I was the only one of Feagan's brood not to see a stint in prison."

"Your eyes, no doubt. I suspect even if you'd been caught you could have persuaded a judge to let you go."

"I've been told they're my finest physical attribute."

"Told? Surely you own a mirror."

"I don't often gaze into it, and certainly I don't linger there."

Fascinating. He'd never known a woman who didn't take up residence in front of a looking glass. "Why have you an aversion to gazing in the mirror?"

"Because within a mirror I can't avoid looking into my own eyes. The life I've lived is reflected in my eyes and there are parts of it that I wish to forget."

"Yet, it has made you the fascinating woman you are."

And he was fascinated with every aspect of her. Perhaps he would prolong the moment of taking her to his bed simply so he could have more moments like these, but even as he thought through that strategy, he knew he wanted her too desperately to wait for very long before having her.

The coach rolled to a stop in front of the Royal Italian Opera. When he'd left England, it was the Covent Garden Theater. It seemed nothing remained the same. The footman opened the door, Sterling stepped out, then handed Miss Darling down.

"Have you ever attended the opera?" he asked as he offered her his arm.

"The previous Earl of Claybourne brought me once. I thought it was quite amazing, the costumes, the performers, and their singing was not to be believed."

"I'm glad to hear that." He led her into the lobby, wondering why he hadn't remembered what a crush it was as people waited to take their seats. He regretted that for a while he would have to concentrate on his surroundings rather than her. "I abhor the opera."

She stopped walking, forcing him to do the same. With any luck they could stand there until most people had gone in search of their seats.

"Then why did we come?" she asked.

"Because it was the only thing I could think of that I thought you might possibly agree to."

He couldn't tell if she was flattered or incensed.

"Luke's grandfather couldn't stand it either. We left halfway through the performance. I've half a mind to make you sit through it all," she said, a saucy grin falling into place.

"If it would please you, I shall accept my punishment without complaint and even applaud when it is over, although I must confess that having you near will make it bearable."

"You're well practiced when it comes to flattering a lady."

"I must admit that I excel at the gentlemanly art. However, do not make the mistake of thinking that I don't mean the words I speak."

"You must want what you . . . want very much to sit through opera."

"Quite honestly, Miss Darling, taking the picnic this afternoon with you was the most enjoyable time I've had since returning to England. I wished only to extend it, so here we are."

He had no idea if his words pleased her, because something just beyond them caught her attention and she smiled. He turned in the direction and saw Marcus Langdon—Claybourne's cousin and once heir to the title—bearing down on them with Lady Charlotte Somner, daughter to the Earl of Millbank, at his side. The man favored Claybourne very little. Sterling suspected it had to do with him having a childhood of ease, while Claybourne had grown up in the criminal world.

With his silver eyes reflecting as much merriment as his smile, Marcus Langdon approached and bowed low. "Your Grace."

"Mr. Langdon. Lady Charlotte."

Lady Charlotte beamed up at him. "Your Grace."

"And Miss Darling." Mr. Langdon took Miss Darling's hand and brought it up for a kiss. "What a pleasure to see you both here." He turned toward the lady at his side. "Lady Charlotte, allow me to introduce Miss Frannie Darling."

Lady Charlotte didn't acknowledge the introduction. Rather, she gave her full attention to Sterling, her smile growing brighter. "Your Grace, I can't tell you how lovely it is to see you here. You must join us for dinner some evening and regale us with tales of your travels."

Langdon appeared flummoxed by his lady's rude behavior. "Lady Charlotte, you're familiar with my cousin, the Earl of Claybourne. Miss Darling is one of his dearest friends."

"So, she's one of those people, is she?"

Before Sterling could champion the lady at his side, she said, "And which people are those, Lady Charlotte? Those who care about the poor and indigent of our society? Those who see the criminal justice system as anything except just?"

"Those who carry the dirt of the streets on their skirts. If you'll excuse me, I need to visit the ladies' toilette. Standing here has made me feel dreadfully unclean." With that, she spun on her heel and marched away.

"Oh, my goodness," Langdon stammered. "My sincerest apologies, Miss Darling, Your Grace, I had no idea—"

Miss Darling touched his arm. "Don't concern yourself, Mr. Langdon. It's unfortunate that some have a very low opinion of me, but I assure you I don't lose sleep over it."

"But still, my cousin—"

"Shan't hear of this incident from me."

He nodded, seemingly relieved, and Sterling

realized he might have had concerns about dealing with Claybourne's wrath. Having suffered through a visit from Dodger and Swindler, Sterling hardly blamed him.

"You're most gracious, Miss Darling," Langdon said.

"I'm nothing of the sort. You can't be held responsible for another's actions. Enjoy the opera."

"You as well." He nodded at Sterling. "Your Grace."

Then he walked away to find the rather unpleasant Lady Charlotte, who, Sterling thought, would find herself falling out of favor with Mr. Langdon. A pity for her, as Sterling had heard the rumors that Langdon was now employed by his cousin at a very advantageous salary.

"Do you get that often?" Sterling asked quietly, turning his attention back to Miss Darling.

"No. Because I stay away from the aristocracy as much as possible."

"We don't all behave as abominably."

"Not all, no. But a good many. May we find our seats now?"

"Would you rather leave?"

"Absolutely not. I may be bloodied, but I can still carry a sword."

"You're quite remarkable, Miss Darling. I'm quite honored to be with you tonight." Extending his arm, he welcomed the feel of hers entwined with his.

"We'll see how you feel tomorrow, when rumors have had a chance to spread."

"You're quite the cynic when it comes to the aristocracy."

"No, simply a realist."

Her words jarred him. Had he not said the same to Catherine?

He escorted her toward the stairs, grateful to realize that with her on one side of him, navigating the other was not nearly as difficult. "At my sister's wedding, when your friends circled around you, that's what they were seeking to protect you from, the unkind regard of others in attendance."

After they'd found their way to his box and taken their seats, she said, "When I was much younger and lived in Claybourne's residence, Luke's grandfather arranged an afternoon tea in the garden with a few of the girls my age. They arrived in coaches and carriages and they were so beautiful. Their laughter was soft and sweet, so very different from the harsh laugher in the rookeries. I thought, 'Oh my goodness, I'm going to be like them.'

"They hurt me that day without touching me. They taught me that words can slice like a knife. They wanted to know about life in the rookeries, and I made the mistake of telling them that I slept with Luke and Jack and Jim. And sometimes at night, I still slept with Luke. They made it into something ugly. It was really rather innocent. To lie in the circle of someone's arms while you sleep can be very, very nice. But I never slept with them again. Never told them why. Those girls took that from me. And I let them."

While she recited the facts without emotion, still he knew she must have experienced a world of hurt. She possessed a kindness that went beyond anything he'd ever experienced before. He couldn't imagine her intentionally bringing harm to another person. He was ashamed to admit that he knew several acquaintances would see her as a bit of sport.

"Tell me who they are and I shall see that matters are put to right," he told her.

She gave him a whimsical smile. "It was long ago, Your Grace. And I do not hold a grudge. Although I must admit that sometimes, I miss having someone to sleep with."

Reaching out, Sterling trailed his gloved finger along her bare arm. "We could remedy that. Tonight if you like."

"I suspect, Your Grace, that you want to do a good deal more than sleep."

"You should take it as a compliment, Miss Dar-

ling. Since returning to England, I've not propositioned one lady."

"On the surface, admirable." She gave him an
impish grin. "But then I suspect you don't consider all women ladies."

"Very few, in fact."

The lights were doused, and Sterling cursed
the darkness. Even the lights that illuminated the
stage did not push back the shadows in his box. He
couldn't clearly see Miss Darling. He could only
smell the sweetness of her, memorize the shape of
her silhouette, and become increasingly aware of
the warmth of her body so near to his.

Leaning near her, he whispered, "Rest assured,
I do consider you a lady."

"One you wish to bed."

Tugging off his glove, he skimmed his finger
along the shoulder exposed when her shawl
fell slightly. "That is not an insult. I'm very
particular."

He was near enough that he heard her swallow,
before she said in a low voice, "As am I, Your
Grace."

Stilling his caress, he sat back. She wasn't going
to come to him easily. Fortunately, he enjoyed a
challenge.

Chapter 11

Halfway through the opera, Frannie decided to be merciful and suggested that they leave. She wanted to avoid the press of people, and she wasn't able to truly enjoy the performances, as she was well aware of Greystone watching her rather than the performers. She wasn't bothered by his perusal. Truth be told, she was quite flattered that he seemed unable to take his eyes off her, but she was finding it difficult to relax, wondering where dinner might lead.

When the coach pulled into the wide circular drive, she caught her first glimpse of Greystone's residence. She'd always thought Claybourne's house was magnificent, but this was monstrously large and unbelievably elegant. The coach door clicked open and Greystone gracefully exited before extending his hand to her. Shoring up her resolve, she placed her hand in his and allowed him to help her out of the coach. Glancing around at the grandeur, her hand on his arm, she followed him up the wide sweeping steps, with the sudden realization that Catherine had once lived here. She and Catherine were friends now, so in a way it was like being invited into a friend's home.

A friend who had a very charming and dangerous brother.

Inside, as he escorted her through the hallways, she fought not to gawk at the portraits, but she could see him in the faces of so many of his ancestors. How wonderful it must be to know from whom he came, while for her she knew nothing more than that she existed. Someone—she had no idea whom—had given birth to her. Had she been married? A servant? A lady? Had someone loved her? Or was it as Frannie feared: was she the result of a violent encounter her mother hadn't wanted, and so neither had she desired the child?

Greystone led her into a small room that seemed out of place in such a large residence. It contained thickly padded chairs and a sofa. Near the fireplace where a fire lazily crackled was a small lace-covered round table. The flames from strategically placed candles flickered, casting most of the room in shadows except for the area where they would dine. The draperies were drawn open to reveal a lantern-lit garden. In the corner of the room, a man stood silently holding a violin. Her heart gave a little flutter. She wasn't exactly sure what she'd expected. Dinner formally served in a large dining room, the way she'd eaten every night when she lived at Claybourne's. She'd certainly never expected anything with such romantic overtones. She knew Greystone wanted her in his bed, but this hinted at something more than a hasty mating.

She gave a little jump when Greystone's fingers skimmed over her shoulder, as he slowly removed her wrap. He must have given some signal, because the soft strains of the violin began to float through the room.

"Easy, Miss Darling," he whispered near her ear, coming from behind her, "we're going to share only dinner."

Nodding, she turned to face him. All his preparations made her more nervous because she feared she'd vastly misjudged exactly what he had in mind for her. If he romanced her, would she be able to walk away from his bed without feeling an immense loss? "You went to a great deal of trouble."

"I went to none at all." He gave her a devilish grin. "My servants, however, did. I take it you approve of their efforts?"

"It's all exceedingly lovely."

"I'm pleased that you're pleased." Lifting her hand, he began to peel off her glove.

"I can do that," she said, breathlessly.

"I'd rather, if you've no objections."

She shook her head, the pulse at her wrist jumping as his warm fingers trailed over her bare skin. She hadn't even noticed him removing his gloves. It seemed he might be as light-fingered as she was. While she was not yet regretting her decision to join him tonight, she was well aware that he could be more dangerous than any of the men she might encounter on the street when she went in search of orphans.

When her hand was bared, he placed a light kiss on her fingertips before turning his attention to her other glove. She imagined him doing the same if he removed her clothing, kissing every spot that was revealed.

When he'd removed both gloves, he laid them on her wrap, led her to the table, and pulled out the chair for her, selecting the one that provided her with a view of the garden.

"The music is a nice touch," she said as she took her seat, striving for nonchalance and fearing that she'd failed miserably. For him, she wanted to be sophisticated.

"I'm not fond of silence. In the jungles it's a signal that danger is near." He gave a nod and suddenly wine was being poured and food was being served.

"What's a jungle truly like?" she asked.

"It's hot. A lot of trees, plants, vines, monkeys tittering, insects chirping. Then suddenly everything goes quiet and you know a predator is near."

"Were you terrified?"

"Invigorated, actually. It was challenging. Physically and mentally. We had guides, of course, but Lord Wexford—with whom I was traveling—and I would sometimes strike out on our own. Nearly got killed a time or two. Even that was thrilling."

"You were thrilled by the possibility of being killed?"

"Sounds silly, I know, even reckless. My father wouldn't have approved, but it was as though we were reduced to our most elemental struggle to survive. Victory was intoxicating."

"Did you truly ride an elephant?"

"I did. And a camel, which was ghastly jarring. I thought I was going to lose all my teeth."

She laughed. "I can't even begin to imagine how different it all must have been from what we have here."

"I have some sketches of my travels that I can share with you after dinner if you like."

She was vaguely aware of a servant refilling her wineglass, her plate being removed, another brought in.

"You're an artist, then," she said, as she sampled the beef.

"Amateur, I assure you. Wexford is somewhat of a photographer, but he had a bit of difficulty getting creatures in the wild to remain still. He *was* able to get some rather nice landscapes. Now enough about me, Miss Darling." He watched her over the rim of his wineglass as he took a long swallow. "I'm much more interested in hearing about you."

"I fear after all your exciting travels, you'd find me boring."

"I can honestly say that I've never been as intrigued by any woman as I am by you. The rapscallions who were with you today, Mr. Byerly in particular, had a bit of the devil in them. How did they come to be in your care?"

"If a child is arrested and Jim believes he can be turned about, he'll bring him to me. The four today have seen the inside of a gaol. I want them to know life is more than the rookeries."

He slowly stroked the back of her hand with his thumb. It was comforting, mesmerizing as she gazed into his serious blue eyes. "I must admit to having an interest in children who are being led into criminal activity. They're the most vulnerable. If they're caught, their punishments can be severe, even when their crimes are hardly worth bothering with." She remembered what Jim had insinuated. "May I ask you, Your Grace, have you ever stolen an apple?"

His thumb continued its leisurely motions as he studied her while taking another sip of his wine. He nodded. "Yes. What of it?"

"Didn't you think it was wrong?"

"I believe I was eight at the time and . . . it was a game." His last words were delivered more quietly as though he'd come to a sudden realization. "Your criminal children believe they're playing a game."

"For the most part, yes. When a child is very young, what he is taught is the way he assumes it's supposed to be. The purpose of a pocket is to hold items that are to be picked. The grocer's stall is set up for amusement. Take an apple and see if the grocer can catch you—it's a game he wants to play. If you have no one telling you that what you're doing is wrong, how are you to know?"

"If it doesn't belong to you—"

"The children have no possessions. They don't understand ownership. When they're caught, they're sent to prison or even transported for stealing an apple or some trifling trinket the value of which is not even sixpence. Their punishments are often severe. The state of affairs where children are concerned is unconscionable. I was brought up in that world. Fortunately, my kidsman was not one who beat children. But he did teach us to steal and he used us to put coins in his pockets." She shook her head. "It's difficult when you love someone whom you know on some level is wicked."

He skimmed his knuckles along her cheek. "I've effectively ruined what was supposed to be a pleasant evening."

"No, it's I who have ruined things. The children are my passion, and I get carried away when I speak of them."

His face grew incredibly serious. "It is your very passion that intrigues me so much. May we take a turn about the garden before I return you home?"

He'd meant it, then. Opera and dinner only. She should have felt relieved. Instead, she feared he was luring her toward his bed by not flagrantly inviting her to it. But not tonight. Tonight she was safe. "May I see your drawings first?"

Sterling ordered the table cleared away, sent the violinist on his way, and retrieved his sketches and two snifters of brandy. He'd never before offered brandy to a woman, but Frannie Darling took it without objection. He imagined she drank from time to time. After all, she worked in an establishment where spirits were sold in abundance.

They sat on the small sofa. His seduction was not turning out exactly as he'd expected. He'd thought to have her in his arms by now, but he couldn't deny that he couldn't recall an evening he'd enjoyed more.

"A lion," he said as she studied the first sketch.

"I can see that. He appears so . . . regal."

It pleased him that she saw what he'd attempted to capture: the essence of the beast. "It's little wonder he's called the king of the jungle. When he roars, my God. It doesn't matter where you are, a chill races down your spine. And to see him—there is an immense amount of pride about him."

"I thought the same of you when I first saw you at the wedding reception." She peered at him, a slight flush on her face. "You carry yourself with a great deal of confidence that Luke is only just now beginning to exhibit. You don't question the deference owed to you."

"Not to me, to my title."

"But you are the title now, are you not?"

He gave a short nod of acquiescence. He'd never questioned that he'd one day hold the title, but now he wondered if she would be more amenable to his holding her if he weren't titled.

"You know who your family is," she said, "from whom you come through the generations. You must appreciate the legacy that's been handed to you. For me, it's as though there were no one before me."

He couldn't imagine not knowing his ancestry.

How empty would it feel to believe you'd sprung forth from nothing?

"There must be a Darling family to whom you might belong. Your inspector could surely make inquiries."

Her self-deprecating laughter touched his heart. She was enticingly without guile or arrogance. "No. I have absolutely no idea of my true name. I was simply called Frannie darling, as an endearment, and I thought Frannie Darling must be my name. It's quite easy for people to move about London, take a different name, and begin over. When Feagan took in a child, he always changed the child's name in an effort to protect him, to give him a new start."

Placing his arm on the back of the sofa, he trailed his finger along the creamy skin of her bare shoulder. Now he had an inkling of what treasures those drab clothes of hers hid. "So you know nothing at all about your ancestry?"

"Nothing. I don't know if it's a blessing or a curse. Luke is the son of nobility. Jim's father was hanged. We know only that Jack's mother sold him. So were my parents upstanding citizens and was I stolen? Or were they the dregs of society? I don't know."

Had he been considering anything permanent with her—which he wasn't, but if he had been—

her words would have caused him to reconsider. It was the nature of the nobility to wed the nobility, to wed those with whom a person shared a common heritage, along with an understanding and appreciation for one's place. He didn't necessarily consider himself better, but he stood on the shoulders of those who'd come before him, and their deeds assured him special privileges and required of him certain duties and behavior. Expectations were never in short supply.

"Do you want to know?" he asked.

"I suppose it depends on the answer."

"Which answer would you prefer?"

"I'm not really sure. Both leave a lot to be desired." As though she wished to leave the subject of her past behind, she returned her attention to the sketch pad and turned the page to reveal a small monkey.

Discussion of his travels had suddenly become incredibly boring. He wanted to continue to discuss *her*, because he wanted to know every aspect of her life. But more than that, he wanted to see her smile again, so he accepted her wish to steer the conversation onto safer and less exciting ground. "This little fellow adopted us, sat on my shoulder from time to time."

"You're very skilled at capturing images."

He'd always been observant of the world

around him, had always enjoyed sketching what he saw. He assumed that his pastime was one of the reasons he'd begun to notice a shift in his world. It came upon him gradually, but eventually he became aware that the scope of what he was seeing was diminishing.

"I've always enjoyed drawing." He skimmed his finger along her collarbone. "I should think I'd find a great deal of pleasure in drawing you."

"I'm not certain I'd fancy posing for a portrait."

"Perhaps I can convince you otherwise, during my quest to convince you of *other* things." He circled his hand around her neck. Her green eyes widened slightly before narrowing provocatively. He'd promised to behave this evening, but he asked the impossible of himself. He'd judged her lacking in innocence, but now and then he caught glimpses of it: in her smile, in a hesitant flirtation. She was a combination of survival and goodness, daring and inventing her own rules when those that existed didn't suit her. With his thumb, he stroked the soft underside of her chin, felt her pulse quicken. "I would like to amend our plans for the evening."

"Oh?"

She sounded breathless and her pulse tripled its rhythm. Fear didn't enter her eyes, but anticipation did, encouraging him to continue. "The opera, dinner . . . and a kiss."

She gave an almost imperceptible nod. Any other man might have missed it, but he was accustomed to scrutinizing the world around him, to hoarding the tiniest bits and pieces of it for the day when it would all be lost to him.

He'd intended to go gently, but her enticing gown had caused provocative images to flit through his mind for most of the evening, so when his mouth settled over hers, it was with purpose. It was strange, the way his own heart sped up when she welcomed him. During his travels, he must have taken a thousand women into his arms, or at the very least a hundred. Exotic women. Women of every country on which he'd set foot, yet he'd wanted none of them with the ferocity that he desired this one. As he swept his tongue through her mouth, he thought no one had ever tasted as sweet, no one had ever been as hot. Easing away from her lips, he tasted her throat, heard her moan, was aware of her head dropping back to give him easier access. He nibbled his way to her ear. "I want to let your hair down."

"Yes," came out on a sigh as though she could already feel the silken strands tumbling around her shoulders.

And they were like silk against his fingers as he searched for the pins that held her hair in place. Someone had gone to a great deal of bother with the ribbons, but even those he was able to work free and toss to the floor. Her hair began to fall and he gathered it in his hand, before leaning back and draping it over one shoulder. It pooled in her lap.

"Gorgeous," he whispered.

"It's unruly."

He grinned. "I like unruly."

Hungrily, he returned his mouth to hers. He knew she wasn't innocent. God knew, she couldn't work in a place like Dodger's and remain innocent, but sometimes there was a hesitancy in her movements as though she wondered if the stroke of her tongue over his teeth was allowed, if he would object to her exploring his mouth as he did hers. He almost told her that he would find fault with nothing she did, but he didn't want to break the spell of the moment. Bringing his hand up, he cradled her breast in his palm, relishing the weight of it. He skimmed his thumb over her nipple, felt it pearl in reaction to his touch. He wanted to feel it gliding across his tongue. He licked and kissed his way along her throat, dipped his tongue into the hollow at its base, before journeying farther down, slipping his finger into her bodice and lowering it, giving his mouth access to her creamy breast and her pale pink nipple.

Gasping, she dropped her head back, lost in bliss.

With practiced ease he turned her slightly and laid her back on the sofa as he knelt on the floor, then cursed himself because he wanted nothing with her to be what he'd done with a hundred others before. He wanted nothing to come easily. She was different, his Frannie Darling, in ways he couldn't comprehend but wanted to explore at his leisure.

Cradling his face, she brought his mouth to hers and kissed him deeply, almost greedily. She'd put up so much resistance that he'd begun to doubt that she wanted him with the fervor that he desired her—but it was there: the passion, the desperation, the *need* to be touched.

He broke off from the kiss and nipped at her chin before giving his full attention to her one exposed breast. "Perfection," he whispered on a heated breath before he closed his mouth over it.

She turned into him, her fingers clutching his shoulders. She was as untamed as the animals he'd observed in the wilds. She was not a proper miss. She held nothing back as she ran her hands into his hair, along his chest, beneath his waistcoat, as though she wished to touch all of him and was frustrated that so little of his flesh was available to her. But he knew if he began removing his clothes he'd be unable to stop. He'd break his promise. He'd take her here and now and damn the consequences. Unconvinced that she wanted the full measure of what he could give her, he reached down, slid his hand beneath her skirt, and skimmed his fingers up her leg.

She jerked and whimpered when he reached his destination: the honeyed center of her womanhood.

"Shh, shh," he cooed as he rained kisses over her face. She was so wet, so hot, so ready to take what he couldn't yet give without remorse. Never before had he hesitated with a woman, never before had he questioned his actions, never before had he wanted a woman to initiate what he would gladly finish. She was lost in passion, fevered with desire, and he wanted her to have no regrets, wanted it to go no further than she expected.

She clung to him, writhing against him as he used his fingers and mouth to heighten her pleasure. As her back arched, she gasped and he blanketed her mouth with his, swallowing her cry of pleasure, acutely aware of her heated body throbbing against his fingers, pulling from him a deep groan of satisfaction.

He'd never given pleasure without receiving in kind, but tonight it seemed imperative that he not take complete possession, even though it left him with an almost unbearable ache. Drawing back, he saw the wonder and tears in her eyes. She averted her face.

"Don't turn away from me," he pleaded.

"You said only a kiss."

Cradling her face and turning her back toward him, he gave her a wry grin. "I fear I got carried away with wanting to bring you pleasure."

She squeezed her eyes and a tear rolled down her cheek. Leaning in, he gathered it up with a kiss.

"It's nothing to cry over, sweetheart."

"I never . . . I didn't know." Her voice was rough, as though her throat was clogged with tears.

Astounded, he asked, "Has no one ever brought you pleasure before?"

She gave her head a quick shake. He shifted his gaze to where he'd raised her skirts, to her slender legs . . .

She was a virgin? How could that be? She worked in Dodger's.

As a bookkeeper, not a whore, you stupid clod.

"What about you?" she asked softly.

He dragged his gaze back to her eyes. "Pardon?"

"You're not . . . you didn't." Her cheeks burned a bright scarlet, obliterating her freckles.

"No, I didn't, but I promised to take no more than a kiss. Tonight it is a promise I'll keep." Bringing her hand to his lips, he pressed a kiss to her fingertips. Little wonder the others were so protective of her.

* * *

Inside the coach, he held her as though he was loath to let her go. Frannie hadn't expected that. But then there was little about him that did meet her expectations.

"I want to see you again," Greystone said quietly.

"I'm not certain that's wise. We are of different worlds, Your Grace. In yours, I am but one night and in mine you are destined to be merely a memory."

"I should think after everything we've shared that you could call me Sterling."

As much as it hurt, she said, "We are not equal."

They traveled the remainder of the journey in silence, which confirmed that she had the right of it. No matter what feelings might begin to blossom between them, their places in society, as determined by their birth, would always serve to separate them.

Once they arrived, he walked her up the stairs to her flat.

"Thank you for sharing the evening with me, Miss Darling. Your little hellion is now quite safe from being arrested."

She took her key from her reticule and unlocked her door. Glancing over her shoulder at him, she said, "Quite honestly, Your Grace, I suspect he was always safe from that fate."

Before he could confirm or deny the truth of her words, she slipped inside and closed the door behind her. It was long moments before she heard his tread on the stairs, very long moments when she almost opened the door and invited him in.

He'd given her an extraordinary gift tonight. Her feelings toward him had deepened. If anything more had happened, she wasn't certain how she would have managed to close the door on him.

As she prepared for bed, her skin felt more sensitive. Before she got into bed, she reached into the pocket of the dress she'd been wearing at the Great Exhibition and removed the handkerchief that she still needed to wash and iron. She crawled into bed, turned out the lamp, and rolled to her side, pressing the handkerchief against her nose, inhaling Greystone's scent. It was no doubt the closest she'd ever come to being with him through the night.

Sadly, as comforting as it was, it wasn't enough.

Chapter 12

"**Y**our Grace, how splendid of you to visit," Lord Millbank said as he strolled into the parlor where Sterling was waiting to be announced.

"My lord."

"I say, I've been wanting to catch up with you to hear about your travels. Please, have a seat, make yourself comfortable, and tell me everything. I have a servant fetching tea—"

"I fear this isn't a social call."

Millbank brushed what little hair he had back over his balding pate. "No?"

"No. I attended the opera last night."

"Ghastly business that. I do believe it was designed by women to torment men."

"Be that as it may, your daughter was also in attendance."

"Which one?" He narrowed his eyes as though he didn't quite trust Sterling to know his daughters.

"Lady Charlotte."

"Ah, yes, she was no doubt there with Mr. Marcus Langdon. I do believe he fancies her, but if you have an interest" —he winked— "she should be back any time from making her morning calls. Her mother would be most delighted to accompany you as you take Charlotte on a turn about the garden."

"My interest in your daughter stems only from the fact that she insulted the lady on my arm, which is no different from insulting me. I do not take kindly to insults."

His eyes widened. "Of course not. I don't know what Charlotte was thinking."

"Please inform her that should our paths cross again, she is not to approach me."

He bobbed his head. "I'll have a word with her. Yes, thank you."

"Good day, Millbank."

He'd taken three steps toward the door before Millbank asked, "Might I inquire as to who the lady was?"

Sterling didn't stop or look back as he said, "All that matters is that she is *my* lady."

Which—he mused later in his coach as he traveled back to his residence—were rather bold words, considering that Frannie had indicated he wasn't to call on her again. He would have to do what he could to change her opinion on that matter, because he fully intended to finish what he'd only begun last night.

When he arrived home, he was surprised to find Catherine and her husband awaiting him in the library. He could tell by their stern expressions they hadn't come to make a social call. Unfortunately for Sterling, Claybourne had taken up a post near the window with his arms crossed over his chest, as though he were there to provide support for Catherine regarding whatever matter she'd come to address. She stood in front of his desk. In her usual style, she got straight to the heart of things.

"Sterling, I've heard a rumor that you were seen accompanying Frannie to the opera last night."

Taking the chair behind his desk in a negligent pose as though he couldn't be bothered, Sterling looked at Catherine, which meant losing sight of Claybourne. Damnation. Without repositioning himself he couldn't keep both within his sight, and distancing himself so he could properly see them would seem odd. He was fairly certain that his father had never told his sister about the condition that his father had deemed "an embarrassment and disgrace on the family heritage," as though Sterling had purposely taken measures to diminish his vision. He was like a horse wearing blinders. Why would he wish that disadvantage upon himself?

"Shouldn't you be in the country by now?"

"The estate manor was involved in a fire. Until the repairs are completed, we're staying in London."

"Ah, that's right." He turned his head to the side to give Claybourne a raised brow. "Avendale died in that fire, as I recall. What I can't understand is the reason he would visit you in the first place. It was no secret that he did not believe you were the true heir to the Claybourne title, and advocated for it to be given to Marcus Langdon."

"We're not here to discuss Avendale," Claybourne said. "We're here because of the rumor regarding Frannie."

Sterling glared at him, then gave his attention back to his sister with an impatient roll of the eyes. "This rumor—did it come from someone reliable?"

She pursed her lips. "Lady Charlotte."

He should have known. *Making her morning calls, indeed.* In spite of the late hour, Sterling should have visited Millbank immediately after he'd delivered Frannie to her door.

"I do hope you don't consider that rather unpleasant woman your friend."

"Is it true then? Whisperings are going about that she's your mistress, because you were there with her without benefit of a chaperone."

Damnation. He didn't like hearing that, although truth be told, he suspected the rumor had more to do with their disparate places in society than the lack of a chaperone. He would have to find a way to stifle the rumors. He wanted her, but not at a cost that embarrassed her or ruined her reputation. But he wasn't about to admit that to Catherine or her husband.

"It's my understanding that she's near thirty, the arbitrary year, as far as I can tell, when a chaperone is no longer required."

He could see that he had her there. It was a silly bit of etiquette, but there it was.

"But Sterling, you're only twenty and eight."

"Are you implying I'm the one in want of a chaperone?"

"Don't be obtuse. You're younger than she is."

"I don't see that my youth is of any significance."

"Men don't generally look to older women with matrimony in mind. Hence, further fodder for the gossipmongers."

Another bit of silliness. He was well aware that men tended to take an interest in women younger than themselves, but it wasn't the law. Hearing the clinking of glass, he jerked his head around to where his liquor cabinet stood. Claybourne was standing there pouring whiskey into two tumblers. "Do feel free to make yourself at home."

Claybourne prowled over to the desk, very much reminding Sterling of a panther he'd once witnessed taking position right before it struck its prey. Holding one glass, Claybourne set the other in front of Sterling and sat on the edge of the desk. "Drink up. You may have need of it."

Sterling might not have been hardened by the streets, but he'd had some harrowing experiences during his travels and come close to death a time or two. They tended to make a man develop a keen understanding of his limits and a profound respect for his strengths.

"Did you slip in some poison? I assure you the threat is quite unnecessary. I've already received warnings from Dodger and Swindler."

Claybourne tapped his glass against Sterling's— which he had yet to touch—and downed the whiskey. Sterling could see both his sister and his brother-in-law now. Catherine looked as though she was tempted to interfere. What she did instead was turn her back on him and walk beyond his field of vision, which worked well because Sterling wanted to concentrate on Claybourne. Marrying Catherine didn't make him immediately trustworthy.

Claybourne leaned forward, his forearm pressed against his thigh. "Did you ever wonder why I killed the Earl of Claybourne's second son—a man I didn't realize at the time was my uncle and now refuse to openly acknowledge as such?"

There it was. Confirmation for what most of

London believed to be true, but as the man had never actually endured a trial and been convicted, in some corners of London, doubts lingered. Did anyone want to welcome a murderer into the ranks of the aristocracy?

"I assume a dead man's possessions are easier to pluck."

"He brutally raped Frannie."

The words couldn't have been delivered with more force if they'd been accompanied by a swift kick to his gut. What little vision remained to Sterling threatened to blacken completely.

"She was twelve," Claybourne went on, his voice flat, but the fury still simmering just beneath the surface. "Sold to a house of ill repute, one known for specializing in virgins. He was her first. As far as I know, her only. So yes, the four of us circle around her the way one might an injured butterfly, never touching it for fear of damaging it more, forever hoping that a day will come when it will again fly. If you harm her, in any manner, no matter how slight, you will answer to us. And while Graves might not have stopped by to issue a warning, don't underestimate him. With that scalpel of his, he could slice out your heart and you'd never feel it."

Sterling repeated to Claybourne what he'd told Dodger and Swindler. "It's never been my intent to hurt her."

Claybourne nodded. "Sometimes we harm without intending to. So be forewarned. She is more precious to us than the Crown Jewels are to the queen."

Claybourne got up and began striding from the room.

"Claybourne!" Sterling called out, rising to his feet as Claybourne stopped in his tracks and faced him. "In my world travels, I saw a good many varieties of butterflies. They're incredibly delicate creatures, but they shouldn't be underestimated. Observing them as I did, I learned a valuable lesson. Sometimes if you surround a butterfly too closely, it couldn't fly if it wanted to."

Claybourne studied him for a moment as though searching for a compelling argument. Eventually he gave a brusque nod and turned his attention to the side, to await his wife, Sterling realized, who had approached Sterling. The room was large enough and Claybourne had walked far enough away that he'd be unable to hear whatever the brother and sister said to each other.

"She's not of the nobility, Sterling."

"I'm well aware of that, Catherine. You needn't worry. I have very strict requirements when it comes to a wife, and Miss Darling doesn't suit." For his own sake. He didn't want to see the disappointment in her lovely green eyes, as he'd seen in Angelina's when the truth of Sterling's situation came out. No, he needed a wife for whom he wouldn't care if she went on her merry way.

"I just don't want to see you—or her—get hurt. Frannie" —she glanced back at her husband briefly— "Claybourne first asked for her hand in marriage. She refused him. One of her reasons being that she had no desire to be part and parcel of the aristocracy."

Sterling narrowed his eyes. "Do not ever think for one moment that he *settled* for you, Catherine. It's obvious he adores you."

She bestowed on him a radiant smile, reached out, and squeezed his arm. "I'm well aware of that, Sterling. I just felt the need to share with you what I knew. While you might not be considering her for a wife, I know that sometimes feelings can overcome all rational thought. I think the world of Frannie, but I also truly believe that if you pursue anything other than a platonic relationship with her you may both be miserable."

"Your concerns are duly noted."

She rose up on her toes and gave him a kiss on the cheek before going to join her husband. As they left, Sterling wondered if they'd expressed their concerns to Frannie. He doubted it. He was the one doing the pursuing, so they'd brought him a clear message. Stop the pursuit . . . or else.

He dropped back into his chair and, with a shaking hand, reached for the glass of whiskey that Claybourne had poured for him. He downed it in one long swallow. Leaning back, he closed his eyes and worked to control the tremors going through him. Not because of the dire threats Claybourne had made, but because of what he'd revealed about the man he'd killed and what that man had done to Frannie.

It had happened years ago, and she'd been a child—she'd been a child!

Coming out of his chair with such force that it nearly toppled over, he searched frantically for something to pound his fist into. He settled for grabbing a vase he'd brought back from China and hurling it into the hearth.

"Oh, God." Dropping into a chair, he buried his face in his hands. "Oh, Frannie, sweet Frannie." He wanted to hold her. Her innocence stolen. He thought of the wonder in her eyes, the tears as he's brought her pleasure . . .

He wanted to change her past, but even as he thought it, he realized it was her very past that had shaped her into a woman who fascinated him. Sweetness and steely determination. Even as he accepted that he couldn't have even one night with her, he realized he wanted a thousand.

Chapter 13

Sterling sat in his library, no lamps lit, only the fire in the hearth to provide any semblance of light. It had been nearly a week since the opera. He'd sent Frannie flowers, but had included no note. He hadn't known what to say. She'd grown up in a world of violence that he couldn't truly comprehend. Oh, he had troubles, but their lives were so very different that they couldn't compare.

He should quit London, go to the country. Attend to his estates, make an appearance at a country party or two, look over the ladies . . .

He shoved himself out of his chair. It was after midnight. He was going to Dodger's. Lose some money and think about Frannie counting it.

He strode into the hallway and staggered to a stop. Damnation. The lamps had been put out. Whose idea was that? He was about to return to the library where he could use a bellpull to wake the butler to light the damn place and ready a carriage, when he heard someone creeping around.

Knowing the hallway would be clear as long as he walked down the center, he strode as quickly and quietly as he could to the foyer. The thumping grew louder as he rounded the corner—

"Ah, blimey!"

Based on the size of the person and the timbre of his voice, he was a child, silhouetted by a lantern that was covered on three sides and cast light in only one direction. With an uncanny speed that reminded Sterling of Charley Byerly, the imp darted off, and Sterling rushed after him. "You there! Halt! Wedgeworth! We've a thief in the residence!"

The little bugger dropped his lantern, extinguishing the flame, but from the area of the kitchen, pale light emerged to push back the shadows. The cook, thank God, must have heard Sterling's cry for help and the commotion that followed. She barged out carrying a lamp and a rolling pin, her wide girth effectively blocking the doorway.

The boy screamed, turned, and began running an erratic path down the hallway, dodging from side to side as though he thought he could maneuver his way around Sterling with a few fancy steps. Engaging in his own darting around, Sterling managed to grab hold of the back of a jacket and soon found himself holding nothing but discarded clothing. Slippery bugger!

Sterling charged after him, determined not to let him escape.

"Jenkins got him, Your Grace!" Wedgeworth's voice echoed through the residence.

With the cook providing the light, Sterling walked briskly in the direction from which Wedgeworth's voice had come. He found him back in the hallway leading to the library. A footman wearing only trousers, his hair rumpled, was holding the squirming lad.

"We'll send 'round for a constable," Wedgeworth said.

"No," Sterling answered sternly. "I have something else in mind for our little thief."

I have come into possession of something which I believe may belong to you. My coach is at your service.

Greystone

Sitting at her desk in her office at Dodger's, Frannie set down the neatly written message and stared at the gold pocket watch that had arrived with it. She was not familiar with the coat of arms of every noble family, but this one she recognized. It had been nestled against her palm when she lifted it from Greystone's waistcoat during the wedding breakfast.

What could he possibly have that belonged to her? Why didn't he bring it here instead of insinuating with his unwritten words that she should go there? She knew that was what he wanted, knew it was the meaning behind the inclusion of his watch. That she was to return it to him in order to gain what he possessed.

A trade.

She closed her fingers around it and imagined she could feel the warmth that would have come from it being nestled in his pocket. She knew it was unlikely. It had been a while since it had been in his possession.

Why now, when she was finally beginning to dream of him with greater infrequency, to look for him in the gaming area less often, to no longer consider the pleasures she'd experience if she were to slip into his residence—into his bed—at midnight? With nothing more than a few written words, she was remembering everything about him that she'd fought so valiantly to forget, wanted to see him again with a desperation that was almost frightening.

This time of night no one would see her climbing into a coach bearing his ducal crest. Even if someone did see, what did it matter? For a child of the streets, chaperones, etiquette, and proper behavior were as foreign as an abundance of coins.

She looked up at the wide-eyed young man who'd brought her the missive. Thomas Lark had been at Dodger's for only a few short months. Another child of the streets taken in by Jack, who often provided employment for promising lads. Only for Thomas, he'd been providing a place to hide.

"The gentleman who gave this to you. I assume he came in through the front door."

"Yes, m'am."

"Does anyone else know about this?"

"No, m'am."

So no one was likely to interfere. She nodded, her decision made. "Tell him to bring the coach 'round to the back."

He gave his head a quick bob and dashed out to see to her bidding. He was so eager to please.

She closed the ledger with which she'd been working. The remaining calculations could wait until tomorrow. For now, she was anxious to determine what Greystone was up to.

Or at least that was the excuse she was willing to admit to. She didn't want to give credence to the fluttering in her stomach that had more to do with anticipation than worry. Since the night he'd introduced her to the wonders of passion while denying his own needs, she'd not seen him within Dodger's. He'd sent her flowers, but nothing more. He'd not pressed her to become his lover. She couldn't deny the disappointment that had slammed into her when she realized that he'd given up his quest to possess her. Where he was concerned, however, her resolve had been weakening.

She knew marriage between them would never be an option. As a noble, he'd never ask a woman of the streets, a bookkeeper in a gaming establishment, for the honor of marriage. Even if he did, his wasn't a world in which she wanted to live permanently.

But to visit for only one night, to lie within his arms, to be smothered in his kisses, to touch his skin as he'd touched hers, to bring him pleasure as he'd brought her . . .

What was she thinking? Nothing she hadn't thought of every night as she drifted off to sleep, clutching his silly handkerchief as though it had the power to return him to her.

She shook her head to clear it, got up from her desk, and strode across the room. She snatched the cloak hanging near the door and draped it around her shoulders before closing her door and striding down the hallway to the far end. Once outside, she lifted her skirts and headed toward the nearby coach, where the footman stood beside the closed door that bore the ducal crest. Without a word he opened it and assisted her inside.

Disappointment rammed into her when she realized Greystone wasn't waiting for her, that she would be traveling alone. The footman must have delivered the message. Warmer inside than she'd anticipated, she realized a heated brick was resting on the floor. Of course, Greystone would have insisted she travel in comfort. He was thoughtful in that regard.

With a sudden lurch the coach took off. Vanity slapping at her, she wished she'd taken a moment to freshen up, perhaps to change her dress and unpin her hair. If she took it down now, without a brush in hand, she'd look like the very devil when she arrived. Why did she care anyway? What did it matter what he thought?

But it did. The part of her that longed to be desired wanted him to see her as the woman she could be—not the woman that each of Feagan's lads saw when they looked at her. They loved her, yes. They cared about her. But they didn't *desire* her.

While Luke had offered for her hand in marriage, she was fairly certain that he'd never actually envisioned bedding her. And Jim. Now and again, he dropped his armor and she saw how much he wanted her, but it was in the same manner that a child might want a puppy—to care for and look after. Not to share trials, tribulations, joys, and sorrows with. And certainly not to get lost with in wild, sexual abandon.

None of them had ever looked at her the way Greystone did—as though he would like nothing more than to slowly peel the clothes from her body. She knew how talented his mouth and hands could be, and she envisioned him using them to elicit even greater pleasure, envisioned them lying in a tangle of naked limbs.

As she grew unbearably hot with her thoughts, she wished they hadn't put a warming brick in the coach. Pressing her cheek against the glass, she welcomed the coolness against her skin. She didn't want to arrive with her cheeks flushed. All of a sudden she didn't want to arrive at all. What if she no longer had the strength to resist him?

But it was too late. The coach came to a halt, and she realized that they were going to take her in through the front, not usher her in through the servants' door as though her arrival was to be kept secret. Did this action mean that he held respect for her? Or did he care so little for her reputation that he didn't care who saw her coming into his residence long past midnight?

The coach door clicked open and the footman held out his hand. Shoring up her resolve, she placed her hand in his and allowed him to help her out of the coach.

After the footman opened the door, Frannie preceded him inside. The butler was apparently awaiting her arrival. He bowed slightly. "Miss Darling, His Grace is waiting for you in the library. If you'll be so good as to follow me?"

Surprised by the number of servants still about at this time of night, she nodded and followed him down the wide hallway. A footman opened the door to the library. Inside the massive room, a movement near the far window caught her attention, and there he was. Greystone.

For the span of a heartbeat, as she crossed over to him, she thought she saw pleasure in his face at her arrival, but it quickly vanished. She indulged in the luxury of feasting her eyes on him. She'd never seen him absent a waistcoat and jacket. His shoulders were broad, even without the outer layers of clothing. She remembered clutching them in the throes of passion, how powerful they had felt beneath her fingers. His mussed hair made him appear much younger, and she felt a sudden burst of jealousy hoping that his fingers—and not a lady's—were responsible for the dishevelment.

"Would you care for some refreshment?" he asked, so damned formally that her heart lurched. Was this the man who had swallowed her cries of pleasure?

"I don't believe so. Thank you." She wasn't opposed to spirits, had drunk with the lads many a time, but she wanted to keep her head about her for this encounter. Something between them had shifted, and not in the direction she'd hoped. "Your missive said—"

"We'll get to that in a moment. Please, sit down." He indicated two chairs near the window. They were no doubt safer than a sofa, but in all honesty, she was no longer certain she wanted safe. She took the one farthest from him. He promptly sat in the one left vacant.

"How have you been? I'm assuming since you arrived so quickly, they found you at Dodger's."

With the flatness of his tone, they might as well have been strangers. She fought to sound just as disaffected by his nearness. "Yes, I was working on the books. I usually go to the orphanage during the day. I have staff there at all hours." Why was she rambling about inconsequential matters when more important ones preyed on her mind? "I haven't seen you at Dodger's of late."

"I thought it best to stay away."

She almost asked him why—why now, when he hadn't before. The ease that had existed between them was no longer there, had been replaced with stiff politeness. "I received your flowers."

"I don't recall sending them with a message."

"You didn't, but who else would send me flowers?"

"I hope you enjoyed them."

"Very much. Thank you." Why was it so awkward? Why were they so formal?

"Oh, your watch." Removing it from her pocket, she held it out to him.

He took it from her, dangled it in front of his face, and studied it. "It was my father's. A gift from my mother, I believe. As I recall, she was rather fond of being a duchess."

"I can't imagine."

He shifted his gaze to her. "Being a duchess?"

"Having a fondness for the position. I daresay, I don't envy those of you in the nobility. I can think of nothing worse than living your life."

"And I can think of nothing worse than living yours."

Why did his gaze roam over her as though he was searching for some evidence . . . ?

Oh, God, her stomach churned, because she knew what the difference was. He looked at her as Feagan's lads did: as though she might shatter, as though she shouldn't be touched. Although his perusal was so much worse, because she was fairly certain he regretted the time they'd spent together, the intimacy they'd shared. "Claybourne told you," she said quietly, knowing he was the one affected as much by that horrible time as her. "About the unfortunate incident in my youth."

"Unfortunate incident? That's how you refer—"

He shoved himself out of the chair, grabbed a porcelain figurine, stormed over to the fireplace, and hurled into the hearth. Its shattering echoed obscenely loudly through the quiet library. Bowing his head and gripping the mantel, he stared down at the destruction.

She rose from the chair and walked over to where he stood. "Sterling, it's all right."

He spun around, and her heart nearly broke at the anguish reflected on his face. "All right? I swear to God that if he wasn't already dead, I'd kill him."

Trembling with the evidence of his raw emotion, she reached up and placed her hand against his bristly cheek. Laying his hand over hers, he turned his mouth into her palm and kissed it. "It's all right, Sterling. It was a long time ago."

"You were a child."

"But I'm not a child any longer."

"If you'd told me, I'd have taken greater care."

She shook her head. "You were the first to look at me as though I were desirable. Why would I want to lose that?"

In near desperation, he suddenly took her in his arms and slanted his mouth across hers. He tasted of brandy as he kissed her hungrily. A thrill shot through her. He still desired her. It was evident with every sweep of his tongue, every low groan that reverberated up through his chest, every press of his hands along her back. She yearned for him as she'd never longed for anything else. She didn't care that he might not want her for always, he wanted her now.

She ran her hands over his shoulders, feeling the strength in him as his muscles bunched with his effort to hold her near. She wanted this, wanted him.

Drawing back, breathing harshly, he pressed his forehead against hers. "This is not the reason I sent for you."

He glanced toward the doorway as though he were considering lifting her into his arms and carrying her through it. She realized with astounding certainty that she wouldn't object. In his eyes, she could see him deliberating: did he remain a gentleman or did he take advantage of whatever reason had caused him to send for her?

She knew the moment that his noble character declared victory. A hint of regret mingled with loss briefly touched his eyes before acceptance took hold and he returned his gaze to hers.

"Make no mistake, Miss Darling. I still desire you as I've never desired another. But now is not the time."

Determined not to reveal her own disappointment with his decision, she kept her voice steady when she reminded him, "Your missive said you had something that belonged to me."

He traced his finger around her face as though he would memorize every aspect of it. "I believe it does. Come along. I'll show you."

Offering her his arm, he led her out of the library. They walked through numerous corridors until they reached the kitchen. Inside, stuffing a meat pie in his mouth at the servants' table, was a boy who was more bone than skin.

"Oh!"

Sterling watched as Frannie rushed over and crouched beside the boy. He couldn't imagine the strength of purpose it had taken for her to put her past behind her. Yes, what had happened to her had occurred long ago, but still she had experienced it, lived through it. The more time he spent in her presence, the more she humbled him. Did she ever put her own wants and needs before others?

She combed her fingers through the boy's long dark hair as though it probably wasn't infested with lice. Someone—the cook or Jenkins—had scrubbed the boy's face clean. It was pink and so damned pale.

With a thousand questions reflected in her green eyes, Frannie looked at Sterling.

"He broke into the residence," he explained.

She returned her attention to the boy. "What's your name?"

He stuffed more pie into his mouth, so much more that Sterling was surprised his cheeks didn't burst.

"Poor thing," Sterling's cook said. "He's been eating like that ever since I set food in front of him. That's his third pie."

"Chew your food, then answer the lady, lad," Sterling ordered.

The boy swallowed. Sterling was surprised he didn't choke.

"Jimmy," he grumbled and shoved more food into his mouth.

"Who's your kidsman?" Frannie asked.

The boy shook his head.

"I know you didn't plan this burglary on your own."

He simply shook his head again.

"Do you know Feagan?" she asked.

He bobbed his head.

"I used to be one of his crew. My name is Frannie Darling."

The boy's eyes widened in horror. "Sykes says ye be the very devil."

Considering the sudden hard set of her jaw, Sterling assumed she knew this Sykes fellow and didn't think much of him. Or perhaps she didn't like being compared to the devil. Although, God help him, Sterling thought the same thing, in a more flattering way. She was dressed as plainly as he'd ever seen her, but the hour was late and her hair wasn't quite as tidy as it might have been earlier. The back looked as though it was struggling against the weight of the heavy strands and might lose the battle at any moment and tumble down. He desperately wanted it to lose the battle. He wanted to bury his hands in it.

He wanted to loosen the buttons at her wrist and place his mouth on the pale flesh he'd find there. He wanted to feel her pulse quicken beneath his lips. He wanted her to be as tender with him as she was with this lad. He wanted to be as tender with her.

Frannie unfolded her body and strolled over to Sterling. He was acutely aware of the worry in her eyes, the delicate pleat between her brows. "What are you going to do with him?"

"Give him to you, I suppose."

So much relief and gratitude filled her eyes that he wished he'd discovered a thousand boys in his residence.

"I would like to take him to the children's home. Would you allow me to make use of your coach?"

"I'll do better than that. I'll accompany you."

Chapter 14

As his coach rumbled toward the outskirts of London, Sterling knew it was pointless to prolong his time with her. Her thoughts were not on him. They were on the young lad stretched out on the bench, the one whose head was in her lap while she slowly combed her fingers through his dirty hair. The boy was like a mongrel pup, filthy and ill cared for. He'd stuffed himself with so much food that he'd brought a good deal of it back up on the way to the coach. Sterling wanted to believe he was just a greedy little bastard, but he suspected he was quite simply starving. His arms were little more than sticks. Sterling wouldn't have thought he could have carried his ink blotter out of the residence, but his pockets had told a different story.

"It was very kind of you not to have him arrested," Frannie said quietly.

To ensure that she was comfortable with him

in the coach, and to ensure that the lad didn't find a way to disappear from it—Sterling certainly wouldn't put it past him to be artful in the ways of escape—he'd had the footman light the coach lantern. Besides, it gave him the opportunity to see her a little more clearly, even if the shadows worked against him.

"I decided your Scotland Yard friend would liberate him and give him to you anyway, so what was the point?"

She smiled at that, giving him reason to believe some truth resided in his words, and looked back at the boy, who appeared to be asleep.

"So who is this Sykes fellow?" Sterling asked quietly.

Rather than answering him, she murmured, "How old do you think he is?"

He was not a student of children, but based on the boy's size—

"Somewhere in the neighborhood of five."

"I put him at eight, possibly nine." She sounded confident of her answer.

"He's too small."

"That's the way Sykes likes them." She lifted her gaze, and he saw not only profound sadness but fury as well. She was a woman of far-ranging passions and the ability to feel them simultaneously. Knowing of her past, was he a bastard for still wanting her in his bed? Knowing he could never marry her, was he a blackguard for wanting her in his life? "He scours the streets for the smallest of lads, and then works very hard to keep them small. He feeds them only enough so they survive. I suspect this one either came down one of your chimney flues or through a window that is seldom locked because it's considered too small to allow anyone entry. It's the very reason Sykes works so very hard to keep them so small."

While she spoke, not once did she stop or slow the journey of her fingers through the lad's hair.

"He terrorizes them so they do as they're told. Under his care, they know not the gentle hand of kindness. If they fall ill, they get no comfort, no food, because they're no longer earning their way."

"And he refers to *you* as a devil?"

She smiled fully then, and he realized she was pleased that Sykes had gone to the trouble of calling her anything at all.

"The devil takes on all sorts of shapes," she said.

"You're jabbing sticks at him."

"I give his lads a home when I can find them. And yes, I've put out word that I provide a safe haven."

"He sounds like a rather unpleasant fellow. He can't appreciate what you're doing."

Determination washing over her features, she angled her chin. "I know what it is to be fearful for your life. I will not cower from what I know is the right thing to do."

"Even if it puts your very life at risk?"

"Don't be so melodramatic. There are many children. Sykes can always find another." She gazed down on the child still asleep on her lap. "This one now belongs to me."

"You think to reform him?"

"He's young enough that his soul is not yet lost. It's the older ones, the ones who have been in prison who are more difficult to reach."

"I'm familiar with the London streets. There are hundreds of children scouring about. You can't save them all."

She gave him a wistful smile. "No, but I can save this one, and for now, that's enough."

And what about you, Frannie? he wanted to ask. *Who will save you?*

She gave so much of herself to others. He wanted her to be like him, to put her own pleasures first.

He gazed out the window just as the coach rounded the curve and went through the gates of the orphanage. The gas lamps lit their way up the cobblestone path. When the coach came to a stop, the boy stirred.

"I'll carry him," Sterling said as the door opened and he stepped out. He reached back in and took the boy, who clung to him instinctively like a little monkey, his arms tightly wound around Sterling's neck, his legs around his waist. Sterling stood there, astonished to realize that the child weighed almost nothing. He knew he was thin, but this . . . he couldn't possibly be as old as Frannie thought.

"Sterling?" she prodded, indicating the path to the well-lit door.

"I do hope he doesn't have fleas or lice," he muttered as he fell into step beside her.

"I think you're quite safe. I didn't notice any."

Withdrawing a key from her pocket, she unlocked and opened the door. Stepping inside, he was taken aback by the change in the place. It had a very homelike feel to it, with plants dotting the floor and paintings on the walls. Lamps burning low were sprinkled throughout. A large man with beefy fists rose up out of a chair as though ascending from the depths of hell.

"Miss Frannie."

"Good evening, Mr. Bates. How are things?"

"Quiet. Looks like you're bringing in another one."

"Yes, I am." She turned to Sterling. "Mr. Bates keeps an eye on things at night."

Like Cerberus guarding the gates of Hades,

Sterling thought, although he suspected that here they were closer to heaven.

Frannie touched Sterling's arm. "We'll put him in a room down here. Tomorrow when we have a chance to clean him up and explain things, we'll put him in a room with another boy."

She guided him along a hallway to a room that contained a bed and a very soft-looking chair. She lit the lamp on the table beside the bed while Sterling carefully laid down the boy who'd sought to steal from him. The irony didn't escape him.

Moving back, he watched as she removed the lad's scruffy shoes which—when his black-soled feet were revealed—were much too large. As though reading Sterling's thoughts, she reached into a shoe and pulled out crumpled newspaper. She shrugged as though to signify that at least he had shoes.

She left his clothing in place and brought a blanket over him. Once again she touched the boy's hair, then leaned down and bussed a quick kiss over his temple. "Sweet dreams."

The boy muttered something indecipherable and promptly began to snore.

With a tilting of her head, she led Sterling back into the corridor. "Whenever I come here at night, I always take a walk through. I'd like it very much if you'd accompany me."

As it would prolong his time with her, he nodded. She lifted a lamp from a nearby table and directed him toward the stairs.

"Do you come here every night?" he asked as he followed her up.

"Not often. Depends how late I work on Dodger's books. I'll usually stay at my apartment there and come here during the day to check up on things, visit with the children" —she glanced over her shoulder at him and smiled— "and look over the books. It seems I'm forever looking over books."

They reached the landing and he could see all the doors were open. She walked through the first one. Inside, two boys were sprawled on separate beds. Two small chests were at the foot of each bed, chests which he imagined contained their possessions. Leaning over, she gave first one boy and then the other a kiss. Neither stirred, and Sterling imagined they were accustomed to receiving angel kisses while they slept.

She went through the same ritual in each room. Eventually, feeling utterly useless, he took the lamp from her so that he could at least contribute in some way. Besides, he was able to direct the light so it shone more on her than the children, giving him a clearer portrait of her. She possessed no pretense. She didn't put on airs. She truly cared about these children, was seeking to provide them with a better life. Children she'd not given birth to. How much more might she love her own children? Or was her ability to love infinite?

The number of children astonished him.

"Where do you find them?" he asked, when she'd delivered her last kiss and they were walking down the stairs.

"Mostly they find me. While Sykes might call me the very devil, there are others who refer to me as an angel. Word passes along the street that here they will find sanctuary and no harm will come to them. Some don't trust it. Others are to a point that they feel they have nothing to lose. And of course, Jim knows who has been arrested. He'll bring children here after they've suffered their punishment."

Of course. The inspector from Scotland Yard. Sterling had never thought he'd find himself competing with a commoner for the affections of . . . God help him. A commoner. Not that he found anything about Frannie Darling to be the least bit common.

Leaving the lamp on an entryway table, he went outside, grateful that she accompanied him. Every moment in her company left him wanting one more.

"I didn't notice the little scamp who tried to steal from me at the Great Exhibition. Charley wasn't it?" he asked.

She smiled warmly. "Charley Byerly, yes. I managed to find a decent family willing to take him in."

"God help them."

"He's not as bad as all that. I managed to find time to visit him just the other day. He's adjusting quite well actually."

"So in addition to everything else you're doing, you're striving to find them homes?"

"Yes."

"You're remarkable. May I escort you back to Dodger's?" he asked.

She shook her head. "I'm going to stay with Jimmy. He'll be frightened when he awakens in these strange surroundings."

He didn't want to leave her here, but he knew she'd not appreciate if he insisted that she leave. "Then forgive me an indulgence."

Not giving her the opportunity to fully comprehend the meaning of his words, he took her into his arms and lowered his mouth to hers. She released a low moan, but no objection. He kissed her more gently than he had in the library when desperation had clung to him. He wanted more from her than he could have, more than he deserved. She wanted him to desire her, and by God, he did, with a fierceness that was almost terrifying.

Drawing back, he clamped his hand beneath

her chin. "Much remains unresolved between us, but never think for a single moment that I don't desire you. Sleep well, Frannie."

Later, leaning back in his coach, Sterling slipped his thumb into his waistcoat pocket and smiled. His pocket watch was missing. Her taking of it was an invitation, if he'd ever received one. He was looking forward to accepting.

Sitting in a chair beside the bed with the lamp turned low, Frannie watched as Jimmy slept. Poor lad. She was familiar enough with Sykes to know that Jimmy would worry about retribution if he didn't return to his mentor. Sykes had been a bully as a lad, a monster as an adult. He cared for no one save himself, and while Frannie had not seen him since she was twelve, she walked the rookeries often enough in her search for orphans to hear stories about him.

She slipped her hand into her pocket and withdrew Greystone's watch. She wanted to see him again, and she hoped that by taking his watch she'd sent him the message. A message he would understand.

He might never realize how deeply it touched her that he'd sent for her instead of a constable. If only she could get others to do the same. If these children never had to experience gaol or prison or any sort of punishment. If only her work could make a difference.

She wasn't aware of falling asleep, but she awoke with her neck aching and sunlight filtering into the room. Jimmy was still asleep.

"Miss Darling?"

With a smile, she looked to the doorway, where Mrs. Prosser, the headmistress of the orphanage, stood. "Good morning."

Mrs. Prosser gave a quick curtsy. Frannie couldn't convince her that she wasn't deserving of one. "I'm sorry to bother you, ma'am, but a gentleman is here to see you."

She felt her smile grow. Greystone had wasted no time in returning to reclaim his watch. Perhaps he'd join her for a bit of breakfast. But when she stepped into the foyer, it wasn't Greystone who waited for her, but a small man with a ruddy complexion and a balding pate that was only visible because he'd removed his hat and was squeezing it between his chapped hands.

"May I help you, sir?" she asked.

"I'm here to help you, ma'am. I'm a cobbler. His Grace, the Duke of Greystone, has hired me to see that all the lads here have proper fitting shoes."

Frannie felt the tears sting her eyes at yet another example of Greystone's generosity. "He did, did he?"

"Yes, ma'am. Whenever a lad needs new shoes, you just send word to me and I'll be by to take measurements. His Grace will pay for all the shoes you need."

"That's very generous of him."

"Aye, ma'am. I've brought plenty of paper with me. If you'll line the boys up, I'll start taking their measurements, so I can get to work back at my shop."

After setting some of the staff to work gathering up the boys, she returned to the bedroom where Jimmy had been sleeping to discover he wasn't there.

"Mrs. Prosser?"

Mrs. Prosser hurried into the room. "Yes, ma'am."

"The boy who was sleeping here, did you do something with him? Send him for a bath perhaps?"

"No, ma'am. When I left he was sleeping."

Frannie was fairly certain it was futile, but she had everyone search the building and grounds for more than an hour. No one caught sight of a scraggly boy who answered to the name of Jimmy. She felt that she'd not only let Jimmy down, but Greystone as well.

Chapter 15

Standing in the darkened alleyway, Sterling reached into his waistcoat pocket for his watch before remembering that its absence was the very reason he was here now. It was habit to take out his watch, flip it open, and look at the time—even though he'd not be able to see its face in the darkness. He'd instructed his driver to park his coach on the street at the end of the alleyway. If Swindler or Dodger was about, he didn't want either of them to know that he was. There was also the possibility that he'd misread Frannie's taking of his watch. Perhaps she intended to pawn it in order to acquire the few coins needed to feed the little urchin who'd stolen into his residence.

Or as he hoped, perhaps it was an invitation. He'd gone into Dodger's briefly and cornered one of the lads who ran errands. He'd confirmed that Miss Frannie was seeing to the books. With any luck, she'd be finished shortly and Sterling would approach her and invite her to join him for a late-night repast in his residence or a late-night ride in his coach. She'd initiated this encounter and he was content to let her dictate the pace of things. Since Claybourne's visit, Sterling wasn't quite sure what he wanted of her any longer. Considering her past, seducing her for his own pleasure seemed inherently wrong. He couldn't deny that he still wanted her, but he recognized that he wanted her for more than one night. He wanted to undo the harshness of her past, he wanted to introduce her to the sensual pleasures that she should have known all along.

He could make her his mistress, provide for her orphanage, get her out of Dodger's. For years. They could find a satisfying happiness. Yes, eventually he would have to marry some lord's daughter, but he knew many men who had a wife and a mistress. It was the way of things. Of course, there was still the problem of saddling her with a blind man, denying her marriage, which she deserved, and her own children, who deserved her. No, making her his mistress was not the way to go. It was dreadfully selfish, and while he'd always seen to his own pleasures first, where she was concerned, he was more interested in hers.

The back door opened and she stepped out onto the stoop. After she locked the door, she brought the hood of her cloak up over her head. A strange thing to do when her apartment was so near. It was certainly chilly out tonight, but . . .

She hurried down the alleyway, passing by the stairs that led up to her apartment. Where was she going?

By nature he was not in the habit of sticking his nose where it didn't belong. But her movements were those of someone not wishing to be discovered. He told himself it was none of his business as he began walking briskly yet quietly in her direction. Coincidence, on his part. His coach was just around the corner, after all.

Frannie had finished with her books as quickly as possible. She wanted to get to the rookeries while children were still out and about, while men were not completely foxed, while women hadn't taken their last customer to bed. She'd spent most of the day prowling the area for Jimmy with no luck. But the atmosphere was different at night. Sometimes Feagan also haunted the streets. If she could find him, she was fairly certain she could persuade him to help her. He knew every nook and cranny. He might be bent with age now, but he was still clever.

As she drew near the end of the alley, her heart picked up its tempo. She would find a hansom—

Someone snagged her from behind and hurled her against the brick wall. Before she could react in self-defense, he was pressing his body against hers, pinning her in place, one of his hands gathering up her skirt, lifting it—

"I'm 'ere to deliver a message from Bob Sykes," he rasped, his breath rancid from too much drink and rotting teeth. "Leave his boys be."

"Let me go," she demanded, trying to buck him off.

He jammed his thigh painfully between her legs. "Not until I get payment fer delivering the message. I've always wanted a taste of a fancy skirt."

He clamped his hand on her jaw, his mouth smothering hers, his other hand touching her—

No, no, no!

She was twelve again, fighting, fighting—

Everything happened in a heartbeat. Struggling against the dark abyss into which she wanted to fall, she pulled out the knife and thrust it—

He yelled and was gone. She heard a thud, even as the knife hit something hard, and the impact reverberated up her arm.

A strangled groan sounded.

Labored breathing echoed around her.

Fingers dug into her shoulder. In the pale glow of a distant gas lamp, she found herself staring at

Greystone, his hand pressed to his side. She could barely make out the inky blackness flowing between his fingers.

She heard a scrabbling motion and was vaguely aware of the other man running away. "This ain't over, Frannie Darling," her attacker called out as he disappeared in the deep shadows and around the corner of the building.

Releasing the knife, she pressed her hand over Greystone's. He ground out a strangled curse, and she felt the warm blood oozing between her fingers. So much blood.

"Dear God. How badly are you hurt? Can you make it up the stairs? I want to have a look, see how—"

He wrapped his hand around her neck, surprisingly strong, holding her near. "If I'm to die," he rasped, "let me do so . . . with the taste of you upon my lips."

Without his usual finesse he planted his mouth over hers. She told herself that he couldn't be mortally wounded if his hand still held such strength and his mouth such passion.

A strange fluke of fate that he'd jerked her attacker off her just as she was plunging a knife toward his midsection. Greystone, with his heroics, was now spilling his blood over himself and her. So damned much blood.

She pushed against him. "You fool. You're going to bleed to death."

"It's a mere scratch."

"Then you're an even bigger fool for making me worry. Have you the strength to climb the stairs?"

"Yes."

She snaked her arm around his back, while his landed hard on her shoulders. They staggered toward the stairs, the weight of him increasing with each step as though he were losing strength along with the blood. It wasn't a mere scratch. A mere scratch wouldn't drench her hand in blood. They were halfway up the stairs when he dropped to his knees.

"Seems I misjudged," he said.

"It would be undignified for you to die here."

He chuckled low. "I'm nothing if I'm not dignified."

"I'm glad you find this humorous."

"Not in the least."

Grabbing onto the railing, he pulled himself up. They lurched up the steps. Anyone seeing them might have thought they were drunk. When they reached the top, he leaned against the wall while she dug the key out of her pocket. Once she opened the door, she led him into the apartment.

Like her office, it was sparsely furnished. She considered the sofa, but decided on the bed. It was far more comfortable and he might need to lie down. He sat on the edge of it while she gathered some towels. She came around and knelt in front of him. His clothing was soaked. So damned much blood. That's all Frannie could think as she tried to staunch the flow of blood. "This doesn't look good."

"I think it's just a gash. Hurts like bloody hell, though. Remind me . . . to never try to rescue you again."

"I can't believe the timing, that you stepped in just when I was thrusting. I didn't see you."

"I didn't see the knife, so we're even."

Hardly. "May I . . . may I unbutton your waist-coat and lift your shirt?"

He nodded. He was growing paler by the minute. She was gentle but as quick as she could be. The gash was horrible. Long and deep, it ran up his side. Thank goodness nothing was spilling out except blood.

"Lie down. I'm going to send someone to fetch Bill."

"Bill?" He was taking short breaths as though anything more was painful. With a low groan he stretched out on her bed.

"William Graves. He's a physician."

"Right. He looked after Catherine."

"Yes. Just wait here. I'm going to fetch him."

He gave her a crooked, endearing smile, as though her order made him want to laugh, because he couldn't go anywhere if he wanted.

She took a step to leave, then turned back to him. "What were you doing here?"

"Came for my watch. Thought your . . . taking it was an invitation."

She'd forgotten all about that. Reaching into her pocket where she'd been carrying it all day, she removed it, placed it in his hand, and folded his fingers around it. "It was," she whispered quietly, before brushing a kiss over his forehead. But it certainly hadn't been an invitation for this.

After sending someone to fetch Bill, she found Jim and Jack in Jack's office. They came with her as she returned to Greystone's side. Pressing towels against his wound, she watched in horror as the blood soaked through them, little by little.

He was still having difficulty breathing, grimacing and taking shallow breaths. His jaw was clenched so tightly she feared he'd break a tooth. It would be so much easier to endure the guilt if he didn't keep his eyes on her. They were such a lovely blue, but filled with such pain.

"I'm so sorry," Frannie said.

"What are you sorry for?" Jack asked, standing at the foot of the bed, arms crossed. "You were trying to protect yourself. It's not your fault he got in the way."

A corner of Greystone's mouth twitched and she wondered if he wanted to laugh. She was fairly certain this was an incident that he wouldn't laugh about in later years—if he survived to have later years.

"Would you rather I hold cloth to his wound?" Jim asked.

Greystone, watching her so intently, clutched her wrist and held her hand in place, as though to signal that he wanted her to stay. He needn't have worried. She had no plans to leave. She shook her head. "No. I'm responsible here. I should see to him."

She wanted to run her hands through his hair, cradle his face, press her forehead to his, and apologize again. But she didn't want him to survive this only to be set upon by Jack and Jim. "Where's Bill?"

As though her words summoned him, he strode through her door. "What's going on? I got word that Frannie was hurt."

"Not Frannie," Jack said, then, "Good God, are you hurt, Frannie? Didn't even think to ask."

"I'm fine." Except for some bruises and scrapes, but she held her silence because she didn't want any attention taken away from Greystone. He was the one in need of immediate assistance. She twisted around slightly to look at Bill and explain what had happened. Her movement jostled the bed, and Greystone groaned, sounding as though he was strangling trying to hold back the evidence of his pain.

Bill came around to stand beside her. "Let me see, Frannie."

"There's so much blood."

"Sometimes the shallowest of wounds gives the appearance of a great wound. Let me have a look here, all right?"

With a nod, she eased back, her pressure on the wound easing. As she stood to give Bill more room, she felt arms come around her and she buried her face in Jim's shoulder, grateful for the comfort he gave. He urged her away from the bed. As much as she wanted to go with him, she couldn't bear the thought of leaving Greystone to suffer alone.

"No, I'm staying near," she said, suddenly breaking free and walking back to the bed. "Do you need more light, Bill?"

"Yes, please."

She lifted the lamp from the bedside table and held it aloft over Greystone so Bill could have a better look. "Oh, it's ghastly."

"I don't think it's as bad as all that." Bill pressed against the duke's chest and Greystone sucked in air through his clenched teeth. "Did that hurt, Your Grace?"

The duke glared at him.

"Yes, I suppose it did. Silly of me to ask. May have bruised your ribs a bit. You must have smashed him pretty hard, Frannie."

"I was trying to kill him." She grimaced. "Well, not Greystone. The man who attacked me."

"And who was that?" Jack asked.

"I don't know."

"You don't know? You know every man who comes in the club."

"He wasn't one of our customers."

"What did he want?"

"What does any man want who throws a woman up against a wall?"

"Would you recognize him if you saw him again?"

Now she was the one glaring, glaring at Jack. "Can't we wait for this inquisition?"

"The sooner we go looking for him, the more likely we'll find him and have an opportunity to deal with him."

She looked at Jim. He was with Scotland Yard. He should be asking the questions.

"Doesn't matter when we get the questions answered," Jim said quietly. "I'll find him. I'll take care of him."

"Don't do anything foolish," she said.

"Just try to remember what he looked like."

"It was dark. I couldn't see and I had survival on my mind."

"Maybe the duke saw him."

"No, too dark and shadowy," Greystone ground out, then hissed at whatever Bill was doing to him.

"Try to stay still, Your Grace," Bill said. "I'm going to remove some of your clothes here, then stitch you up and bind those ribs."

Greystone gave a quick nod.

With Jim's help, Bill removed Greystone's finely tailored jacket, waistcoat, and shirt. She supposed she should have been embarrassed at the sight of a man's bare chest, but she was too concerned about his wound to give it much thought—except for the passing realization that he was as finely made as his clothing.

"What the devil is that?" Jack asked.

Frannie eased around to see what Jack was staring at. Greystone's back bore a painting of an unusual creature with fire coming out of its mouth and wings spread wide.

"Tattoo," Greystone ground out, as he moved to lie back down.

"Never seen anything like that."

"Go to Japan." He arched a brow as though Jack wouldn't know where Japan was. "Far side of the world."

"Bring the light a little closer, Frannie," Bill said,

snapping everyone's attention back to the matter at hand.

"Oh, yes, sorry."

She knelt beside the bed, holding the lamp so it provided adequate illumination for Bill to properly handle his task, but her stomach went all squeamish at the sight of him working. She averted her gaze and found herself staring into Greystone's pain-filled eyes. She wanted to apologize again, but apologies after a while became irritants. She wanted to take his hand, but she'd have to move around Bill or go to the other side of the bed, and with Jim and Jack both watching, she was suddenly very self-conscious, wondering what she might be giving away. She couldn't overlook the fact that he was a duke. She'd not wanted to marry Luke because he was an earl, and a duke was so much more. Greystone especially, because he'd been bred and led toward the position. The manner in which he held himself. His every stance, movement, his complete bearing spoke of noble blood. Even now, he bore his pain with an occasional grimace but nothing more.

"All right, Your Grace, let's try to sit you up. I want to wrap your ribs, simply as a precaution," Bill said.

Frannie veered slightly away so he could swing his legs over. Her bed seemed so small with him in it. As soon as he was situated, his gaze came back to hers, as though she had the power to ease his suffering.

When Bill was finished, he gave Greystone some laudanum. "I'm sure you're experiencing a great deal of discomfort. This should ease your pain on the journey home."

"Are you saying he's fit to leave?" Frannie asked.

"I'm sure he has a well-sprung coach. The journey shouldn't be too unbearable."

"I'd rather he stay here so I can look after him."

"He's not in danger of dying. Granted, the wound could get infected, but—"

"It's my doing. I should tend to him, at least for a few hours."

"I've no objections," Greystone said, and Frannie nearly leaped out of her skin. His deep voice still harbored an undercurrent of pain.

"Then it's settled," she said.

"I'm not certain that's a good idea," Jim said. "Your reputation—"

"Dear God, my reputation? Are you going to run about London spreading rumors?"

"No, but, Frannie—"

"Oh, God, Jim, not now," Frannie said. "Help me change the bedding."

When they were finished, Greystone lay back down and closed his eyes. His breathing wasn't as harsh, but he was still pale. It took a bit of arguing, persuading, and insisting, but she finally convinced Jack and Bill to leave. They were worried about her and she appreciated it, but she didn't need them hovering around like mother hens. Jim was a bit more hardheaded.

"Are you sure you're not hurt?" he asked, his gaze running the length of her.

Looking down, she realized her dress sported almost as much blood as Greystone's clothes. "I'm going to freshen up. Keep an eye on him."

She wasn't at all uncomfortable with the notion of going behind her screen in order to change into clean clothes after washing away the blood with Jim near. They'd slept in the same room, taken their yearly bath in the same tub. And Greystone was asleep.

Sterling didn't remember drifting off to sleep, but when he opened his eyes, he didn't see any of the men about and was certain they were gone, because what he did see was a silhouette of Frannie behind a screen. She raised an arm high over her head and stroked her other hand along it. She was washing up, he deduced. He could see only the shadow of her, but it was enough for him to realize she no longer wore a dress. His body tightened painfully—nowhere in the vicinity of his wound—as her hands moved along her shoulders, lowered—

"I'd close those eyes again if I were you."

Sterling jerked his head to the side to discover his worst nightmare sitting there. Swindler's gaze bore into him.

"It would be unfortunate if Graves misjudged the seriousness of your injury, and you were to suddenly expire on the spot. Frannie would be terribly disappointed," Swindler said.

"And you don't like to see her disappointed."

"It's the only reason you're still breathing."

"For someone who is supposed to uphold the law, you threaten an inordinate amount."

"When it comes to matters involving Frannie, I have my own laws."

"As I've mentioned before, I have no intentions of harming her. Tonight I might have very well saved her life. I'd expect a bit of appreciation for that."

"That's the difference between us, Your Grace. If I'd saved her life, I'd have expected no thanks whatsoever. Wouldn't have even wanted them."

Sterling shook his head in frustration. "Doesn't matter what I do, Swindler, you'll find fault with it. Rot in hell."

Swindler chuckled low. "I'll be taking you with me."

"I'm already there, man."

Swindler seemed taken aback by that, his eyes

narrowing. "I didn't think the wound was that serious."

"This" —he glanced at the bandages wrapped around his chest— "is nothing. You flatter yourself into thinking the devil only visits the impoverished and destitute. Quite honestly, Inspector, you're beginning to bore me with your self-righteous view that only you can know what hell truly is."

Whatever retort Swindler may have wanted to make went unsaid as Frannie walked out from behind the screen in a black dress, as though Sterling was already dead and she was preparing to go to the funeral. He wanted her in the green gown or nothing at all. Yes, nothing at all was preferable.

"You're awake," she said.

"Barely."

She smiled at Swindler. "Thank you for seeing after him while I tidied up. I think you can go now."

"Frannie, I don't think it's wise to leave you alone—"

"Jim, I retrieved my dagger." She patted her side. "He's aware I know well how to use it. Besides, he put himself in harm's way earlier. I think he deserves a bit of trust."

Swindler gave Sterling one last glare, designed to kill a lesser man, before pushing himself to his feet. Heading for the door, he stopped momentarily to touch Frannie's cheek. "Just watch yourself."

Frannie followed him to the door, gave him a reassuring smile and a gentle nudge onto the stoop. After closing the door, she turned the lock. Sykes's man might have run off, but nothing prevented him from returning at his leisure.

With a weary sigh, she walked toward the bed, coming up short when she saw that Greystone was watching her with those cobalt-blue eyes.

"That inspector . . . he's in love with you," Greystone said quietly.

"All of Feagan's lads are." Brushing off his words, she walked to the chair and sat.

"Not like he is."

"We're friends, nothing more."

"Why did you lie to them?" Greystone asked, swinging his legs over the side of the bed and pushing himself up to a sitting position. "You did know who attacked you and you knew what he wanted."

"I didn't know who he was. And they would just worry."

"I wasn't close enough to hear everything, but I did catch the name Sykes. Has this anything to do with the boy?"

"Possibly. He ran away. I spent much of today in the rookeries searching for him. I came away with four children but none of them were Jimmy. I'm assuming Sykes was outside your residence last night and probably saw us taking the lad to the orphanage. He may have seen me going into your residence, recognized me. I don't know. Perhaps the boy told him."

"Why didn't you explain all this to Swindler? He could arrest this Sykes fellow—"

"For what? It's not against the law to threaten."

"He sent someone to hurt you."

"What proof do I have that he was behind it? I didn't get a good look at the fellow, so there's no one to testify. And even if I did know who attacked me and Jim located him" —she shook her head— "Sykes is not someone anyone would testify against. He is the devil incarnate."

She didn't appreciate the way he was scrutinizing her, as though he could read her thoughts. "You didn't tell them what you knew because you knew they'd try to take care of it."

"I thought they might get hurt trying to take care of it. And because . . ." Her voice trailed off.

"Because?" he prodded.

She gazed at him intently. "How many of them have threatened you?"

A muscle in his jaw jumped. Men. So damned proud. They wanted to handle their own affairs, not show any weakness, not ask for help. Why couldn't they understand that sometimes a woman felt the need for the same considerations?

"All of them," she said with conviction.

"No," he responded quickly.

She nodded thoughtfully. "Bill didn't. He wouldn't. That's because he's a healer. He can't stand to see anyone suffering. But the others . . . I love the lads. I've always loved them, but sometimes I feel as though they're suffocating me."

"You need their help here."

She nodded. She knew she did, but just once she wished she could be as independent as she wanted.

Reaching out, he took her hand and skimmed his thumb over her knuckles. It seemed he welcomed any excuse to touch her, as though he relished her nearness as much as she did his. "Come to my residence for a few days."

"And to your bed?"

"No. Not unless you want to." With a low moan, he reached back for his shirt and began putting it on. "You were attacked tonight and that had to be . . . difficult."

She felt the tears stinging her eyes and blinked them back. In most ways it wasn't like before, but still it had brought back the horrid memories.

"You nearly killed me, which would have been tragic."

She bit back her smile. How could he make her want to laugh and cry at the same time?

"You're bound to be feeling guilty about it. And now you have to worry about this Sykes fellow. How can you think clearly, Frannie? He won't think to look for you at my residence. Even if he saw you come there last night, he won't think I've invited you back."

"My orphans—"

"Can survive for a few days without you. You have staff to look after them. And I need a nurse to help me with my recovery. I'd think you'd suffice. When was the last time you had a few days of not worrying about anything?"

But being in his residence would bring with it another set of worries. Could she remain near him and not want him?

"My coach is waiting down the street."

"Your poor driver—"

"He's accustomed to waiting until dawn on some occasions, and I pay him well enough not to be bothered by it." He folded his hand around his waistcoat and jacket. "Come with me. Otherwise, I'll have to stay here, and no offense, but you're lacking in amenities. Dodger obviously is taking advantage of your goodness. He needs to increase your salary. I can have my solicitor discuss the matter with him."

"I have no complaints regarding my pay." For the first time, she viewed her accommodations through his eyes. They were rather . . . depressing. "I believe my money is better spent on the orphanage."

"But to sacrifice everything—"

"I don't sacrifice anything that I truly want." Although she truly wanted him, and here she was arguing against going when there was nothing she desired more.

"Come with me. My servants will pamper you and so shall I."

"You're the one who's hurt, the one who should be tended."

He grinned as though she'd fallen right into his trap. "Fine. You may pamper me."

"I'll at least escort you home," she conceded.

"And stay."

"Until dawn. Just to make certain you're all right."

He smiled a devilish grin that seemed to imply that she'd granted him exactly what he wanted. It wasn't until they arrived at his residence and he was helping her out of the coach that he said in a low, sensual voice, "Fortunately for me you didn't specify which dawn."

Chapter 16

I t was nearly two in the morning, but Greystone's butler greeted them in the entry
hallway to take Frannie's wrap and Greystone's
bundled jacket and waistcoat. His bloodied shirt,
however, remained on his person.

"Good God, Your Grace. I'll send for your physician immediately."

"No need, Wedgeworth. I've already been
tended and it's really nothing to worry over. Miss
Darling will be staying the night in Lady Catherine's room. Assign one of the maids to see to
her needs while she's here."

"Yes, Your Grace."

It was strange, but as Greystone led her up the
sweeping stairs, she didn't feel the least bit uncomfortable approaching the floor that contained
the bedchambers, and yet she thought she should
have. She thought of the last time she'd been here
and all that had happened. He might tell her that

he expected nothing from her, but she knew it was a lie—and she wasn't bothered by it. The one person with whom she'd always been honest was herself. She was here because there was nothing he wanted of her that she wasn't willing to give.

"Have I mentioned that I'm very glad you're here?" he asked.

Raising her gaze to his, she smiled. "I don't believe you have."

"I want you to be glad to be here, Frannie."

The top of the stairs opened into another huge corridor. It was so large that tables and chairs lined the walls, yet people could still walk easily four across. She imagined during balls that ladies tittered as they came up here to see after their toilette.

"This bedchamber here," he said, leading her to an open doorway.

She peered in at the artwork on the ceiling, the grand canopied bed, the luxury she'd not experienced since leaving Claybourne's. "It's gorgeous."

"It's not to your taste, though, is it?"

She shook her head. "No, but I'll manage."

From the corner of her eye, she saw a woman walking sedately down the hallway, having come up the servants' back stairway. She was surprised Sterling didn't turn toward the approaching girl.

"Your Grace," she said with a bobbed curtsy.

Only then did Sterling choose to acknowledge

her. "Agnes, you're to serve Miss Darling's every need while she's here."

"As you wish, Your Grace."

"Miss Darling will be making use of Lady Catherine's wardrobe."

"That's not necessary," Frannie said.

"Suit yourself. Just know that Catherine left behind clothing that she'll no doubt never use again, and her clothes—like everything within this residence—are here to serve at your pleasure." He took a step forward, took her hand, and brought it to his lips. "And now, Frannie, I fear I must retire and shall leave you to do the same."

He appeared exhausted and she realized his discomfort was taking a toll on him. "I came to watch over you."

"Get some sleep first. If you fall ill, Swindler will kill me. Besides, I need to wash up and get out of these bloody clothes."

Giving a nod, she watched him cross over to a room opposite hers. She truly hadn't planned to stay beyond dawn, and she hadn't anticipated sleeping here. Hearing a drawer open, she turned to see Agnes taking out a nightgown. With a shy smile, she said, "Would you like me to have a bath prepared?"

"Oh, no, it's too late to bother with that."

"It's no bother if that's what you wish."

Frannie took the gown, surprised by the softness of the cloth. It would be like sleeping in a cloud. "Return to bed. I can see to myself."

"But His Grace—"

"Will never know."

Agnes gave a quick curtsy. "Yes, ma'am. Thank you, ma'am."

After changing into the nightgown and brushing out her hair, Frannie crawled into bed. She stared at the canopy for a while. Then she rolled over and studied the light coming in through the window. Was it moonlight or lamplight? Did it matter? She was in Greystone's residence. If she was staying only until dawn, she certainly didn't expect the sunlight to find her in this bed.

Throwing back the covers, she got up, lifted the lamp from the bedside table, and went into the hallway. She laid her hand flat against his door. She thought of him entertaining the lads with his stories at the Great Exhibition, thought of him sending for her instead of a constable when he'd discovered a thief in his residence. She thought of him putting himself in harm's way tonight. She thought of the pleasure he'd brought her the night of the opera.

He'd given her confidence that she was a woman a man might desire. While he would never marry her, perhaps another would. But life was precarious and opportunities were never guaranteed. Here was a man for whom she cared a great deal. Whatever they could share, it would be enough.

As she opened the door and walked in, she felt Greystone's gaze come to bear on her so quickly that she was fairly certain she hadn't awakened him. She glided over to the bed. "I wanted to check in on you. Are you in much pain?"

He shook his head. "My valet spooned me up some laudanum."

"You should have no trouble sleeping, then."

"What about you?"

"I should be fine now that I know you're all right."

"You told me once that you took comfort in sleeping—just sleeping—with someone. I'm wearing trousers if you want to—" He lifted the covers in invitation.

"You knew I'd come."

"I hoped you would."

She set the lamp on the table, slipped into bed beside him, and laid her head on his shoulder. His arm came around her, cocooning her in comfort.

"You see? I told you we'd find more comfort here," he said slowly as though he had to push the words through the fog of drowsiness brought on by the medication. "I want to know how you truly are, Frannie. You act as though what happened earlier affected only me, but you must have been terrified."

She skimmed her finger over his chest. "I think I was furious, more than anything else. I've been so careful when I go about the rookeries, yet there I was caught by surprise. When he mentioned Sykes I wanted to tear into him with everything I had."

"These trips you make to the rookeries—do you make them at night?"

She had yet to lie to him. He nudged her arm. "Frannie?"

"Sometimes."

"Alone?"

She nodded.

"Dammit, Frannie, do you know how foolish that is?"

"Children won't approach me if I'm not alone."

"They are not more important than you. Hire someone, for God's sake, who can skulk about without being seen, but can keep an eye on you."

"You're getting as bossy as Feagan's lads."

"Because you've become very precious to me." He pressed a kiss to the top of her head. "Please don't go there alone anymore."

She nodded. It was easier to break promises when they weren't voiced.

"What's that creature on your back?" she asked quietly, hoping to turn the subject away from her.

"A dragon."

"Did you see one in your travels? Does it exist?"

"As far as I know, only in legend. Are you not familiar with Saint George? He slew one, you know."

"I don't know him."

"Perhaps I'll tell you the story some day."

"Will it fade? The tattoo?"

"No."

"Why would you want it on your shoulder like that, something that will forever be there?"

"As I recall, I was quite drunk at the time and thought it a good idea."

"Why a dragon?"

"Symbolic. We all face dragons in one way or another, at one time or another."

"So it's not a good thing."

"Depends whether or not we slay them. It all made perfect sense when I was drunk."

"Did you slay yours?"

"I thought so at the time."

His hand was gently strolling up and down her arm, and she found herself wishing that the gown had no sleeves. Lying with him was nothing at all like lying with the boys when she was a young girl. His scent, his body, the length of him was that of a man. "I could have killed you."

His hand stilled, his arm tightened around her.

"But you didn't, and if you had it would have hardly been your fault."

"They might have hanged me anyway—for killing a lord."

"Swindler wouldn't have let that happen."

He was right, there. Jim would have protected her. He did it for so many others.

"I shouldn't have liked it if you'd have died," she said quietly.

"I wouldn't have liked it much either." She felt his chest rise beneath her cheek as though he were in the midst of a sigh that stopped abruptly as his wound protested. "I'm not certain I could have said the same a year ago."

Rising up on an elbow, she gazed down on his heavy-lidded expression. "That's an odd thing to say. At the worst times of my life, I've never wished for death."

"You've no doubt seen worse things than I have. How can you remain so optimistic?"

"Feagan used to say, 'No matter how bad things get, Frannie darling, they can always get worse and they can always get better. Expect worse and you'll never be disappointed. Expect better and you'll always have something to look forward to.' I prefer living in anticipation of the better."

"Where were you when I was an angry young man?"

"Probably at Claybourne's knowing that what he was giving me was better than I'd ever had and not liking it one bit. I missed Feagan. Claybourne forbade us from visiting Feagan while we lived under Claybourne's roof." She nestled back into the comforting crook of Greystone's shoulder. "I'm fairly certain it didn't stop Jack, though. He never was one to take orders well."

"I'd take that wager."

"Have you heard that he recently married?"

"No. God, who would have him?"

She released a small laugh. "Truly, you must think better of my friends."

"When they stop threatening me, I shall."

"Are they still threatening you?"

"Not lately. So who is the unfortunate lady?"

"Lovingdon's widow."

"Olivia? That's a surprise."

"I daresay that's an understatement, but I believe they're very happy."

"You take delight in others' happiness."

"Of course. Shouldn't we all?"

"I don't suppose I've really given it much thought."

With her finger she lazily drew circles on his chest. "I should probably let you sleep."

He closed his hand over hers, stilling her actions. "Stay with me while I do."

She listened as his breathing quickly became slow and even. She knew if he woke up first, he'd not take advantage of her. Luke had ensured it by telling Greystone about her past, but she suspected he'd have not taken advantage without the knowledge. Yes, he was a lord. Yes, he was accustomed to power. But he was also a gentleman.

As she drifted off to sleep, her final thought was that he was *her* gentleman.

Sterling awoke to find himself resting on his good side, his arm curled around Frannie, his hand nestled innocently against her breast. Not a position he had ever been in before with any other woman. He always touched a woman with purpose, with desire. He had to admit that he wanted to touch her that way again, but it had to be at her pace, when she was ready. Her backside was spooned against his hips, and his body's reaction there wasn't innocent at all. He eased back a little because he didn't want her to awaken to find herself being poked—

Only with a sigh, she snuggled back against him.

Lovely. Here he was, trying to be a gentleman, and she was ensuring that he not be. He concentrated on the sound of the rain pattering against the window, which made him think of water, and subsequently, his thoughts turned to her bathing, her silhouette behind the screen, and he grew achingly harder. He began cataloging all the treasures he'd brought from his travels: vases, pottery, statuettes, jewels. His body began to respond to the lack of exciting images. He thought of the bone-jarring trek on the camel. He thought of the fear that had fissured through him when a tiger attacked him and Wexford had shot it. If Sterling had died, he would have missed out on lying here with Frannie in his arms, her scent gracing his pillow, her delicate body separated from his by nothing more than a thin layer of cloth . . .

He cursed under his breath as the ache returned.

"Do you always awaken in such a foul mood?" she asked.

"How long have you been awake?"

"Long enough."

She rolled away from him and off the bed. The drapes were drawn, but the lamp still burned and he could see her clearly. "In spite of what happened when I was a girl, I don't fear intimacy. I fear a lack of honesty. Always be honest with me."

Running his gaze along the length of her, he said, "I want you. Desperately."

She gave him an impish smile. "I know. Unfortunately for you, at the moment I want breakfast."

He rolled over to his back, started to laugh, then cursed that unfortunate reaction that caused his side to ache.

"Perhaps it's fortunate for you that I want breakfast," she said.

He slid his gaze over to her. "Don't make me laugh."

"I'll stay until dawn tomorrow."

With that she quit the room. Sterling stared at the deep purple canopy. He planned to have the speediest recovery on record.

Sterling had promised her pampering so he saw to it that she was served breakfast in bed—even if it was in his with a tray of food between them. She sat at the foot of the bed wearing one of Catherine's simple day dresses, while he leaned against a stack of pillows at the headboard. His valet had changed his bandage, then helped him into trousers that didn't look as though they'd been slept in and a billowing shirt that made him feel more carefree than he had in some time.

"I suppose, working at Dodger's, that you're acquainted with all sorts of naughty behaviors," he said, spreading marmalade on his toast.

"I'm also sworn to secrecy regarding what I know. Jack has always had a very strict policy regarding the confidentiality of our customers."

"Pity. I imagine you have some rather fascinating stories."

"Well . . . I suppose I could share one." She gave him a sly smile.

He sat up a little straighter. "Go on."

"One night . . . it must have been around midnight" —she shook her head— "I don't know if I should tell you."

"I'm not going to tell anyone."

"Promise?"

"Promise."

"All right." She set her face in a mask of determination, and his anticipation grew as he waited for her to reveal her scandalous story. "It was rather shameful, but I added a column of numbers incorrectly. Jack discovered it. I was mortified."

"Numbers," he stated flatly.

She smiled saucily. "I am the bookkeeper, after all, and as a rule the numbers don't behave too badly."

"So that's the game you're going to play. You keep your nose buried in ledgers and never peep through the peepholes? Is that what you're claiming?"

"People are entitled to their privacy and their secrets."

"That's disappointing. I, on the other hand, have seen women dancing with hardly any clothes on at all."

Now it was her turn to sit up. "Really?"

Nodding, he took a bite of his toast. "They can make their stomachs undulate as though they're snakes. Very entertaining. You should consider inviting them over to work at Dodger's. I suspect gentlemen would never leave."

"It's a thought." Setting her plate aside, she brought her knees up and wrapped her arms around them. "I can't even begin to imagine all the sights you've seen."

"They were wondrous. My father didn't agree with my decision to go. We argued about it. He told me if I left, he never wanted to see me again. He thought I was selfishly putting my wants above my duties. In a way I suppose I was. He told me I could always see the world later. He didn't understand."

"I'm sure he didn't mean it—about never seeing you again."

"I returned to England four months before he died. I went to visit him, when Catherine wasn't there. He was infirm, had lost the ability to speak, but his nurse told me that he could communicate with his eyes. He refused to look at me. I believe he did mean it when he said he never wanted to see me again."

Sterling's father had also been ashamed by Sterling's limitations, although he had no desire to share that facet of his tale with Frannie. Perhaps he was as ashamed as his father. She worked within the dark shadows of London, and there he might as well be blind for all the good his limited vision did him.

"At least you know who your father was," she said.

"Yes, I suppose there is some comfort in that."

She placed her chin on her knees. "So now that you've returned you'll see to your duties."

"Precisely. I shall have a boring wife, hopefully not boring children."

She laughed, but it sounded rather forced, and he realized that under the circumstances, he probably shouldn't discuss with her the kind of woman he wanted to marry. But she had demanded honesty. "I won't make a good husband, Frannie."

"I think you underestimate yourself there, but I expect nothing lasting from you, and rest assured that becoming a duchess has never been one of my dreams."

"I thought all girls dreamed of marrying a duke."

"Oh, no. I'd much rather marry a king," she teased.

"I suspect Anne Boleyn felt the same."

She laughed. He loved hearing her laugh. "Oh, you're horrible."

Grinning, he shrugged. "All right, then. Queen Frannie."

"Sounds silly, doesn't it? Truthfully, I don't see myself getting married at all."

"Will your orphans keep you content?"

"I believe so, yes." She looked toward the window. "I should be out searching for more."

"In this miserable weather? Surely, they'll all be indoors."

"If they have places to go." She sighed wistfully. "It's good reading weather, isn't it? Do you read many books?"

"Not as many as I used to. Reading has begun to give me a headache of late."

"Spectacles might help."

They didn't, but he didn't want to follow this path. "I should probably look into it."

"Do you enjoy Dickens?" she asked.

"I find his stories rather bleak."

"I think he writes about that which he knows. Perhaps I'll read to you this afternoon."

"I'd enjoy that very much."

She slid off the bed and began gathering up the empty dishes.

"Call for a servant," he told her.

"I can do it easily enough."

Reaching out, he grabbed her wrist. "Why do you do that, Frannie? Why do you seek to remind me that our stations in life are so different?"

"I'm not reminding you, I'm reminding myself to remain honest with you about who I am and what I am. The only time I've ever pretended to be what I wasn't was when I wanted to fool someone into giving me something. Do you know there are people who will kindly take in a soldier down on his luck? The soldier and his young daughter. And while the generous family was sleeping, we'd gather up their valuables and slip out into the night. You should never forget, Your Grace, that I was once one of the light-fingered people you wanted to keep out of your house."

"And I was once a young man who put his own pleasures ahead of his duties. We all change, Frannie. We make up for our past failures. You stole, I disappointed my father. Now you do good works and I will honor my responsibilities and my title. It's the woman you are now who intrigues me, the one I . . . care about as much as I am able to care."

"I don't want to become something to you that I'm not or that I'm not capable of being. I don't want to fool you."

"You think so little of me as to believe I can be easily fooled? You've discouraged me at almost every turn, and yet here you are at last in my bed. At my invitation as I recall."

"It could all be part of my well-conceived plan. That's how we work, you know. We lure you into believing exactly what we need you to in order to take advantage."

Releasing his hold on her wrist, he settled back against the pillows and spread his arms wide. "Then by all means, take advantage."

Her gaze slowly wandered the length of him, and his body reacted with fierceness that he couldn't control. He watched as she swallowed and licked her lips. Then she picked up the tray and gave him a saucy wink. "You see? Now you are no longer in a position to stop me from removing the dishes—which is exactly what I wanted."

He laughed. He didn't believe her, not for one minute, but if it was the game she wished to play, he would concede defeat in hopes of gaining a decisive victory later.

"You should rest now," she told him. "Regain your strength."

He watched her leave the room, then closed his eyes. She was correct. He needed to regain his strength and quickly. The minutes were ticking away, and he suspected once she left his residence, he'd have a devil of a time getting her to return.

Chapter 17

While Greystone rested, Frannie retired to the morning room. Jutting out into the garden, it was three walls of windows with a glass roof that the rain pattered and exploded against. She wanted honesty not only from him, but also from herself. Could she look herself in the mirror if she gave herself to a man who would never marry her, a man she would never marry? Was it wrong, just once in her life, to know what it was to be truly desired?

Greystone was a man of passion. He was a man of adventure. He was a man who desired her. That much had been evident this morning when she'd awoken to find him fully aroused and pressing against her bottom.

His nearness exhilarated her.

He didn't care about her past. He didn't care that she'd once been a pickpocket and thief. She'd never enjoyed the times when Feagan would pretend to be a soldier, when people were kind to them, and they repaid the kindness by taking their possessions. She'd innately understood that everything they were doing was wrong—and yet she did it anyway in order to please him.

She used the excuse that Luke's grandfather had forbidden them from visiting Feagan to explain her never again seeing him. But the truth was that she was ashamed of the things he'd asked of her. It was part of the reason that she spent so little money on herself and she had so few possessions. She'd taken that to which she wasn't entitled when she was younger and now she wanted to give back as much as she could. If she could teach children not to break the law, if she could provide them with good examples to follow, if she could undo the lessons they'd been taught . . .

Perhaps she wouldn't feel quite so tainted by her past, by her association with Feagan.

"I was hoping for a sunny day so that we might have a picnic in the garden," Greystone said as he sat in the chair beside her.

She smiled at him. "I enjoy the rain. I'm probably the only person in all of England who does."

"It seems melancholy weather."

"I prefer to think of it more as weather designed for reflection."

"You are the eternal optimist. And what are you reflecting on?"

"Nothing of any importance. How are you feeling now?"

"Still a bit achy, but I'm confident that survival is in my future."

She studied him for a moment, the lines fanning out from his eyes, the crease in his brow. He was still experiencing discomfort. Why did men feel that they always had to give the impression of being strong?

"I want to thank you again for sending the cobbler."

"Did it make you think better of me?"

"Yes."

"Then it was worth the expense."

"I'm thinking of listing our benefactors on a plaque on the wall. Would that be a nice acknowledgement, do you think?"

"I prefer to be anonymous. I did it for you, not for the glory."

"And here I thought you did it for the boys."

He gazed out at the rain, a slight flush on his cheeks that she thought had nothing to do with his injury. He had done it for her, to please her, to gain her favor. Another bouquet of flowers would not have worked as well. It meant a great deal to her that he'd come to realize what was important to her and what wasn't.

"Will you dress for dinner tonight?" he asked quietly.

"I thought I might. I found a gown of Catherine's that fits me rather nicely."

He shifted his gaze over to her. "I'm pleased to hear that. I've asked Cook to prepare something special. Is there anything you don't fancy?"

"Growing up as I did, I'm thankful for any food that comes my way."

"You're too easy to please, Miss Darling."

"I prefer when you call me Frannie."

His beautiful blue eyes warmed. "Frannie, it would please me immensely if you'd call me Sterling and no more of this Your Grace business while we're here."

She wanted to tell him that she thought it was important that she remember he was a duke, but suddenly with the rain locking them inside, it was almost as though the real world was no longer surrounding them. They could pretend for just a few hours that they belonged in the same world.

"We have some time before dinner," she said. "Shall I read to you?"

"Only if we sit on a sofa together and I can rub your feet while you read."

She smiled. "Sterling, I do believe we have a trade."

*   *   *

Dinner was served in the same intimate setting as before, although no one was there to surround them with music. Fewer candles flickered. Fewer words were spoken. Fewer breaths were taken.

Or so it seemed to Frannie.

She considered that perhaps her corset was too snug or maybe Catherine's gown was a little too small for her, but she suspected the true reason for her difficulty rested in the way that Sterling looked at her, as though he fully intended to have her for dessert.

He was dressed as formally as he had been for the opera and he struck her as being as wickedly handsome. Over the rim of his wineglass he perused her with a leisurely wandering of his gaze, which caused pleasure to light and darken the blue of his eyes. It was a strange and heady combination to know that she affected him so.

She had bathed earlier and sampled all the bottles of perfume that adorned Catherine's vanity until she found one that brought forth images of nymphs cavorting in a garden. She preferred light scents, perhaps because in her youth she'd favored heavier fragrances that masked the stench of the rookeries. Everything in her life now she weighed against what her life had been then.

Yet she felt ill prepared for this moment.

"Relax, Frannie," he said in a voice so calm that it had the power to calm her thundering heart. "Nothing will happen tonight that you don't wish to happen."

"And what if things you wish to happen don't?"

"Then they don't. I'll be disappointed, to be sure, but I can live with disappointment. You shouldn't have to live with the feeling that you were forced into doing something you didn't want."

He seemed to realize the significance of what he'd said. "It won't be like before," he added.

"I wouldn't be here if that was my expectation."

He tapped his wineglass against hers where it rested near her plate. "Thank you for seeing to my recovery."

"I'm just grateful your wound wasn't as severe as I thought."

"I'm doubly grateful. I suppose Swindler will be searching for the culprit."

"Probably. Even without a description, I suspect he could find the offender. He's very skilled that way."

"You admire him."

She scowled at him. "I admire all of Feagan's lads."

"It seems to me they're as much Claybourne's lads as Feagan's. Claybourne took you all in, didn't he?"

"Yes. But Feagan taught us himself while Claybourne hired tutors. It's very easy to accomplish something when you have the means with which to purchase it."

"You admire this Feagan fellow."

"I'm not sure *admire* is the correct word." She thought about it for a moment. Some aspects of him disappointed her, but she couldn't deny that he'd provided well for the children he took in. "I suppose it is. Yes, he taught us questionable skills, but he gave us a home of sorts. I've been thinking of naming my children's home after him, actually."

"Feagan's Children's Home? Is that an honor he deserves?"

She took a sip of wine, and then another. She knew that Greystone wanted nothing more from her than a night in his bed, but still she felt obligated to ask, "Would you think less of me if you knew that I believe he might be my father?"

Swirling the wine in his wineglass, he seemed to ruminate the implications. "I may give credence to a person's elevation in society based on his ancestors, but of late I've learned to judge the individual on his own accomplishments and merits."

She smiled at him. "Then I find you to be rare indeed."

"If he were your father, wouldn't he claim so?"

"I would have thought. I asked Jack once. Jack knows so many secrets."

"What did he say?"

"He avoided answering. I'm not sure if it's because whatever the answer, he thought I'd find it disappointing or if he was trying to protect me."

"Secrets have a way of always coming out."

"Have you secrets, Sterling?"

"We all have secrets."

But she couldn't imagine that his were nearly as dark as hers.

Dressed in one of Catherine's nightgowns, Frannie sat at the vanity brushing out her hair. A hundred strokes. It had been one of Feagan's rules. She'd often wondered if a lady in his life had brushed out her hair for him. Had he loved her? Had she loved him? He was so secretive about his past. But tonight she didn't want to reflect on where she'd come from. She was interested in only where she might be going.

Sterling had said good night to her at the bedchamber door, giving the impression that he truly meant good night. He would not come to this room. He wouldn't come for her.

The choice as to whether or not they'd ever lie together was hers—because he would never marry her, and so he was leaving the decision to her. She met her gaze in the reflection in the mirror. To willingly go to a man who would not make an honest woman of her . . .

But was it more dishonest to deny herself the pleasure of his bed when she wanted it so desperately? Following the opera, he'd given her a taste of the pleasure she'd find in his arms.

It had been eighteen years since a man had taken possession of her. She'd locked away the disgust of those pudgy hands pinching and pulling. She'd forced into darkened corners the memory of his body ramming into hers, the pain, the blood, the echo of her screams, the reverberation of his hideous laughter . . .

But they were there, waiting to be replaced by something strong enough to destroy them.

Chapter 18

Within his bedchamber, Sterling sat in a chair near the fireplace, staring at the dying embers, watching them diminish until they were nothing, similar to the way that his eyesight was diminishing. Other than the faint light emitted by the hearth, the only glow came from the low light in the lamp near his bed. He wore only trousers and the bandage on his wound. Because he was breathing more easily, he'd removed the narrow strip of binding around his chest.

From the moment he'd kissed Frannie in Claybourne's library, he'd sought to seduce her, to lure her to his bed. Yet he'd been the one seduced into being a better man than he was. He'd decided to let her go without ever knowing the full taste of her. She humbled him beyond measure with her Dickens, and her orphans, and her ability to ferret out noble intentions even in those with a criminal past. In his world, there was right and wrong, good and evil. Hers contained no absolutes. Hers was a world of grays. Hers was what his was truly becoming. The irony didn't escape him. At night, nothing was clear. Lines blurred. Shadows removed definitions.

Her dreams led her to the darkest parts of London where he couldn't follow and keep her safe. His dreams had ceased to exist long ago. He would carry out his duties and he would see to his responsibilities. But none of them would include her—even if he wanted to include her, she didn't want the life of an aristocrat. He couldn't turn away from the legacy that had been handed down to him. He'd pay a much higher price to honor his title than his father had ever imagined.

He heard the click of the door opening. Satisfaction swamped him. Even if she was here to only sleep in his arms, he would take contentment with that. He would adopt her tendency to find joy in the smallest of pleasures. Sleeping with her nestled against his side was the sweetest of all.

Setting aside his brandy snifter, he rose and turned. She stood at the foot of his bed, one hand wrapped around the post. On bare, silent feet, he walked across the thick carpet until she was a whisper's breath away.

She lifted her gaze to his. Within her green eyes, he saw no fear, no apprehension, no doubt.

"I want one night with you," she whispered softly.

He was unprepared for the force of her words—as though she'd punched him in the heart. Until that moment he'd been deceiving himself into believing that he could live without her because he'd never expected to truly possess her. And now here she was, her mixture of innocence and bravado charming him as no other lady ever had.

"Then one night you shall have." Because he couldn't deny her any more than he could deny himself. Sliding his arms around her, he brought her up against him and lowered his mouth to hers.

Frannie welcomed him as she might air to breathe or sun to warm. His brandy taste was an aphrodisiac, igniting the flames of desire until they were spreading through her body, heating her core, licking at her fingertips. She glided her fingers up his bare arms and felt the muscles rippling beneath her palms. His strength was palpable, his determination evident. His kiss was more aggressive than any he'd ever given her, as though with her surrender, whatever beasts of pleasure that had been lying in wait were now unleashed.

Breathing harshly, he trailed his hot mouth along her throat, his tongue swirling over her skin, his teeth nipping. "Stop me if I frighten you, but know that I will not hurt you, but neither can I go gently. I want you too badly, have been patient too long."

He'd once warned her that he was no longer civilized. It was here she realized where his warning held the most credence as the gown that separated their flesh was ripped asunder, pooling at her feet before she'd even realized what he'd intended. And then, as though the beast had been satisfied, he touched her with the gentlest of hands that skimmed over her curves. Strange that she didn't feel exposed, that she had no desire to cover herself. Rather she wanted to light additional lamps, gather up lighted candles and reveal all she had to offer him. She who had once been shy about her womanhood was now glorying in it.

"Dear God, but you are beautiful. I knew you would be." He lifted his gaze to hers and held it. "Tell me what you don't want."

"I don't want you to treat me as though I'm vulnerable or might shatter. I want you to treat me as you would any other woman you've known."

"You are nothing like any other woman I've ever known. Never make the mistake of thinking that you are or could ever be."

His mouth came back to hers, kissing her deeply. Her breasts flattened against the warm plane of his chest. She glided her hands down his thighs, then glided them up between them until she cupped through his trousers what she'd felt pressing against her that morning. He released a gravelly groan, broke off the kiss, and stood perfectly still as though giving her leave to explore, to do as she would.

Licking her lips, her mouth suddenly dry, she lowered her gaze to the hard bulge in his trousers. She had no misconceptions regarding the power presently leashed behind a few straining buttons. It was a wonder they weren't popping off and spinning on the floor.

"It won't hurt you," he rasped as he skimmed his mouth along her temple.

"I know. Because you won't hurt me."

His mouth went still, and she was incredibly aware of the tension in his muscles, the light beads of sweat that coated the cords of his neck. His hand moved to the top button—

"I'll do it," she said quickly, placing her hand over his and nudging it aside. The buttons popped free as though grateful for the freedom, and she realized he wore nothing except trousers. But her fingers didn't falter. Instead they hastened to reveal what cloth held hidden. He shucked his trousers down until he stood before her, erect, proud, and utterly magnificent. She lifted her eyes to his. "You're beautiful as well."

The worry she'd seen in the deep blue of his

eyes dissipated. He laughed and lifted her into his arms.

"We're going to have a jolly good time, Frannie," he said as he laid her out on the cool satin sheets.

She was more beautiful than Sterling had expected, more bold than he'd dared hope for. Whatever experiences may have tarnished her past, she'd not brought them with her to his bed. She was coy. She didn't turn away from him or pretend embarrassment. She received him as the most highly paid courtesan might, with a seductive smile and welcoming arms.

But she was there not because of any coins he might have given her. She was there solely for the pleasure they could bring each other. He'd never wanted a woman more. His body ached with the need to possess her, but he had no plans to rush the moment. He'd have only one night with her, but he wanted it to be one that would last his lifetime. He was fairly certain he'd never find another woman as courageous, determined, and intriguing as she was. Any moment not spent in her company was an empty moment. As he stretched out beside her and skimmed his hands over her, relished the gliding of her hands over him, he didn't want to contemplate the never-ending spectrum of empty moments that might lie ahead.

"I wonder what would happen to your fair skin if the sun kissed it in the desert," he murmured.

"You mean remove my clothes outside?"

Giving her a devilish grin, he arched a brow at her. Her eyes scanned the length of him. "Did you do that?"

"Once or twice."

Her fingers trailed up his thigh, skimmed around to his buttocks, stopped. Tickled. "What's that?"

Sitting up she leaned over and looked at his buttocks. Gently, she feathered her fingers over the five ragged scars that ran from his hip down as though the wounds were fresh and still causing him pain.

"Tiger," he said. "I didn't see him until he was upon me. Fortunately, Lord Wexford is an amazing shot."

"You could have been killed."

"And instead, now a tiger skin adorns the floor in Wexford's study. I thought women found scars rakish."

"I don't mind their appearance. I just don't like that you were once so badly hurt."

Powerful words from a lady who carried her scars inside. Cradling her neck with one hand, he brought her back down to the pillow. "How can you have so much compassion and no bitterness?"

She gave no answer to that. He expected none, truly wanted none as he kissed her. He'd explored many women during his travels but none with the intensity that he wished to explore her. The others were merely passing fancies. She was more. She was the reason he skulked around in alleyways and had food prepared for little thieves. She was the reason he now understood the sentiments that drove a man to kill.

It was as though before her, each of his emotions had lain dormant. He'd never known such intense anger, or jealousy, or joy, or . . . love.

His thoughts faltered. No, it was not love that he felt. Infatuation, adoration. But not love. Nothing as binding. She would walk away from him and he'd allow her to take nothing of him with her. But while she was there, in his bed, he would strive to give her much by which to remember him.

Frannie had known he was a man of passion. What she hadn't expected was the way he touched her as though he could never have enough of touching her—not only with his hands, but with his mouth.

He swirled his tongue around her nipple until it pebbled, then closed his mouth greedily around it. She raked her fingernails through his thick hair, dug her fingers into his shoulders, skimmed the sole of one foot up his calf. Pleasure ebbed and flowed until she thought she would go mad with the wanting for release. Patiently his mouth journeyed to her other breast. She, a child of the streets, had never known such reverence, had never expected it, especially of a man whose life was so above the squalor.

Here, in his bed, she found what she'd never hoped to hold—unselfish giving and receiving, a sense of evenness that was difficult to explain. He knew of her past, but because he hadn't witnessed it, he wasn't obsessed with guilt over what he'd been unable to prevent. He didn't treat her as though she was fine china that would shatter with too much pressure. He squeezed and he coaxed and he trailed his mouth along her stomach, across her hip, down her thigh.

He lifted his head to give her the most wicked smile she'd ever seen, one that promised adventures, delight, the sun kissing her skin. He gently nudged her thigh and she opened herself to him. He moved this way and that until he was nestled between her legs, his open mouth heating her stomach. And then he journeyed lower and lower . . .

She thought she should have been afraid or at the very least wary, but she realized with startling clarity that she trusted him to never hurt her, to never cause her discomfort, to never betray these tender feelings that allowed her to come to his bed when she'd never gone willingly to the bed of another man.

Then his tongue stroked and swirled intimately. She released a sigh of pleasure as her back arched and her hips jerked. She felt as though her body was the world and he was traveling across it, sampling every aspect. She wanted to do the same to him. Would he think her bold or wanton?

Did it matter? Did anything matter when he was causing her body to sing? Oh, she felt as though she were an operatic song, rising in crescendo. Her breathing became harsh and rapid. Her breasts tightened, her stomach grew taut. His mouth and fingers were creating sensations more vivid than what she'd experienced on his sofa. Where was her selfish duke who cared only about his own pleasures? Was he enjoying this as much as she?

Then the questions dissipated as the pleasure spiraled . . .

"Oh, God, you should stop now," she rasped, digging her fingers into his shoulders.

He laughed, his breath tickling her, before he returned to where he'd been. She wanted to weep, she wanted to laugh . . . the cataclysm slammed into her and she was screaming, screaming for him to stop, for him to go on, screaming his name as pleasure shot through her.

When she came back into herself, she was trembling and he was licking his way up her body until he reached her mouth and kissed her hungrily, so hungrily, as though he could taste what she'd just experienced.

He brushed his lips over her cheek, nibbled on her ear. "I love the sounds you make."

He said it as though her screaming were a wonderful thing. He moved until he could look into her eyes, and she saw, in his, absolute joy, as though he were pleased with what he'd just given her. Dew glistened on his throat and shoulders. She skimmed her hands up his back and felt the tenseness in his muscles.

"This isn't . . . all," she panted.

"No, but it will be if that's all you want."

Studying him, she tried to make sense of his words. He would grant her pleasure and forego his own yet again? The words he'd spoken in the library so long ago took on new meaning. He'd asked to be her lover. To give with no expectation of ever receiving?

She shook her head. "I want everything. I want you."

A slow, triumphant smile flashed across his face. "Then you shall have me."

He shifted his weight, leaned toward the bedside table. She heard the scraping of a drawer being opened. He pulled something out—

A condom, she realized.

It was an odd moment to be disappointed, yet she understood the wisdom of it. She even appreciated his effort to protect her from scandal, but she couldn't deny that she had a sudden desire to bring his child into the world.

She watched in fascination as he covered himself. Their eyes met as he rose above her and began to very slowly ease his body into hers. There was a tightness but no discomfort, a sensation of pleasure unfurling as he went deeper and deeper. This satisfaction, this possessiveness, was what it was to want to have a man share his body. He groaned low as he stilled. With heavy lidded eyes he grinned at her. "No pain?"

She shook her head. "No."

"Good, because I want to hear you screaming my name again—but I want it to be from pleasure, not agony."

"Again?"

His grin grew. "Again."

She was replete, had thought she'd be able to do little more than run her hands over him as he rocked against her, but his movements awakened something deep within her. The surprise of it had her gasping. He increased his rhythm, the power of his thrusts, until the bed was banging against the wall and she was holding onto him, digging her fingers into his buttocks, feeling the strength, the power . . .

His movements contained a wildness. He was uncivilized as he carried her to new heights. She did scream his name again.

Then he was growling hers through clenched teeth, his head thrown back, his body arching and thrusting, trembling and jerking.

Collapsing, he buried his face into the curve of her shoulder. She heard his harsh breathing, felt the tremors cascading through him, was aware of her own body's quivering. Each time was more than the last. She wondered if a person could expire from too much pleasure.

Relishing the weight of his body on hers, she lightly trailed her fingers up and down his back.

"Tickles," he muttered.

Naughtily, she skimmed her fingers along his sides. He jerked upright.

"You are a witch. Wait here."

As though she had a choice. She would have laughed, but she had no energy. He rolled off her and padded into what she assumed was the dressing room. He returned with a towel and gently wiped the dew from her body. Then he climbed into bed and brought the covers up over them.

Lying within the curve of his arm, she listened to the steady pounding of his heart. When his breathing evened out, she lifted her head slightly and gazed down on his face. His hair was disheveled. In sleep, he had fewer lines of worry. She felt the tears sting her eyes as she realized she'd made a dreadful mistake in coming here.

She feared she'd fallen in love with the Duke of Greystone.

Frannie didn't know what time it was when she awoke, lying on her stomach, sprawled over his bed, barely opening her eyes. What she did know was that he was no longer in bed with her. She felt his absence without even looking. Was he finished with her then?

"Don't move."

She opened her eyes fully. He was sitting in a chair near the bed, one leg crossed over the other in such a way to provide support for his sketch pad.

"What are you doing?" she asked.

"Drawing you."

"Do you draw every woman you bed?"

He glanced up then, looking as though something significant had dawned on him. "No, actually. You're the first I've ever cared about remembering."

His words delighted her, made it more difficult not to move when she wanted to crawl into his lap and kiss him soundly. "How much longer must I remain still?"

"Just a few more moments. Then I'll show you what I've done."

"You won't show anyone else, will you?"

"Absolutely not. These go into my private collection."

"These?"

"You've given me one night. I didn't intend to spend most of it sleeping."

She wanted to smile or laugh, but she fought to stay completely still. She'd never known anyone who made her feel quite so appreciated. Certainly, Feagan's lads appreciated what she did, but they didn't make her toes curl when they looked at her.

"Can you do a self-portrait?" she asked.

"No. Why would I care for that?"

"So you could give it to me."

He grinned. "I'm sure we could find something around here that would suffice."

"All the paintings around here are so large that it would make it difficult to place it in a private collection."

He winked at her, and her entire body threatened to curl into a ball of pleasure.

"We'll find something."

She was surprised by the drawings when he fi-

nally returned to bed to show her. They sat back
against a mound of pillows while he revealed
them one by one.

Her feet, one crossed over the other.

"You rub your feet together while you sleep,"
he said.

"Probably a habit. They were always cold when
I was younger. Coal was a rarity at Feagan's."

"If they get cold before you leave my bed,
simply press them against me. That should warm
them."

*The sheet draped over her back, one bare
shoulder exposed.*

"You have lovely shoulders," he said. He leaned
over and kissed one.

"You're a very good artist."

"I've had a lot of practice. My efforts will never
be on display in a museum, but they relax me."

"And you needed to relax after what we did
earlier?"

He began wrapping her hair around his finger.
"No, I was fairly melting into the bed."

Her hand curled beneath her chin.

"That's my favorite," he said. "A bit innocent, a
bit sultry. I wonder what you were dreaming."

"About you, probably."

"Probably? Don't you remember?"

"I seldom remember my dreams."

He gave her a funny look before tossing his papers to the floor and pulling her beneath him. "One night, you said, but the night's not yet over."

As his mouth blanketed hers, she sighed. *No, no, it's not.*

Frannie had planned to leave at dawn, but just before the sun began easing over the horizon, he was making love to her again and he didn't rush it. They both knew it would be the last time, the final time, and they savored every touch, every stroke, every kiss. When she did finally leave his bed, breakfast had been readied.

They'd gotten dressed and walked down to the breakfast dining room together. He was telling her about his adventures in learning to ride a camel. She was laughing so hard that she couldn't eat. She loved his smile and the joy that lit his eyes. She loved—

"Your Grace, I'm sorry to disturb you, but an Inspector Swindler from Scotland Yard is here," the butler announced.

Frannie felt her stomach knot up. Her magical world was about to clash with reality.

"Send him in," Sterling said, just before he reached out and squeezed her hand. "It'll be all right."

She nodded, rising to her feet as he did. Jim strode into the room and came to an abrupt halt as his gaze fell on her. She saw the disappointment sweep over his face. She suspected it didn't take a genius to determine what had happened here. Was it evident in her blush, which she had no ability to control?

"Inspector, would you care to join us for breakfast?" Sterling asked.

"No. I just . . . we were worried about you, Frannie. We didn't know—"

"I left a note on Jack's desk." All she'd said was that she was going to see after Greystone, but still, it had given her whereabouts. There'd been no cause for worry. Well, except for the part where she'd promised to return yesterday.

Jim nodded. "You're all right, then?"

"Yes, I'm very well. Thank you."

"Sorry to have disturbed your morning." He spun on his heel and strode out.

"Jim!" Tossing down her napkin, she rushed out after him.

"Frannie!" Sterling called after her but she ignored him.

She ran down the hallway, catching up with Jim in the foyer, grabbing his arm. "Jim."

He spun around. She could see the concern and hurt in his green eyes. And anger, too, as though he didn't know what exactly to feel any more than she did. "He won't marry you, Frannie."

"I'm well aware of that."

"I would." He dropped his gaze to the floor as though he couldn't bear to see whatever her eyes might reveal. She was acutely aware of him struggling to get his emotions in check. She wanted to reach out and touch him, comfort him, but she was fairly certain he wouldn't welcome either at that moment. He lifted his eyes to hers, and all the love he'd ever felt for her was there. "Even if his babe is growing in your belly, I'll marry you."

He headed for the door. The footman opened it and Jim strode through it without a backward glance.

Oh, God, what had she done? Why had she never seen that before, why had she never recognized the depth of his feelings?

"Are you all right?" Sterling asked, coming up behind her and putting his hands on her shoulders.

Tears burned her eyes. "I should leave now."

"I'll have the coach readied."

She nodded, as the full measure of what they'd done and what they must now do loomed before her. Slowly, he turned her around and held her close. She inhaled his scent, absorbed his strength.

Then he tipped her head up. His eyes met hers, and he began to leisurely lower his mouth—

"Thank you, *Your Grace*," she said softly.

He stilled. She watched his throat work as he swallowed. His arms moved slowly away from her. "It's been my pleasure, Miss Darling."

Leaving him standing in the entry hallway, she headed for the stairs so she could change into her clothes and return to her world. Her chest ached so badly that she thought it might cave in on itself. She wouldn't cry here, but later, in her apartment where no one could hear her, she would let the tears fall. And she prayed that eventually they would stop.

Chapter 19

With a sigh, Frannie placed her elbow on the desk and her chin on her palm. She was supposed to be adding numbers and instead she'd been writing *Greystone, Sterling, Duke* on a piece of paper at random angles. Once, she'd even written *Duchess*, but she scratched it out. She wouldn't be his duchess—ever.

It had been two nights since she'd gone to his residence. She'd visited the secret balcony at least half a dozen times trying to catch a glimpse of Sterling at the gaming tables. If he was there, he was as hidden as she was.

If Jack had a problem with where she'd gone for two nights, he didn't say anything. He'd become a little more accepting of the nobility since marrying into it and perhaps not as judgmental. Jim hadn't stopped by. She rubbed her brow. She was dreading that encounter when it finally happened—if it ever happened. Jim might be having misgivings about how much he'd revealed regarding his feelings for her. He'd laid them bare. And dear God, help them both, she couldn't return his affection in equal measure.

She considered going to talk with Luke. He'd once asked her to marry him, but he hadn't loved her, not truly, not in the way that a man loved a woman. His love was the love of youth. Thank goodness, Catherine had come into his life and shown him the error of his ways.

She supposed she could talk with Catherine. After all, Sterling was her brother, but she sensed that they weren't as close as they might have once been.

Frannie was tired, not sleeping well, because she'd begun to dream, to remember the dreams, and in every one of them Sterling was doing wicked things to her and she was screaming out his name. In some, she was being equally wicked and he was screaming out hers.

She rose from her chair and took a last look around her sparsely furnished, tidy office. She should probably move her books to the orphanage. She could work on them there and be with the children every night, instead of only visiting with them during the day. It didn't matter where she worked on the books as long as she worked on them.

Strolling down the hallway, she removed her dagger and reached into her pocket for the key that unlocked the door to the outside. She wasn't about to let one of Sykes's footpads frighten her into cowering. Let someone try to attack her again. She was in the mood for a fight.

Once she was on the steps in the dim glow of a lantern hanging nearby, she closed and locked the door. She gave her eyes a moment to adjust to the shadowy and foggy gloom.

"Frannie?"

She heard the soft whisper, the almost desperate need to be heard and not heard at the same time. Turning toward the shadows, she reached up and lifted the lantern from the hook. Because she recognized the voice, she wasn't afraid, but she was incredibly curious and cautious. "Nancy?"

A woman stepped out of the shadows. She was only two years older than Frannie, but the years had not been kind to her. Her face was hollowed-out cheeks and eyes, dark circles and smudges that might have been dirt but were most likely bruises. "How ye be?"

They'd been friends on the street, although they were under the care of different kidsmen. When Nancy turned twelve, she moved in with a boy three years older—Bob Sykes. It wasn't uncommon for young girls to attach themselves to boys only a bit older than they were. They offered protection. For the boys, having a girl was a symbol of achievement. Frannie had always been able to tell which boys had taken in a girl because they had such large swaggers when they walked about, their status among the other boys raised by the apparent evidence of their manliness.

Frannie hadn't seen Nancy since the night Frannie had been abducted and sold into prostitution. She and Nancy had planned to sneak into a theater to see a play that Nancy had been talking about incessantly. Instead disaster had struck. Fortunately for Nancy, she'd managed to escape, while Frannie had been carted into hell.

"I'm doing well, Nancy. How are you? Still with Sykes?"

"Caw, yeah. 'e's not somebody yer loikely to leave, now, is 'e? Ye still working for the Dodger?"

Nancy was stooped over, cowering from the light, so Frannie pulled it back. She knew what it was like not to want to be seen under too harsh a light. Nancy's clothes were worn and frayed, but Frannie could tell they'd been recently pressed as though she wanted to make a good impression. Although it was night, she wore a hat that sat askew on top of her piled-up hair.

"Yes, I'm still with Dodger," Frannie said. "We

have a cook who prepares food for the gentlemen all night—anything to keep them playing at the tables. Come inside to the kitchen, and I'll find you something to eat."

"Nah, thank ye, I'm fine. That ol' gent taught ye how to speak right."

"He taught me a good deal."

"So everything wot 'appened that night, I guess it weren't so bad after all."

Frannie had been brutally raped. To even think that it wasn't "so bad" was the same as comparing a knife through the heart to a pinprick of the finger. "I survived." She glanced around. "It's all damp out here with the fog rolling in. At least come up to my apartment, get out of the weather."

"I 'eard yer taking in orphans," Nancy said quickly.

"Yes, I—"

"Then take this 'un." Nancy reached back into the shadows, then slung a boy against Frannie's legs. "He's one of Sykes's boys. I ken bring ye more if ye'll take this 'un."

"Nancy—"

"Please. 'e's my boy, too. I want something better than the streets fer 'im. 'is name's Petey. 'e's a good boy."

Wrapping her arm around the lad, Frannie drew him up against her skirts. While he wore a jacket, she could still tell that he was little more than bones. Sykes was a burglar by trade, and she knew he worked hard to keep the boys small so they could fit through tiny places in order to get into a house and open the front door for him.

"You come with us, too, Nancy. I can provide a safe haven for you and the boy."

Nancy scoffed. "I been with 'im since I was twelve. 'e ain't likely to let me go easy."

"I can find you employment in the country—"

She watched Nancy's face crumple. "Ye was always so nice. I didn't want to do it, ye know. Ye gotta believe that. I didn't want to do it."

"What are you on about?"

"It was Sykes. 'e made me. 'e said we'd make good money selling ye to that old woman. I never saw a 'apenny."

Frannie's insides felt as though an ice storm had hit them. The old woman? The gray-haired woman who'd run the brothel where she'd been taken? Suddenly she found herself clutching the boy to keep herself standing.

"Ye look loike yer about to bring up yer supper. Ye didn't know?"

Frannie shook her head. "No."

"Ye was always so smart that I figured ye figured it out. Don't hold it against my boy."

"I'd never take the sins of the mother out on

the child. Do you know what they did to me, Nancy?"

"I can well imagine."

"No, I don't think you can."

"I imagine it's pretty close to wot Sykes does to me ev'ry night. 'e's an animal, that one is. A dog. Someone should put 'im down. I'll bring ye more boys if I can."

Before Frannie could respond, Nancy was running off into the darkness, her rapid footsteps muffled by the thickening fog. Frannie lowered the lantern and looked at the boy who'd been left behind.

He was the boy who went by the name of Jimmy.

The little thief was again in Sterling's kitchen, sitting at the servant's table, stuffing food into his mouth as though he hadn't had a nibble since he'd last visited.

That Frannie had brought him here and not to her orphanage spoke volumes. Unfortunately, she wasn't saying quite as much, and Sterling sensed that whatever was troubling her was far more worrisome than discovering the lad's parentage.

"So he's Sykes's son?" he repeated.

"According to Nancy, yes."

"I suppose that explains his inability to appreciate your taking the lad."

"I'm afraid if I take him back to the orphanage that Sykes might come after him there."

Sterling shifted his gaze to her. She was looking up at him with absolute certainty in her eyes that he would offer the solution without misgivings.

"If he's to stay here and sleep in one of my beds, he's to be bathed first. I don't care the hour."

She gave him a beatific smile that warmed the cockles of his heart. Blast her. Was there anything he could deny her? He'd let her go once and he didn't know if he'd be able to do it again. To watch her walk away had been the hardest thing he'd ever done.

"I also think you should stay the night." He didn't like the idea of her being out on her own. Besides, knowing her, she'd head to the rookeries to confront this Sykes fellow. As much as he disliked her friends, he was considering alerting them to the situation. No, she'd see it as betrayal. He should see about hiring guards to follow her around.

"If you don't mind—" she began.

"I wouldn't have offered if I minded. You should quit working at Dodger's."

She released a half laugh. "Dodger's provides me with the means to do as much as I do for orphans." She nodded toward the urchin. "We probably shouldn't let him eat as much tonight."

"I concur. One pie is all he's getting."

She squeezed his hand, may as well have squeezed his heart. "I know you don't like light fingers in your residence, but I'll see that he doesn't steal anything."

He touched her cheek. "He brought you back. He can steal anything he wants."

Her laughter was soft and for a moment it erased her worries, but he could see them return with force. Once his company was abed, Sterling would seek to entice out of her what was truly troubling her. It was more than the boy. Of that he was certain.

He awoke the youngest of his footmen and had a bath prepared in the kitchen for the lad. While Frannie was scrubbing the little devil clean, Sterling went to his boot-boy's room and grabbed a few items. The clothes would be a trifle large but should suffice.

When he returned downstairs to the kitchen, the boy was out of the tub and Frannie was toweling him off.

"Caw, blimey! Yer scraping off me skin!"

"Stop your complaining," Sterling demanded, before Frannie could reply. "I'll have you know I've paid good money to have beautiful ladies towel me off."

She jerked her head around to look at him, and a charming blush crept up her cheeks.

He grinned at her. "Some foreign countries have lovely customs." He held up the clothes. "He can have these." With the toe of his shoe, he nudged the rags on the floor. "These we should probably burn."

"Probably." Reaching for the clothes, she dropped the towel and it pooled on the floor.

Sterling didn't mean to stare, but dear God . . . "He really is nothing more than bones."

"I'm afraid so, yes."

Sterling could see some marks on the boy's side, on his shoulder. He turned him around—

" 'ere now!" the boy bellowed.

Ignoring him, Sterling studied the crisscross of faint scars on his back. "Did someone whip him?"

Turning him around, Frannie had him raise his arms and began working the nightshirt over his head. "The authorities," she said quietly. "He was apparently arrested for stealing sixpence. Rather than sending him to prison, he got the lash."

"But . . . but he's a child."

"Some gent fancied his sixpence more."

"Wot ye bothered fer?" The boy crossed his bony arms over his skinny chest. "I didn't cry."

"How old are you?"

"Don't gotta tell ye nuffin', bloody nob."

"He's eight," Frannie said. "Do we have a bed for him?"

Sterling nodded. "Yes."

The room he chose was just down the hall from his. He thought Frannie might want to pop in and check on the boy from time to time. He stationed the footman inside the room with the order not to let the boy go anywhere.

He looked even smaller tucked into that massive bed with Frannie combing her fingers through his dark hair.

"You need to stay here, Peter," Frannie said quietly. "It's what your mother wants. Tomorrow we'll have a nice breakfast and get you some proper clothes. Everything is going to be all right. I don't want you to be afraid."

"I ain't afraid of nuffin'."

"Don't run away again, all right?"

He shrugged, nodded, rolled over, all at the same time.

Frannie rose and smiled softly at Sterling.

"That wasn't exactly a promise now, was it," he said.

Shaking her head, she headed for the door. Sterling stopped by the footman and said in a low voice, "Expect trouble."

"Yes, sir."

"Fetch me if there is any."

"Yes, Your Grace."

Sterling went into his bedchamber, grateful to

see that Frannie was there, sitting on the sofa in front of the fireplace where a low fire burned on the hearth. Her bare feet were drawn up on the cushion and she was rubbing her arms as though she were chilled. He went to a table where he kept his nightly brandy, poured two generous snifters, and joined her.

She took the snifter from him and drank deeply before balancing it on her thigh and holding it with both hands. Her gaze was far, far away.

"Tell me what's wrong," he stated quietly.

"You don't think that child deserves worrying over?"

He rubbed his thumb between her furrowed brows. "Something else is upsetting you. Tell me what it is."

She shook her head, tears welling in her eyes.

"There is nothing you can tell me that will change . . . the affection I hold for you."

"Do you have affection for me, Sterling?"

He feared he had a good deal more than that, but that admission would lead them toward a road they couldn't travel and would make things so much more difficult in time. "I care for you very much, Frannie. I don't like to see you so unhappy. The boy is clean, fed, and in bed. He's back in your care. That should be a reason for joy. But, Frannie, my darling, you look as though your heart is breaking."

She nodded, squeezed her eyes shut, and took another gulp of the brandy. Shifting around, she faced him. "Nancy . . . she was my friend. She wasn't one of Feagan's children. But she was there, on the streets, one of us. She was two years older. When she was twelve, she moved in with Sykes. Girls do that on the street. You survive the best way you can. But we were friends. *Friends*."

She seemed to be stuck on that word.

"You were friends," he repeated. "Did you play together?"

She laughed and shook her head. "The game we played was called the Lucifer Drop. I had two boxes of matches and I'd walk along offering them to people. Of course everyone ignored me, because I was a beggar. I'd very skillfully knock into someone and drop the matches into the mud. I'd start crying and Nancy would start screaming that our mum was going to kill me. The fellow I bumped into would pay us handsomely to quiet our attention-drawing dramatics. We made out quite well."

"So you feel an obligation to do right by her son?"

A tear spilled over onto her cheek. With his thumb, Sterling captured it. He folded his fingers around her neck. "Frannie . . ."

"One day she told me about this wonderful play

and that she knew a fellow who would let us into the theater through the back door. Feagan had always told me, 'Frannie, darling, the night isn't a place for you. Always come back to me before the dark.' But I wanted to see the play. So I stayed with Nancy until it got dark. And we walked down an alley . . . and someone jumped out at me and put a sack over my head and I screamed for Nancy to run . . ."

She released a strangled sob and more tears fell. He took the glass from her, set it on the table along with his own. He wanted to comfort her, but he knew that she had more to say. She looked at him imploringly, as though he could take away the pain, and God knew he wanted to, but until he knew what was causing it—

"All these years, Sterling, I thought I'd deserved what happened."

"No one deserves what happened to you."

She shook her head forcibly. "I'd been bad. I was where I wasn't supposed to be, doing what I wasn't supposed to be doing. Feagan had warned me not to be out at night, and I'd discarded Feagan's warning. When I was taken, I thought it was my punishment. And dear God, when Luke killed Geoffrey Langdon and they arrested him, I thought they'd hang him, and it was all my fault. You can't imagine how guilty I felt."

"Frannie, you are to blame for none of this."

She wiped at the tears. "Tonight, Nancy . . . Nancy told me that she and Sykes arranged everything. They set things up so that I'd be taken like that."

"Ah, dear God, Frannie." He drew her onto his lap, holding her close, rocking her while she wept.

"They knew what would happen and they did it on purpose."

He tamped down the fury simmering through him. Now was not the time for him to start destroying things or venting his own anger. He had to care for her. Had to console his precious Frannie.

"I was taken somewhere. I didn't know where. My clothes were stripped from me. I was tied to a bed. This horrible, horrible giggling man examined me. I had to be a virgin, you see. Virgins don't yet carry disease. Some men will only bed virgins."

He felt her tears soaking his shirt.

"I thought I'd pushed all the horror away, but somehow it's so much worse knowing someone wished it upon me, made it come to pass."

"If I ever cross paths with Sykes, I shall kill him."

She drew back, and looked at him with her

beautiful green eyes filled with tears. "They'd hang you and he's not worth it. Help me to forget, Sterling. Help me to shove all these horrible memories back into the dark crack where they belong. Give me something beautiful to remember."

She brought her mouth down to his. He wasn't certain this was a wise idea, but he didn't have the strength to deny her anything she wished for as he rose from the sofa, cradling her in his arms, and carried her to his bed.

He was as tender a lover as she could ever hope for. When he'd brought her to his bed before, there had been no shadows of her past. Tonight it was as though he were brushing them away in the same manner that one might cobwebs. Gently, and yet diligently when they stuck to the fingers.

He removed her clothes slowly, kissing her wherever skin was laid bare. His gaze held tenderness mixed with desire. He still wanted her. She knew that. After all she'd revealed, he still yearned for her . . . yet he cast his own needs aside, taking her leisurely, his hands and mouth almost worshipful.

She touched him with equal care. Not because he was fragile, because he most certainly wasn't, but because the reflections of the night required something different from what they'd shared before.

He seemed to sense when to stroke, when to

kiss, when to murmur sweet words near her ear. They were in tune, as she'd never been with any other person.

There was no frenzy tonight, no rush to join.

He rolled her over onto her stomach and trailed his mouth along her spine. He rubbed her back, he kneaded her buttocks, he kissed behind her knees. He massaged her feet, her calves, her thighs . . . until she was languid and thought she might never be able to stand again.

He pulled her up and over until she was straddling him, her wild hair forming a curtain around them. He threaded his hands up through it and brought her down for a kiss that was unhurried, yet passionate. Her mind was filled with only thoughts of him. The way he touched her, reverently, the way he made her feel as though no one and nothing else mattered.

They were in their own world, just the two of them. No nobility, no street urchin. Just Sterling. Just Frannie. No differences. Simply a common goal: to give and receive pleasure.

Cradling her hips, he lifted her up and brought her down until she was enveloping him and he was filling her. Smiling down on him, she kissed his chest, felt its vibration against her lips as he released a deep purr and she imagined that he was imitating the lion he'd sketched.

Then she was rocking against him, riding him, watching the pleasure travel over his face as his fingers dug into her hips. The pleasure intensified, became almost unbearable. She buried her face against his neck to muffle her screams of abandon. Holding her close, he bucked and jerked beneath her.

Where he found the strength to rub her back afterward, she had no idea. As she drifted off to sleep, his hands were still moving gently over her and she took the sweet words of reassurance he was murmuring into her dreams.

Chapter 20

As the sun began to peer through a part in the draperies, Sterling watched as Frannie opened her eyes. "Good morning," he said, trailing his hand around her breast.

She sighed and stretched. "Good morning to you."

He rolled onto her and slid easily into her. He nuzzled her neck. "You feel so good."

Rocking languidly against her, he watched the smile of contentment ease over her face. "This is a fine way to welcome the morning," he purred.

She glided her hands down his back, cupped his buttocks. "I love the way it feels when you're inside me." She released a long, low moan. Turning her head to the side, she widened her eyes, stiffened, screeched, and dug her nails into his skin.

He jerked his head to the side.

"Wot's 'at on yer back?" the little thief asked.

"None of your damned business. What the devil are you doing here?"

"I'm 'ungry."

"What about the fellow watching you?"

He lifted a bony shoulder. "Sleep. Ye ain't doing it roight, ye know."

"I beg your pardon?"

"When yer foikin' 'er, yer s'posed to make 'er cry. Me mum always cries."

"Yes, well, I'm not at all surprised by that revelation, but you see I'm *making love* to her and that requires a certain finesse, which I doubt your father has the wherewithal to possess."

Frannie started giggling and what had begun as one of the loveliest mornings he'd experienced went to hell. Bringing the sheet up to provide her with some semblance of modesty, he rolled off her and sat up, whipping the sheet over his hips.

"Aren't you mortified?" he asked.

She shook her head. "Children in the rookeries often sleep in the same room as their parents, often in the same bed."

It was a wonder they produced more children after the first.

"You there." He pointed at the boy. "Go find the kitchen. Get yourself something to eat. And don't you dare run off. I'll send this beast on my back after you, if you do."

The boy's eyes widened. "Is it real, then?"

"Just mind that you do what I say."

"Can I meet 'im?"

"Depends on whether you're still here when I go down for breakfast."

"I will be. I promise."

The boy ran off, his little stick legs moving remarkably fast.

"Where are you going to find a dragon?" Frannie asked.

"I'll worry about that later. At least for now, I don't think we need to be concerned about him running off."

She tiptoed her fingers along his back. "Were you really making love to me?"

He rolled back over onto her. "If you have to ask, then I'm obviously not doing it well enough. Let me try a bit more diligently before I go searching for a dragon."

He made love to her twice. Yes, he most certainly made love. Afterward, she went to Catherine's room to begin preparing for the day. She had a bath readied and took a leisurely soak.

She didn't want to think about Sykes, but she worried that he'd seek some sort of retribution if he discovered she again had his son. As for Nancy, Frannie decided she'd gotten whatever she

deserved. Just as quickly, she changed her mind.
No one deserved Sykes.

His son might have a filthy mouth, but she didn't
think he was beyond redemption. What surprised
her was the rapport that seemed to be developing between Peter and Sterling. For a man who
proclaimed to despise light fingers, he certainly
seemed to be taking to the boy.

After her bath, she had Agnes help her with
her hair, then selected one of Catherine's morning dresses. A dark blue that seemed dignified
yet provocative. She was fairly certain that Sterling had readied himself for the day much more
quickly than she had.

So she was surprised when she arrived at the
breakfast dining room to find him not there. She
asked one of the footmen, "Has His Grace enjoyed
breakfast yet?"

"Yes, ma'am."

"Can you tell me where I might find him?"

"I'm sorry, ma'am, I don't know. Mr. Wedgeworth might know."

"And where would I find *him*?"

"I believe he wanted to speak with Cook about
luncheon."

Indeed he did. She found him in the kitchen.

"Miss Darling, was breakfast not to your satisfaction?" he asked.

"It was very nice, thank you." Even though she hadn't eaten. She was most anxious to find Sterling. "Do you know where I might find the duke?"

"In the art room. Would you like me to escort you?"

"Yes, please."

The art room was on the top floor in the corner of a wing she'd not yet visited. The outer walls were all glass and the sunlight poured in, creating a halo around Sterling as he sat behind Peter. Peter was in trousers but what she assumed was a shirt someone had scrounged up for him was lying in a rumpled heap on the floor.

Sterling, holding a palette, was painting on the child's back. A dragon, of all things.

"He needs lots of fire," Peter said.

"Yes, well, you'll take what I give you and be grateful for it," Sterling said.

"Please, sir?"

Sterling's mouth twitched as though he were amused and perhaps pleased that he'd acquired a bit of politeness from the boy. "Is fire across your shoulder sufficient?"

"Yeah."

Frannie walked across the room and came to stand beside Sterling. "What are you doing?"

"I have just initiated Master Peter here into the

Order of the Dragon. He has sworn an oath to stay wherever Miss Darling—who is the queen of the order, by the way—determines he is to stay."

"I'm 'oping I can stay 'ere," Peter said, twisting his head around to look at Frannie.

"Need to be still, lad," Sterling said sternly, delaying the need for an answer to be given right away.

Frannie wanted to weep. Staying here was not an option. "I'll have to review my accounts," she said quietly, to delay disappointing him for a while.

"That's quite an impressive dragon," she said. "I didn't know you did oils in addition to sketches." She glanced around at the walls. "Are these your works?"

"Yes." He set the palette aside. "Sit there, Master Peter, while it dries."

"Yes, sir."

Sterling rose and said to Frannie, "Amazing how a knighthood can bring about manners."

"I think he's filled with goodness. It just hasn't been tapped."

"You'll draw it out."

"I'll try."

"You're free to look around if you like."

He followed her as she walked around the room. He seemed to prefer landscapes. She stopped at one that was rolling hills flanked by trees, a pond in the foreground. It wasn't quite as polished, but something about it made it very special. "That's lovely."

"It's the ancestral estate."

She moved down to the next painting. It was the same setting. "Is this a favorite view of yours?"

"Do you see this willow tree here?" he asked, touching a sprig on the other side of the pond. "Father planted it after Mother passed. I always thought of it as her tree, so I began to record its growth. Each year on the day she died, I set up my easel and painted the view."

She walked along the wall where the paintings were lined up one after another. "I like what you've done here," she said when she got to the last one.

"Oh? What's that?"

"Well, in the first paintings you had the whole scope of the countryside. But as the years went by, you began to include less of what surrounded the tree and focused more on the tree as it grew larger."

"Genius, isn't it?" he asked flatly.

She turned to face him, not certain what she was hearing in his tone. "It is, really. You must have been very young when you started painting these. You have well over a dozen."

"Well over, yes. And you're quite right. How I viewed the world began to change during those years." He turned away. "Let's check on the state of this dragon."

"I should probably go to the orphanage for a bit."

"We'll go with you." He glanced over his shoulder at her. "I prefer that you not go anywhere alone."

And she had no intention of becoming a prisoner, but she supposed for today, she could see no harm in it.

Later that night, Frannie closed the ledger. The numbers were all running together, probably because she was so incredibly tired. If they didn't bring in so much money, she could do the books later, but as it was, she knew if she didn't keep up with things, she'd be forever behind. She'd considered turning the books over to someone else, but quite honestly, they all thought the fewer people who knew the true worth of Dodger's the better.

She'd spent the better part of her day at the orphanage making sure all was going well there. Sterling and Peter had gone with her.

"If you force him to stay," Sterling said of Peter, "you're turning this into a prison."

"I know, but I promised Nancy I'd see after him."

"I suppose he could stay at my residence until you find someone willing to take him in."

She'd been deeply touched by his offer.

Glancing at the small clock on her desk now, she saw that it was almost midnight. When Sterling had reluctantly dropped her off at Dodger's, she'd promised him she'd be home by that hour. She knew he'd send a coach for her and that it would be waiting in the alleyway.

Home. Her mind stuttered around the word. It wasn't her home. It was a haven for Peter until the child wasn't so frightened, until he would be content to stay in the orphanage while she looked for someone to take him in.

She caught sight of something out of the corner of her eye, snapped her attention to the doorway, and nearly leaped out of her skin. Taking a deep breath to calm her nerves, she shoved back the chair and rose to her feet. "Hello, Jim. How long have you been standing there?"

She'd not seen him since the morning he'd interrupted breakfast at Greystone's. He looked awful, as though he hadn't slept since.

"A few minutes. I don't know if there's anyone who concentrates on things as hard as you do."

"And I was sitting here thinking that my concentration was sadly lacking. How have you been?"

He shrugged his wide shoulders. "I'm sorry, Frannie, for what I said the other—"

"No, don't apologize." She came around to stand in front of the desk. "I know you meant well. I appreciate your willingness to marry me if I should find myself in a spot of difficulty."

"Even if you don't." He grimaced. "I've always loved you, Frannie. You're the reason I stayed with Feagan, but I knew you loved Luke and Jack ahead of me."

"Don't be silly. I love you all the same . . . like brothers."

"I don't think of you like a sister. I'm sorry for that, too, but I don't think we can help what the heart feels. Do you love him?"

She didn't have to ask to whom he was referring. She pressed her hand to her mouth, felt the tears sting her eyes. "God help me, Jim. Yes, I think I do. I know he won't marry me. You had the right of that. And please, for God's sake don't go deliver a message. I wouldn't marry him even if he asked. He's a damned duke and I'd be a damned duchess. But please remain my friend. I've a feeling I'm going to need my friends."

"I could never abandon you. I'm insulted you'd think I would."

She walked over to him, stood up on her toes, and bussed a soft kiss against his cheek. "Thank you."

They stood awkwardly for a moment and she realized they'd never again share the easy camaraderie they'd once had. "Well, it's getting late. I should probably go."

"Yeah. See you 'round."

He turned to leave and she reached for her cloak.

"Oh," he said, coming back into the doorway. "Do you remember Nancy, from when we were growing up?"

Frannie stilled, clutching her cloak against her stomach. "Nancy who lived with Sykes?"

"That's her. We found her floating in the Thames."

"She's dead?"

He nodded gravely. "Judging by the bruising around her neck, I'd say someone choked the very life out of her."

Chapter 21

Jack Dodger was drifting off to sleep after just having made passionate love with his wife when he heard the whistle. Because Livy was snuggled against him, her reddish-brown hair spread out over his chest, she stirred when he stiffened at the sound.

"What is it?" she murmured.

"Just something I need to check on." Kissing the top of her head, he eased out from beneath her. "Go back to sleep."

"Jack?"

"Shh," he whispered near her ear. "I'm sure it's nothing."

He padded across the room and quickly drew on his trousers and a shirt before heading downstairs. Even now, a few months after he'd inherited this grand residence in St. James, he had a difficult time believing that he was fortunate enough to have Livy as his wife. As he reached the grand foyer, he considered opening the front door and checking outside for the source of the whistle, but Jack suspected the culprit was already inside somewhere.

Locks had never stopped Feagan.

And if Jack knew Feagan at all, and he knew him very well indeed, he suspected he'd find him in the library, where Jack kept most of his liquor. He wasn't disappointed.

In his topcoat that had seen better days and his felted beaver hat that seldom came off, even indoors, Feagan was pouring himself a glass of whiskey.

"Feagan."

"Ah, me Dodger. That didn't take long. 'ope I didn't disturb wot would have otherwise been a pleasant night." He glanced around. "Ye got a fancy place 'ere."

"Which I've no doubt you've already visited when I wasn't about. So, you crafty old blighter, what are you doing here?" he asked as he took the glass of whiskey Feagan offered him.

"I'm worried about me darling Frannie." He downed the whiskey and poured himself another. "Sykes 'as put out word that 'e'll pay well anybody who snuffs 'er out."

"Sykes wants her killed? Whatever the hell for?"

"She's interfering with his business, taking his boys off the street."

"Yes, well, you put out word that if anyone touches so much as a hair on her pretty little head—damnation, she was attacked the other night. I thought it was random, some blighter wanting a toss. She led us to thinking that."

"Probably. She always felt guilty about Luke killing a lord and all. Wouldn't want you lads doing something that might get ye hanged."

Jack cursed again. They should have known. She wanted to protect everyone except herself. "Put out word that your lads will bring hell into the rookeries if she's hurt."

"Already did. Afraid it won't do no good. Yer not in the rookeries anymore, Sykes is. These new lads know wot kind of devil 'e is. They don't know the kind ye be."

Jack cursed soundly again. No matter what they did, how far they climbed, what levels of success they achieved, the rookeries were always dragging them back. "Very well then. I'll get the others. We'll show up at your favorite gin palace tomorrow night and make sure the *new lads* get a taste of what we're capable of."

"Truth be told, I'm afraid it'll be too late by then."

Jack felt his gut clench. "Feagan, what have you heard?"

"They mean to snuff 'er out tonight."

Frannie knew she should have confessed everything to Jim, told him why she thought Sykes might have murdered Nancy—because she had no doubt that Sykes had killed her—but it was all simply gut feelings and she had more pressing concerns. She needed to get Peter and possibly the other children out of London. Jim couldn't help her with that, but Sterling could.

Besides, if Jim knew what she suspected, he'd want to protect her, question her, keep her secure, and she didn't have time for that sort of nonsense right now. The children had to come first. For her, they always came first.

She opened the back door to the alleyway and released a screech at the sight of the tall, dark figure looming there.

"Sorry, darling, didn't mean to frighten you," Sterling said as he put his arm around her.

"I wasn't expecting you."

"Told you I wasn't going to let you travel about alone. Are you all right? You're trembling."

"Sykes killed Nancy."

"*What?*"

She nodded at the disbelief in his voice. "Jim just told me. He doesn't know Sykes did it. They found her body in the Thames, but I know it was Sykes. I shouldn't have let her go back to him. I should insisted—"

"Frannie, love, you're not responsible for every wrong that's done to someone."

"I know. I just . . . I was so angry with her."

"For good reason."

"Still, she didn't deserve what she got. Where's Peter?"

"He was sleeping when I left."

"Did you leave someone watching him?"

"No. He promised not to leave."

"Oh, Sterling, a child doesn't understand promises."

"Come on, then. Let's get home and check on him."

As his coach traveled quickly along the streets, Sterling held Frannie close against his side.

"Sterling, I know it would be a great imposition, but could we take him to your country estate?"

"Do you really think that's necessary? Why would Sykes think we have him?"

"Nancy might have told him. I don't know. I just . . . I don't think he's safe here."

"Very well then. We'll take him to the country."

She squeezed his hand. "And the other children? I want to take them as well."

"How many are there?"

"Thirty-six. I know that's a lot but I'll make certain they don't pilfer anything."

"Oh, Frannie, I don't care about all that. I'm thinking logistics. I have two more carriages—your staff could ride in those. We have a large wagon we use for carting our belongings here for the Season, then taking them back to the estate. I think it'll hold the children. Be miserable for them if it rains, but it's only a day's ride if we start with the sun."

She wrapped her arm around his waist and squeezed him hard. "Thank you ever so much."

"Did you think I wouldn't help?"

"No, I knew you would."

Two months ago, he wouldn't have. That was the thing of it. He hadn't cared about the orphans in the streets. He'd cared about only his own pleasures and given little thought to how others survived. They weren't his concern. What a shallow young man he'd been.

When they arrived at his residence, Frannie dashed up the stairs while Sterling spoke with Wedgeworth about the arrangements he wanted made with the carriages and the wagon.

"Sterling!"

He looked to the top of the stairs, and he could tell by her stance what was coming.

"He's gone."

They searched everywhere. Sterling thought perhaps he'd gone to the art room. That evening Sterling had let him use charcoal to draw a picture before scurrying off to bed.

For a moment Frannie studied the picture Peter had drawn. It was all harsh lines, dark beady eyes, pointed teeth.

"Something that gives him nightmares, I suppose," Sterling said, as uncomfortable now looking at the picture as he had been when Peter showed it to him. *What sort of dark thoughts ran through that child's mind?*

Frannie gave Sterling a sad smile. "That's Sykes." She turned away, heading for the door. "I want to check on the orphanage."

"I can see him coming for his son," Sterling said as he followed her down the stairs, "but the others—"

"You don't understand Sykes. When I was twelve, he told me that he wanted me to be his girl. He tried to kiss me. I kicked him. Told him I'd rather die. He told me there were worse things than death. I suppose that's the reason he arranged my little journey into hell."

"You failed to mention that."

"It only occurred to me tonight when I heard about Nancy."

"I like this fellow less and less. Surely Swindler can do something about him."

"Not without proof, and Sykes is very difficult to find. He hides in the shadows."

Which gave him an advantage over Sterling.

They went outside and started down the steps. The coach was waiting, but Sterling didn't see the driver or footman. Probably having a spot of tea in the kitchen.

"I need to alert the driver—"

She'd reached the bottom of the steps ahead of him, and he realized there were more shadows there. Two of the gas lamps weren't burning.

Where was Frannie? She'd been in his field of vision and then she'd disappeared beyond the hedgerows.

"Wedgeworth!" he yelled at the top of his lungs as he hurried down the steps.

He cursed the darkness that swallowed her. He saw what he thought were shadows . . . moving . . . he heard a feminine grunt.

"Frannie!"

He heard rapidly pounding footsteps coming from the residence. "Your Grace!"

More light was bobbing his way. He could

make out the shapes now. Two men bending over someone—

"Frannie!"

The men took off at a run.

"Get them!" Sterling yelled to his footmen as he knelt beside the crumpled and broken woman.

"Dear God, it's Miss Darling," Wedgeworth said as he held a lamp higher.

Sterling couldn't respond. His throat was thick with tears. Very gently he cradled her in his arms and stood. He swallowed down the knot of fear. "When Catherine fainted, Claybourne sent one of the servants to fetch a Dr. Graves."

"Yes, Your Grace. That would have been Jessup."

"Send him for Graves. Immediately."

She lay so still that Sterling kept his fingers pressed to the pulse at her neck, feeling the slight, faint fluttering. She had a horrible gash on her head. One of the maids had helped him change her into a nightgown so she'd be more comfortable. She was already bruising. It was evident they'd been beating her. If only he'd seen them. If only he hadn't stopped on the stairs. If only he had better vision at night. If only . . .

Sending for Graves was like putting out word using a telegraph. Claybourne, Catherine, and Swindler arrived in short order and were quickly followed by Dodger, who brought along a disreputable-looking chap he introduced as Feagan. The old man leaned on his cane, studying Frannie as she lay with her glorious red hair spread out over the pillow. This was the man Frannie had thought might be her father. Judging by the way he watched her, as though it would kill him to lose her, Sterling thought she might have the right of it.

"She's taken quite a blow to the head," Graves said as he leaned over, opening one closed eye and then the other. He straightened and glanced around. "I need all of you except Lady Catherine to leave so I can examine her more fully."

Several mouths opened—

"You heard him," Catherine said sternly. "Go. You do her no good by delaying this. We'll join you in the library when we know more."

As Sterling heard the others leaving, he stayed where he was—standing beside the bed, gazing down on her. Catherine touched his arm.

"Sterling, you must leave as well."

"I need a moment."

With a nod, she led Graves over to the sitting area.

Sterling bent over and whispered near her ear, "Please, sweet Frannie, don't let Sykes take you.

I swear to you that I'll never let him harm you again." He kissed her temple. It wasn't enough but it was all he could offer her.

"I didn't see them lurking about," Sterling said for what seemed like the hundredth time. He wasn't accustomed to defending his actions. He'd tried to welcome them into his library by offering them a shot of strong whiskey and anything else they wanted. It seemed all they wanted to do was determine how he was responsible for this tragedy.

"How could you not?" Swindler asked, his anger still apparent, his inquisition growing tedious.

"Enough!" Dodger shouted. "What's done is done. What we have to do now is figure out how best to protect Frannie."

"Sykes ain't loikely to fergive 'er," Feagan said. "Only one way to make sure 'e never harms 'er again."

"And what would that be?" Sterling asked.

Swindler looked at him as though Sterling had left his common sense on a sideboard somewhere.

"We kill 'im," Feagan said in the same tone that someone might say, "Pass the marmalade, please."

The next words Sterling spoke were ones he'd

never thought to hear himself say. "How do we manage that?"

"We have to find him first," Claybourne said.

"Can't you just go to his residence? Wait for him in the shadows as he did for Frannie?" Sterling asked.

"Someone like Sykes doesn't exactly give out his address," Swindler said. "He works in secret. He hires people to do the dirty work for him. Unless it's very personal. Then he might see to it himself, but no one betrays Satan, because his revenge is hell."

"We need to lure Sykes out," Jack said. "The problem is that he knows all of us, knows how we feel about Frannie. He wouldn't trust us if we arranged a meeting."

"He doesn't know me," Sterling said.

He thought he'd have been able to hear a feather land on the floor, the room got so quiet.

"Could work," Feagan finally said, scratching his beard.

Sterling did hope there weren't lice living in there, although God help him, he'd welcome the pesky buggers if it meant not losing Frannie.

"What could work?" Swindler asked, the impatience clear in his voice.

"Sykes is not only a burglar, but 'e provides boys for others in the trade. Right? Right. So we get the word going that a Mr." —Feagan looked Sterling over as though trying to measure his worth— "Knight? I think that'll work. A Mr. Knight is in need of a breaking-in boy. And he desires a meet with Mr. Sykes."

"Sykes isn't going to meet with him without checking him out first," Claybourne said.

"Course 'e won't. He ain't a fool. Ye'd be in the shadows watching ev'rything. Eventually, Sykes will show because our Mr. Knight 'ere will insist on doing business only with Mr. Sykes. When Mr. Sykes shows, ye take care of 'im."

Swindler gave Sterling a hard stare. "I think we need to make certain His Grace understands exactly what we're proposing here."

"I assure you that I'm not quite the simpleton you seem to think I am. I'm to serve as the bait. When the prey takes the bait, you're going to kill him. And I assume, Inspector, that you'll investigate and determine it was an accident."

Swindler shrugged. "Or self-defense."

Claybourne leaned forward from his perch on the corner of the desk. "You need to understand, Greystone, that it's not an easy thing to live with the responsibility of a man's death on your conscience. It's not a decision to be made in haste or in anger."

Sterling gave his full attention to the old man. "Get the word out."

*   *   *

Sterling sat beside Frannie's bed, holding her hand, rubbing his thumb over her knuckles. She had yet to awaken. Graves thought she would . . . eventually. She had two broken ribs, immense bruising, but no damage internally. Graves tried to credit Sterling with getting to her quickly and in time.

But everyone in the library had recognized Graves's desperate attempt to shift blame to some nameless, faceless fellow, when everyone knew who truly was to blame for Frannie's dire condition. A man who couldn't see his hand if he held it out straight from his side. A man for whom the dark was the enemy. They didn't know the particulars, of course. And he wasn't about to enlighten them. He didn't have to see Sykes once he lured him out. Unless Sterling intended to shoot him—and that was a real possibility. Mostly he'd shot game with rifles in Africa, but on occasion he'd used a pistol. It would be much easier to conceal.

Sometimes one of the men would come in and offer to relieve him or to report that nothing had yet been heard from Sykes. It would probably be twenty-four to forty-eight hours before a meeting would be arranged.

Sterling knew he was being reckless to be the one involved. But he hadn't protected her before.

He was damned sure going to see that she was protected forever—no matter what the cost.

He heard the soft footsteps. Glancing over his shoulder, he saw Catherine. She pushed a chair over and sat beside him. "How is she?"

"She hasn't woken up yet."

"She will." She squeezed his hand. "You can trust them, Sterling."

"Don't count on it. I wouldn't be at all surprised if Swindler uses this opportunity to set me up to be hanged. He has a rather low opinion of me."

"They all love her."

"She's very easy to love."

"Do you love her?"

He nodded. "She's so good, Catherine. I've never met anyone as unselfish as she is. I want her to be a little bit selfish. I could teach her that, you know. To put her own pleasures first."

"Is that what you and Father fought about?"

"It was part of it." He looked at her. "I did go see him, Catherine. When I got back to London. He wanted nothing to do with me."

"Why didn't you come see me?"

"You were managing things quite well without me, and my presence would have just complicated matters."

She rubbed her hand up and down his arm. "I shall take your word on that."

They sat in silence for several long minutes. He thought about brushing Frannie's hair. Thought about lying beside her and holding her—one last time. After Sykes was taken care of, everything would change. Sterling would see to it. He knew what he had to do and as much as he didn't want to, he would do what had to be done. Strange that it was this wisp of a woman who had changed him into the man his father had thought he'd never be.

"Sterling, I know you want to do this," Catherine said quietly, "but there are incredible dangers. If anything should happen to you, you've left no heir."

"We have our cousin."

"Wilson? You can't tolerate him."

He held his silence. Nothing, not even his title, was more important than the woman lying in his bed.

Catherine wrapped her arm around him and pressed her head against his shoulder. "You know, Sterling, I feel as though you've come home at last."

Chapter 22

Sterling had to admit that he looked every bit the ruffian. Not shaving or sleeping had given him a roughened look. The not shaving had been Dodger's idea. The lack of sleep had come from hours of sitting with Frannie. He desperately wanted her to wake up, but at least he didn't have to lie to her. He knew she wouldn't approve of what he was going to do, but he had to do it. For her sake. And maybe a little for his.

He didn't ask where the bedraggled clothes that Swindler had brought him came from. They made him itch. He didn't look like a beggar, but neither did he look like a man whose clothes normally came from one of the most exclusive tailors in London.

Word had come through Feagan that Mr. Knight should take a corner table at the designated gin palace at ten. Someone would meet him.

"It probably won't be Sykes," Swindler said

as he, Dodger, Claybourne, and Feagan stood in a darkened alley awaiting the arrival of the appointed hour. "It'll be one of his lackeys. You insist that you'll only deal with Mr. Sykes. Try to roughen up the cadence of your speech a bit."

"I'd planned to imitate you."

"Actually, you probably want to go a bit rougher," Dodger said. "Remember, we've all been educated to a certain degree."

"I ken bloody well talk 'owever I damn well want to," Sterling said.

Dodger flashed a grin. "Not bad. We'll make you one of Feagan's lads yet."

"No, thank you. This is a one-night performance." He shifted his gaze to Swindler. "By the by, Frannie is convinced that Sykes murdered Nancy. She'd given Frannie his son to take care of."

"The hell you say."

"We were keeping him at my residence, but the boy ran off. His name is Peter; he calls himself Jimmy, though God knows why. When this is over, you should try to find him. It'll mean everything to her."

"Find him yourself."

"I don't plan to see her again when we're done here."

Swindler grabbed Sterling's borrowed jacket and hauled him back away from the others. He lowered his face until it was inches from Sterling's. "She loves you."

"Yes, well, that's her misfortune. As I recall you told her that I wouldn't marry her and you were up for the honor. So take good care of her and do all in your power to see that she's happy." He shouldered his way past Swindler, taking juvenile satisfaction in almost knocking him to the ground. He strode out of the alley before any of the others could react.

He'd just given his most difficult performance of the night, pretending that Frannie meant nothing to him. The remainder should go fairly easily.

Frannie's head was pounding, the light hurt her eyes. She recognized the canopy. She was in Sterling's bed. Why did she ache so badly?

"She's awake," she heard a soft voice say; then Catherine was leaning over her. "Hello, how are you feeling?"

"Like an eggshell that's been cracked."

"Do you remember anything?" Bill asked as he brought a lamp nearer and looked into her eyes. She tried to turn away but he brought her gaze back to his by clamping her chin. "Hold still and answer me."

"Oh, uh." She tried to think. "We were looking for . . . Jimmy . . . Peter."

"So the last thing you remember is being at the orphanage?"

"No, we were here."

"Where's here?"

"Don't you know where we are?"

He grinned. "I do, but you took a blow to the head and I want to make certain that you know where you are."

"Sterling's. Where is he?"

Bill cleared his throat and set the lamp on the table. "You've been asleep for almost twenty-four hours. I'd like for you to try to eat some warm broth. Catherine, will you see to that?"

"Yes, of course." She headed out of the room.

Frannie felt a sense of rising panic. "Where's Sterling?"

Bill sat on the edge of the bed. "Do you remember what happened?"

She sat up so fast and gripped Bill's hand that her head almost split in two. "Is he dead? Oh, my God, no. No!"

"No, no, he's all right." He squeezed her hand and set some pillows behind her and eased her back. "He's fine. You were attacked. Do you remember that?"

She shook her head. "No."

"Do you remember Sykes?"

"Of course. Who could ever forget that monster?"

"He wants you dead, Frannie."

"He killed Nancy." She suddenly remembered that fact with startling clarity.

"I don't know about that. I only know he has it in for you. So the others are trying to lure him out."

"The others?" She squeezed her eyes tightly, trying to think of their names. How could she not remember their names? "Luke, Jack, Jim." Nodding, she opened her eyes. Yes, the three of them. She remembered thinking that Luke wasn't part of them anymore, but she'd been wrong. He still was, when one of them was in trouble.

She looked at Bill, who was unusually quiet. She'd seen him examine others. He always asked lots of questions. "So where is Sterling?"

"With the others."

This was making no sense. "And where are the others?"

"As I told you: trying to find Sykes."

"Out on the street? In the rookeries?"

"Yes."

"No." She tried to get out of bed and he held her back.

"Careful, Frannie, careful, girl. You're going to hurt yourself."

"He's not one of us. He's never—"

"Which is why he's the perfect mark. Sykes won't know him."

She pounded her fist into his shoulder. He got off the bed and took a step back. "I see you're feeling somewhat better."

"What are they planning, exactly?"

"Frannie—"

"Tell me."

She listened in horror as he explained things. Sterling wasn't like them. At the last moment, he'd hesitate . . . and then he'd be killed.

Sterling sat in the darkened corner looking out. At least it was unlikely that anyone would come from the side without him seeing them. They might start there, but eventually, to take a seat, they'd have to come into his line of sight.

Of course it was crowded. The shiny bar that spanned the width of the place looked new. He sipped slowly on his ale so he wouldn't stand out, but he knew it was imperative that he keep his wits about him. He carried a pistol in his jacket pocket. It occurred to him that if Sykes was the first to show, Sterling could simply take it out and shoot the fellow. If it weren't so crowded in here, that's exactly what he'd do, but as it was, he couldn't put innocents at risk—although in this tawdry place, he doubted there were that many innocents.

Even as he thought that he cursed his narrow-minded attitude. He'd considered Catherine to be marrying beneath herself—and instead she'd married a man willing to deliver retribution regardless of personal cost. He'd considered Claybourne's three friends to be little more than thieves, and he was discovering what Catherine knew: they were loyal to each other to a fault. Would Wexford do whatever necessary to protect Sterling? Or would he only tend to matters if it was convenient?

He knew it was unfair to judge Wexford against the standard set by scoundrels. It wasn't as though their lives would ever carry the same dangers. Sterling had toured the world seeking thrills, and his heart had never pounded as hard as it did right now.

"Mr. Knight?"

He lifted his gaze to the blond-haired man standing before him. Blond. Not Sykes.

"Who's asking?"

"An associate of Mr. Sykes." The man pulled out a chair and sat.

"Ye've wasted yer time taking a seat. I don't deal with associates."

"'n Mr. Sykes don't deal with blokes 'e don't know."

"'e will if 'e's interested in earning ten thousand quid."

"That's a lot o' money."

Sterling gave him a cocky grin and took a sip of ale.

"Wot's the job?"

"Is yer name Mr. Sykes?"

The man glanced around. "Come back tomor—"

"No."

The man looked at him as though he'd suddenly pulled the pistol on him. Sterling shrugged. "I need the boy tonight. I'm on a schedule."

"Don't sound loike ye've planned it well."

"I've planned it very well. I'm doing it very fast. Less chance of discovery that way."

"Yer a cautious man, Mr. Knight."

"And about to become a wealthy one."

Nodding, the fellow grinned and scratched his scraggly beard. "Awright. Meet me out in the alley behind the pub in ten minutes. I'll take ye to Mr. Sykes."

After the bloke left, Sterling downed the remainder of his ale. Out of habit he reached for his timepiece to check the time and remembered that he'd not brought it. The coat of arms might have given him away. He supposed that he could have claimed that he had stolen it, but had decided it was better not to risk it. If he survived, he wanted to hand it down to his son, and if he didn't . . . he'd left it on his desk along with a note to Frannie.

Strange that only with his death would she learn how much he'd come to love her.

When he decided ten minutes had passed, he walked out the front door. Standing for a moment as though gathering his bearings, he turned up his collar against the chill of the night. It was the signal that contact had been made and that a meeting was arranged.

He walked around the corner and between the buildings to the alley. He'd barely stepped into it before he was grabbed and slammed face first against the brick.

"Easy, Mr. Knight," a voice he recognized from ten minutes ago said. "We're jest checking for weapons."

"'n 'e's got one."

They turned him around and he found himself glaring at a giant. Wasn't this just lovely?

"Surely ye don't think I'm coming to this part of London unarmed. Ye struck me as being smarter than that," Sterling said.

The man who'd approached him inside jerked his head. "This way."

He followed him down the alley to some stairs where an ominously large man was sitting hunched over. He was dressed all in black, his black hair falling into his eyes. The likeness in Sterling's art room wasn't perfect, but it was close enough. Here at last was the dastardly Mr. Sykes.

"Hand it over, Tiny."

The man who'd searched Sterling gave the pistol to Sykes.

Tiny? Sterling thought there had to be a joke between them, although Sykes didn't strike him as the humorous sort.

In the dim light of the lantern hanging over his head, Sykes studied the pistol, turning it one way and then the other. "Nice."

He looked up at Sterling and grinned an evil grin. "Take off yer hat, Mr. Knight."

Sterling narrowed his eyes. "Why?"

"Cuz I loike to see a man's face clearly when I'm doing business with 'im."

Sterling shrugged as though it mattered little to him. He took off the hat.

"Jimmy!" Sykes yelled.

Out of the shadows beneath the stairs came a small, skinny boy. Jimmy, otherwise known as Peter.

So much for Sterling's belief that he was the best choice for this ruse.

When Jimmy got near enough, Sykes put his arm around him and pulled him up against his knee. "Ever seen 'im before, boy?"

Jimmy looked up at Sterling and tilted his head from side to side as though looking for the perfect angle by which to view him. "No, sir."

Sterling fought not to show relief. He knew he didn't look the same, but did he look different enough that the boy didn't recognize him?

"Can I go now?" Jimmy asked.

"Yeah," Sykes said as though he wasn't quite happy with Jimmy's answer.

Jimmy ran past Sterling, who hoped to God that Swindler would see him and snatch him up.

"Me boy. I call 'im Jimmy. 'is mum named 'im Peter. Knew I didn't loike the name. Did it anyway. Wot you gonna do with a woman who don't do wot ye want?"

"Kill 'er," Tiny said, and giggled.

Sterling had never known a man to giggle, much less one so large.

"Shut up, Tiny, or I'll kill ye, too," Sykes said, before homing his gaze back onto Sterling. "Ye see 'ow it is, Mr. Knight. I'm not someone ye want to upset. So tell me about this robbery yer planning."

Sterling wished he could see into the shadows, wished he knew if the others were anywhere near. "Are ye familiar with the Koh-i-noor diamond on exhibit at the Crystal Palace? Largest diamond in the world?"

"Indeed I am." Grinning, Sykes stood up. "Ye got a plan for lifting it?"

"I do."

"Let's 'ear it then."

"Send these two on."

Sykes seemed to hesitate.

"Ye've got me pistol. 'old it on me if ye want."

Sykes nodded. "Ye two go back inside."

Sterling listened as their footsteps retreated.

"Well?" Sykes prodded.

"It's very simple. You go straight to hell."

Sterling felt the fire before he heard the thunder. Not that it mattered. He'd flung himself at Sykes and taken him to the ground. His first jab to Sykes's jaw must have numbed him, because he barely flailed.

Sterling didn't know how many times he hit Sykes before someone was pulling him off. "Wait. He's not dead!"

"You don't have to kill him," Claybourne said, kneeling beside him. "We heard him. Swindler says it's enough to get him hanged."

Sterling shook his head.

"No reason to kill him if the law will do it for you," Claybourne said quietly. "Trust me on this, Greystone. You don't want to kill him if you don't have to."

"He hurt Frannie."

"She'll be all right. She never looked at me quite the same after I killed Geoffrey Langdon. She carries the guilt too."

Sterling nodded. If it was best for her—

He was suddenly aware of the pain rampaging through him. "Where's Swindler?"

"Here." He crouched beside Sterling. "We got the boy."

Sterling grabbed his shirt, then cursed himself as he fell backward, bringing Swindler with him. "Never make her cry."

He didn't know if Swindler nodded, because his entire world went black.

Chapter 23

When Sterling awoke with his shoulder aching and his head pounding, the first thing he saw was James Swindler standing at the foot of his bed, his arms crossed over his chest, his face not nearly set in the rigid lines of distrust it usually was.

"Frannie. Is she all right?" Sterling croaked.

"You could ask her yourself," a soft voice said.

He jerked his head to the side, and there she sat in a chair near his shoulder, in a place where any man with normal vision would see her. She combed her fingers through his hair, the way he'd seen her touch so many of the boys she would willingly die to protect. Slipping her hand around his, she raised his hand to her lips and pressed a kiss against his knuckles while her tears splashed against his skin.

"Don't cry," he rasped.

"You could have been killed. You silly, silly

man." She buried the fingers of the hand that had
been so gentle at first into his hair as though she
intended to hold him there forever. She turned her
head to the side, looked at the man who Sterling
knew loved her. "Will you bring him in?"

Swindler left.

"Who?" Sterling asked.

"Peter. He's been so worried about you." Fluff-
ing some pillows behind him, she helped him sit
up.

"How long?" he asked.

"Three days. Your fever broke last night. You
were fortunate. You lost a great deal of blood
when the bullet went through your shoulder, but
nothing was damaged that Bill couldn't repair."

He nodded. He was exhausted. Holding Sterling's head, she brought a glass of water to his
lips. It felt good going down his throat.

He heard the door open and the sound of rapidly approaching footsteps. The boy came into
view and Frannie grabbed him before he leaped
on the bed.

"Ye gonna be awright?" Peter asked.

Sterling nodded. "You lied to Sykes."

Peter bobbed his head. "He ain't a dragon."

Sterling grinned. "No, he's not. You're not to
run off again."

"I wouldn't 'ave before, but they come fer me."

"They won't come for you again. Will they, Swindler?"

Standing at the foot of the bed again, Swindler said, "No. We've got Sykes in gaol. He's not getting out."

And Sterling heard the determination in his voice. Even if the court found Sykes not guilty, he'd never again walk the streets. Swindler would see to it. If he didn't, Sterling would. He hoped he never came to regret not finishing Sykes off when he had the chance.

Frannie hugged Peter close. "Say good-bye to the duke now."

"Bye, sir."

"Be good, Peter."

"Jim, will you take him, please?" Frannie asked.

Jim gave a brusque nod, turned to go, then looked back at Sterling. "You weren't half bad for a bloke not raised on the streets. It was my honor to fight at your side."

Before Sterling could return the compliment, Swindler ushered Jimmy from the room, closing the door in their wake.

Sterling turned his attention back to Frannie. She was so beautiful. He wished he could believe she was safe, but his Frannie continued to live in a very dangerous world. "You'll continue to go to the rookeries, won't you?"

She looked down at her clasped hands and nodded. Lifting her gaze to his, she said, "That's where the children are."

And where he couldn't protect her. He'd been fortunate with Sykes, but he'd played enough cards at Dodger's to know that fortune was a fickle mistress.

The days passed blissfully as Sterling slowly recovered. Frannie brought him his meals. She bathed him. Every night they slept in the circle of each other's arms.

As his strength returned, Sterling took short walks about the residence, and eventually took longer ones about the garden. Peter would often join him there.

They didn't usually talk, and yet there was a camaraderie between them that Sterling couldn't quite explain. He was going to miss the lad when the time came, and he knew it was coming much sooner than he wished.

Frannie sat at a table on the terrace and watched wistfully as the strikingly handsome lord and his waif of a companion strolled through the garden. It was strange, the way attachments between the most unlikely of people could be formed.

She knew her time with Sterling was drawing to a

close. They'd not made love since his encounter with Sykes, but she could sense him pulling away. She knew she was as well, fighting desperately to protect her heart, fearing that it was far too late for that.

From the beginning she'd known that Sterling was a temporary addition to her life, and she had made peace with that knowledge. Sometimes late at night, in the dark, she desperately wanted to tell him that she'd fallen in love with him, but she suspected it would only make their final parting that much more difficult.

That evening, during dinner, she told him, "I need to go to the rookeries. I was hoping you'd go with me."

Sterling captured her gaze. "I believe I've proven I'm an inadequate protector."

"You've proven that you'd risk your life for me. That's hardly inconsequential."

Shaking his head, he returned his attention to the food on his plate. "You should probably ask Swindler."

Only she wanted Sterling with her. "I want to talk with Feagan. I'm fairly certain I'll find him at his favorite gin palace. It won't take long. I'd very much like you there."

As though he understood the momentousness of what she planned to do, he gave her a brisk nod. "I'll have the coach readied."

The journey to the rookeries was as quiet as their days had become, but Frannie found consolation in the fact that Sterling held her. He always seemed to sense when she needed to be held.

With a great deal of jostling, starts, and stops, the driver was able to maneuver the coach through the area until they were very near where Frannie expected to find Feagan. The place had suffered in the years since she'd last been here, accompanying Feagan because he always insisted on keeping a sharp eye on her.

Because she knew his preferred table, it didn't take her any time at all to locate him. Her heart lurched at the sight of him, alone, in the corner. A man who had once been surrounded by children.

Glancing up he gave her a crooked grin. "Frannie darling, to what do I owe the pleasure?"

Sterling pulled out a chair for her and she sat beside her former kidsman.

"Your Grace, will ye buy me a drink?" Feagan asked.

Sterling looked at her and she nodded.

As Sterling walked off, Feagan said, "Nice enough gent, I suppose. Cares fer you."

"You almost got him killed."

"Weren't my idea. Was 'is. Can't blame me."

No, he never took responsibility, her Feagan. Whenever one of the lads was arrested, it was the boy's fault for being reckless, not Feagan's for sending him into danger.

Sterling returned, setting the tankard in front of Feagan, before taking a chair beside Frannie. Beneath the table, he wrapped his hand around hers. She drew strength from the simple act.

Swallowing hard, she took a deep breath and forced out the words, "Feagan, are you my father?"

Chuckling low, he rubbed his hand over his mouth. "Ah, Frannie darling, where'd ye ever get a silly notion like that?"

"I just always thought . . . I don't know. I just always thought you were."

"Nah. Yer much too fine to 'ave come from the loikes of me. I found ye in a basket on a door stoop, so I took ye. Ye know 'ow I am. I see something that's easy to pluck and I pluck it."

She didn't know whether she was disappointed or relieved. "I love you anyway," she said, giving him a soft smile.

"I love ye, too, me sweet girl." He winked at her, lifted his tankard, and gulped his brew.

As though understanding they were done here, Sterling got to his feet and pulled out her chair.

Once outside, she let the cool night air wash over her.

"Do you believe him?" Sterling asked quietly.

She looked up at him. "Did you?"

"I don't know."

She took a deep breath. "Doesn't matter. It's what he wants me to believe."

"Frannie?"

The tone of his voice told her what was coming before he spoke the words.

"I'll be leaving for the country tomorrow."

She nodded. "This is good-bye then?"

"Very soon. Yes."

"What about Peter?"

"He belongs with you. After all, you're the queen of the dragons."

He was striving to make light of something that was breaking her heart. "He's grown very close to you. Have you told him?"

"He knows. He understands."

Then the child was far wiser than she.

That night Sterling made love to her for the first time in ages. There was a roughness to their lovemaking, as though they were both clinging to something that they could never hold forever.

When they lay in each other's arms afterward, it was bittersweet. Frannie had always known the moment would come when she would no longer be in his life. She simply hadn't expected it to hurt so much.

* * *

When Sterling woke up the following morning, he was alone. He knew it was pointless to go searching for her. She wasn't in the residence and neither was Peter. He felt their absence as soul-rending emptiness.

He roared, his anguish reverberating throughout the room, bringing him no comfort.

With a weary sigh, Frannie closed the ledger. A month had passed since Sterling had left for the country. There was at least half an hour every day when she didn't think about him. Tomorrow she'd add another minute to the tally, until eventually she would think of him not at all.

Peter had adjusted well to life in the orphanage. He brought her such joy. She wasn't at all certain how she could have managed without him to provide her with love.

She became aware of someone standing in her doorway, not at all surprised when she looked up to see that it was Jim.

She rose from her chair. "You know you don't have to escort me to the orphanage every night."

"But I like riding in that fancy carriage of yours."

It had arrived a week after she'd silently left Sterling's residence. She couldn't have born saying good-bye to him. Cowardly, but there it was.

The note that the driver had given her simply said:

So you may always travel in safety. And not to worry. I shall handle the upkeep on the horses.

Greystone

Jim helped drape her cloak around her shoulders. "Have you heard from him recently?"

"No, and I don't expect I shall. He's gone to the country. You know how it is with the nobility. They don't like London in winter."

"Don't think much of it myself."

She laughed.

"I haven't heard that sound in a while." Jim said.

"Then you should come to the orphanage. I laugh quite often there. The children are a delight."

Once they arrived at the orphanage, the footman handed her down and she began to walk toward the building. As she got nearer, she quickened her pace. It was always good to be home.

Chapter 24

The Earl and Countess of Claybourne
Cordially invite you to enjoy a reading
By Mr. Charles Dickens
December 15, 1851
Reception and ball to follow
Your donation of a toy to be taken
To Feagan's Children's Home
On Christmas morning is appreciated

The Little Season occurred in December, when the lords returned to London for a quick session in Parliament. Sterling was amused to see that Catherine, with a small nudge from Frannie no doubt, was planning to take advantage of the opportunity to do a bit of good work. He didn't know whether to view the invitation he'd received as a gift or a punishment.

He'd recovered rather nicely from his wound and had gone to the country estate as soon as he was strong enough. He thought being away from London would make it much easier to forget Frannie, but as he walked over his estate each day until near exhaustion, thoughts of her journeyed along beside him.

He'd contacted Charles Beckwith, the family solicitor, and had him draw up papers for Catherine to sign, giving Sterling permission to send her monthly stipend to the children's home as she'd requested. His own donations were made anonymously, except for the shoes provided by the cobbler. He promptly paid the man's statement of accounts owed whenever it arrived. With winter upon them, he hoped the children's feet would stay warm.

In London, when Sterling slept in his bed, it seemed unlikely, yet he swore he could still smell the scent of Frannie adorning his pillow. It was another gift in his life for which he didn't know if he should be grateful because it made him miss her all the more.

As for the invitation that he'd read and contemplated a dozen times since receiving . . .

As Sterling tugged on his white gloves in the foyer while his servants carried out the hundred sets of water colors that he'd purchased, he knew he couldn't possibly *not* go. After all, what sort of message would that send? Catherine was his sister and one simply didn't ignore an invitation from one's sister. Besides, when a man carried a title as revered as Sterling's was, it was important that he support charitable events. It made a statement that the good works were worthy of his time, gave them credence. And since he and Claybourne had been drafting legislation protecting children, it was really imperative that he let it be known he believed in the work he and Claybourne were doing. What better way than attending this function?

All and all it would work out quite nicely. He wouldn't stay long. Simply make a quick appearance, see that Frannie was doing well, ask after Peter, and then be on his way. He could certainly manage that.

In the foyer, along with Catherine, Frannie greeted the guests as they arrived in their finery. As for herself, she wore a deep purple gown that she'd had made just for the occasion because she wanted to do the children's home proud. Her stomach was all in knots but it had very little to do with the fact that so many of the nobility were here. She feared that if Sterling came, she'd be unable to look at him and not give away how very much she missed having him in her life.

Devoted sister that Catherine was, she had informed Frannie that Sterling was doing well in the country. But the information she shared was all superficial. Frannie didn't know how he truly fared. If he had met someone. If he was happy. She wanted him to be happy above all else.

As people arrived, footmen took the toys to the parlor while Frannie directed the guests to the drawing room, where chairs had been set up in rows and a lectern had been placed at its far end.

She spotted a face in the crowd coming in through the door and smiled. "Mr. Dickens. It's so good to see you, sir."

"Miss Darling, you're as lovely as ever."

"You're too kind. Here, allow me to take your hat and coat." She led him away from the crush of people and had the butler take his outer garments.

"I can't thank you enough for coming this evening. We have quite a crowd," she told Mr. Dickens.

"I'm delighted to help your cause." Looking just past her shoulder, Mr. Dickens grinned broadly. "Why, Mr. Dodger, I expected you to be transported by now."

With his wife and five-year-old stepson, Henry, at his side, Jack laughed. "Ah, Mr. Dickens, you always underestimated my ability to get out of a tight spot. Please, Lady Olivia, allow me to introduce Mr. Charles Dickens."

"I'm honored, sir," Livy said.

"And my stepson," Jack said, "the Duke of Lovingdon. Mr. Charles Dickens."

Mr. Dickens bowed. "Your Grace."

"I know children weren't invited, but Henry is quite taken with your work, and I begged Catherine to make an exception," Jack said.

"So you like my stories, do you, young man?"

Henry nodded. "May I ask you a question?"

"Certainly, Your Grace."

He pointed at Jack. "Is he the Artful Dodger?"

Mr. Dickens bent low. "I write fiction, Your Grace. The characters in my books do not really exist, but if they did" —he winked— "I do believe *he* would be the Artful Dodger."

"I knew it!"

"And do you see that gentleman over there?"

"Lord Claybourne?"

Dickens nodded. "He would be Oliver."

"And what about Miss Frannie?"

"She is every sweet girl who appears in the story."

Henry laughed joyfully, and Frannie hoped a day would come when all the children in her orphanage laughed in the same manner, with such abandon.

"I'm sorry to interrupt," Catherine said, "but we should probably get started."

Frannie squeezed Mr. Dickens's hand. "I'm going to introduce you."

"Lovely."

Frannie walked beside Catherine to the drawing room. "Did your brother—"

"No, I'm sorry. I'd hoped—"

"He's probably very busy."

"He may have returned to the country already."

"Of course." It was where he obviously preferred to reside.

They walked to the front of the drawing room. Catherine clapped her hands to get everyone's attention.

"I want to thank you all for coming. I hope you enjoy the evening as much my husband and I enjoy having you. We are avid supporters of Feagan's Children's Home. We will be taking the toys you brought this evening to the children on Christmas morning. For many of them, it will be the first time they've ever received a gift on Christmas morning. I would like to now introduce you to Miss Frannie Darling, who is the owner and overseer of the home."

People clapped politely and Frannie wished they hadn't. It made her terribly nervous to suddenly have all this attention on herself. She wanted to do the children proud.

"Thank you," she said, sounding like a frog. She cleared her throat—

And then she saw him standing at the back of the room, just inside the doorway, looking so incredibly handsome, and she thought all her nerves would go away if she spoke only to him. . .

"I grew up on the streets of London. An orphan who never knew who her parents were. Feagan was the kidsman who gave me a home in exchange for which I was to pick pockets and steal and lie to people so they would give me their coins. I suppose it seems strange to name a children's home after a criminal, but he wasn't a criminal to me, because I didn't know any better. He was the one who fed me and clothed me and gave me a place to sleep. When I was twelve, the previous Earl of Claybourne took me in, and that's when I learned it was wrong to steal. The present Earl of Claybourne doesn't know this, but I recently bought some land where I shall build another children's home, and this one I shall name in honor of his grandfather."

People applauded, and Luke, who had already grabbed a flute of champagne, was standing at the back of the room. With a bowing of his head he raised his flute to her in salute, and she knew her words had pleased him.

"The children on the streets are not only poor in possessions, but they are often poor in spirit. It is my hope that these homes shall give them what every child deserves: a loving place. So along with the Countess of Claybourne, I thank you for the toys you have brought and for the joy they will bring. And now for *your* enjoyment, I present to you Mr. Charles Dickens."

Again everyone applauded. As Dickens neared, he kissed Frannie on the cheek. She'd heard once that he was as uncomfortable with the nobility as she. It meant a great deal to her that he'd come. When they'd met, she'd been a girl and he'd been a young man scouring the rookeries for stories.

Keeping to the wall, she walked past the row of chairs, heading for the back of the room. When she reached Luke, he drew her close and hugged her.

"My grandfather would have liked that," he said, his voice low so as not to disturb the reading of *A Christmas Carol* that Dickens had begun.

Nodding, Frannie glanced past Luke, then searched the room.

"He's left already," Luke said.

She gave him a smile that she hoped hid her disappointment. "I'm going to check on the ballroom. Make certain it's ready."

But once she was in the foyer, she didn't take the hallway that would lead to the large ballroom. She took the one that led to the library. She hesitated at the door because of the memories that rested beyond it, especially the memory of her encounter with Sterling on that gray, rainy day so long ago. But she wanted to remember it, to remember him.

She opened the door, walked in, and quietly closed it behind her. Several lamps were lit as well as the gas lamps in the garden. The curtains were drawn back and at the window stood Sterling, gazing out, his hands behind his back. Glancing over his shoulder at her, he bestowed a half smile.

Her heart was thundering so hard that she feared he'd hear it. As sedately as she could, she walked over to stand beside him. He turned his attention back to the garden, where large snowflakes were slowly drifting down.

"It started snowing. We stopped to assist someone who was having trouble with his carriage. That's the reason I was late."

"I'm glad you came. I was nervous standing up there until I saw you."

"I can't believe you have Charles Dickens here to give a reading. I suppose you met him through the Earl of Claybourne."

"No, actually, Feagan introduced us. Mr. Dickens was researching life in the rookeries, so he interviewed some of us. To hear him tell it, he put us in his stories, but I don't see the similarities."

"I've not read the tale. Perhaps I'll hire someone to read it to me."

"Reading still causes your head to ache?"

"Worse than ever. So how is Peter? Did you find a family for him?"

"No, actually, I've decided that he shall stay with me. I promised Nancy I'd take care of him. I'm going to keep that promise. He and I live in the orphanage presently, but I'm going to have a small cottage built on the land and we'll reside there. He'll be the son I shall never have."

"Surely, Swindler will give you children."

"I'm not going to marry Jim."

"Has he not yet asked?"

"He's not going to. He knows what the answer will be. I don't love him in that manner. It would be very unfair to him." She desperately wanted to reach out and hug him, hold him close. Instead she took a deep breath. "So how have you been?"

Finally he faced her, and she was able to gaze into those beautiful blue eyes that had haunted her dreams these many weeks.

"I was just standing here thinking about the morning of Catherine's wedding and how easily you lifted my timepiece," he said far too quietly.

"Oh, dear God, please don't remember that. I don't know why I did it. I'm so embarrassed—"

He touched his finger to her lips, silencing

her plea that his memories of her be far more pleasant.

"You managed to do the same with my heart, didn't you, Frannie? You stole it, and I didn't even feel it happening."

Tears burned her eyes and her chest ached with the raw emotion she saw reflected in his eyes. Her heart leaped with the possibility that something real and true could exist—did exist—between them. "Oh, Sterling, I—"

Before she could profess her love for him, he was again pressing his finger to her lips. "I thought if I kept my distance that somehow my heart would return to me."

She shook her head. "As long as I have it, I'll not give it back."

"You must."

He returned his gaze to the garden, and she thought she would shatter with the thought of losing him. Since he'd gone to the country, she'd never known such loneliness. Her dreams of helping orphans paled when compared with the dream of once again having him in her life. She wanted to be able to talk with him at any hour of the day or night. She wanted to envision new dreams and share them with him. She wanted to look across a room and see him watching her. She wanted to wake up next to him and fall asleep beside him.

"Sterling—"

"I'm going blind, Frannie."

Frannie felt her heart stutter, her chest tighten into a painful knot.

"Right now, I can't see you," he said quietly. "Are you looking at the garden?"

"No, I'm looking at you."

"Look at the garden."

Only she didn't want to. She wanted to look at him, but she did as he asked.

"Can you see me?" he asked.

"Out of the corner of my eye, yes." She turned back to him, and discovered his gaze on her.

"I can see you now," he said, a self-deprecating smile on his face. "But unlike you I can't see out of the corner of my eye, or even much to the side for that matter. And when the shadows move in, I lose a great deal more than that."

"What happened? Was it because of your encounter with Sykes?" She was horrified to think—

"No. This has been coming for some time. Do you remember my drawings of the willow tree?"

"Yes, and how you began to focus . . . only on the tree."

"I'm not so artistically clever after all. When I was one and twenty, it occurred to me that I wasn't drawing as much of the countryside as I once had, yet I was standing in the same place. I pulled out my previous drawings and began to compare. Side by side the difference was subtle, but when I compared the first with the last . . . I'm a bit ashamed to admit that my first reaction was raw fear."

She reached up to touch his cheek, his hair, but would he welcome her? She lowered her hand. "I can hardly blame you for that. Have you seen a physician?"

"A dozen or more. In various towns across Great Britain, in various countries around the world. There is no hope for it. Eventually my vision will narrow down until it disappears completely."

"When?"

"I don't know. Could be years."

"That's the reason you went against your father's wishes and took your tour of the world when you did."

He nodded. "I don't know how long my window of opportunity will remain open, as the window on my vision is slowly closing."

"Does Catherine know?"

"No. I'm fairly certain my father carried the shame of my imperfection to his grave."

"He couldn't be ashamed of something over which you had no control."

He shifted his gaze to the falling snow. "You're

wrong there. He actually told me that he wished his second son had lived while his first had died. I've never told Catherine. She adored our father, thought he was without fault. He adored her. I won't steal those memories away from her."

And he declared himself a man who saw only after his own desires?

"You told me that you thought you'd loved a woman, but she discovered your failings."

"Angelina. I was courting her. She loved to dance. It's very difficult to sweep a woman across the dance floor when my vision is as narrow as it is. She began to take offense because I wouldn't dance. Finally I explained the reason—and she very quickly began to give her favor to another. As far as I know she told no one. For that I'm grateful."

"She didn't deserve you."

He laughed harshly. "No woman does."

"That's not true."

Facing her, he cradled her cheek. "The night we went after Sykes, I'd left you a letter because if I died I wanted you to know that you'd stolen my heart as easily as you did my timepiece. As I've walked over my estate these many weeks, I thought how very unfair it was to you not to know how very much I'd fallen in love with you."

She placed her hand over his, turned her face

into his palm and placed a kiss against its center. "Sterling, I love you, too, so very much."

"And that, my darling, is why I won't marry you. I won't burden you with what I will become."

"What nonsense! What you will become is a powerful duke, a loving husband, a wonderful example as a father—"

He pressed his thumb to her lips. "Frannie, you go into dangerous places searching for your orphans and I can't even see if someone is about to attack you. The darkness, my sweet, is the enemy."

"Then I'll stop going into dangerous places."

"In time you'd come to resent me."

"I will not. I'll hire someone to go where I can't. There is no problem that you can envision for which I cannot find a solution."

"You did not want to be part of the aristocracy."

"Yet tonight I actually spoke to some of the ladies and they're really quite nice. Nothing like they were as silly young girls."

"If we attend balls, like this one tonight, I shall have to be content to watch you with other men, knowing I can never sweep you across the dance floor."

"Don't be absurd. Of course you can."

"Are you not listening? With me leading, we shall always bump into people—"

"Then I shall lead." She held her hand out toward him. "We can do this, Sterling."

He lowered his gaze to her hand.

"I love you, Sterling, with all my heart."

He lifted his gaze to hers. "So did Angelina."

"No, she didn't, because if she had, she'd have never given you up for something as inconsequential as a dance. Let's try it tonight and if it doesn't work we'll never dance again. I can live without a dance. I can't live without you."

He seemed to consider, then bowed. "Miss Darling, may I have the honor of the next waltz?"

She smiled. "The honor, Your Grace, is all mine."

Sterling had been unprepared for the impact of seeing her again. Her hair was upswept, her gown was flattering, and she appeared completely comfortable in her surroundings. He suspected that not being able to dance wouldn't matter to her, but still he wanted to give it a try.

The strains of the waltz began and he escorted her onto the dance floor.

"Simply keep your eyes on me," she said.

"That won't be difficult. You look ravishing tonight."

"I had this dress made hoping you would be here. I wanted to catch your attention if you were."

"You caught my attention at Catherine's wedding, even though you were dressed in something plain." It was odd letting her lead him, yet at the same time it seemed . . . right.

"My hair probably. I've never liked the shade."

"I like it very much. You're very good at leading."

"I'm very good at the dodge."

He studied her for a heartbeat. "The dodge?"

"It's when you set up a situation to fleece someone of something. There are all kinds of dodges, but you usually have a partner. You have to learn to read the situation very quickly and to know what your partner is going to do. You never want to play a game where Luke and Jack are partners. They always know what the other is thinking. Anyway, dancing is like a dodge. You follow your partner or let your partner follow you."

"I can see over your shoulders that there are a lot of people on this floor."

She smiled brightly. "Yes, there are. And we've not bumped into a single one."

"That's about to change."

She appeared startled when he came to an abrupt halt. He felt someone brush past him. Couples began to give them a wide berth. He dropped down to one knee and Frannie's beautiful green eyes widened.

He was aware of people no longer circling around him. The music came to a stop and he could sense the anticipation in the room. He took her hand. "Miss Frannie Darling, will you honor me by becoming my wife, my duchess, my love?"

Hers was not the only gasp he heard, but hers was the only one that mattered. Tears filled her eyes. She nodded quickly, smiled radiantly. "Yes! Oh, yes!"

He rose to his feet, took her in his arms, and kissed her deeply.

Without her in his life, the past few months had been sheer torment. He'd traveled the world searching for something he couldn't even identify. And tonight for the first time he realized what he had been looking for, what he'd always been searching for: the woman nestled within the circle of his arms.

Chapter 25

The following day, Sterling received a request for a meeting with Claybourne and arrived at Claybourne's residence at the appointed hour. Within the library, he'd not expected to face Claybourne, Dodger, and Beckwith—his family's solicitor. It seemed he worked for at least one of the gentlemen. Frannie was also in attendance, looking a bit frazzled.

"I assumed the purpose of this meeting was to warn me to be a good husband or else," Sterling said, laconically. "I'm not certain a solicitor is in order."

"We thought we needed to come to terms on the settlement," Claybourne said.

"A settlement? Are you gentlemen thinking to provide a dowry? I assure you. One is not necessary. I have no problem with Frannie coming to me with nothing."

"There. You see?" Frannie said. "I told you this was unnecessary."

Claybourne sighed heavily. "It is necessary, Frannie, because you don't go to him with *nothing*."

"Wait a moment," Dodger said, finally uncrossing his arms and relaxing his stance. "You think she comes to you with nothing?"

"Other than whatever pitiful salary you've been paying her to serve as your bookkeeper. I know she likes to do good works with it. Whatever the salary was, I shall match it with an allowance that she is free to do with as she pleases. We can put it in writing if you want. And if she hasn't already, she'll need to give notice that she'll no longer be looking over your books."

Frannie stepped forward and placed her hand on his arm. "Sterling, I'm not exactly paid to look over the books. They're simply my responsibility."

He glared at Dodger. "You bastard. All this time, you've been taking advantage—"

"No, Sterling." She squeezed his arm until he was looking at her again. "The three of us are partners, in several ventures, actually. I look over the books because, well, they're my books. *Our* books. I have a substantial amount of money."

"Which will become yours once you marry her, unless we come to terms on the settlement," Claybourne said.

"I'm recommending that her current finances as well as any future monies she receives from the businesses be placed into a trust," Beckwith said, "that she will oversee and manage."

Sterling shrugged. "I have no problem with that recommendation. I'm not marrying her for her money." He lifted her hand and pressed a kiss to her palm. "I'm marrying her because I love her."

She gave him a beautiful smile. "In all fairness, you should probably know the amount." She rose up on her toes and whispered a number that staggered him.

"Two million?" he rasped.

"Give or take a quid or two."

"You do realize that if that had gotten around, there isn't a lord in all of England who wouldn't have offered for you."

"That's the reason we kept it quiet," Dodger said. "Fewer fortune hunters that way."

Sterling nodded. "Simply show me where to sign." He winked at her. "Although I may not give you quite as much allowance as I'd planned."

She wound her arms around his neck. "I'll never stop loving you, I promise."

He held her tight and whispered, "As long as I can, I'll give you everything you desire."

Dressed in a white gown, with orange blossoms wreathing her veil, Frannie sat in Luke's open carriage as it transported them through London to the church where she was to be married. Catherine was traveling in a carriage ahead of them. Their son, born in the spring, remained at home with his nurse.

Frannie and Sterling had followed all the proper etiquette, waiting for June to arrive for their wedding to take place. No special license needed, nothing hastily arranged for them. No whisper of scandal. No child of theirs to arrive early, although if Frannie had her way, he would arrive nine months to the day after they were married. It had been absolute torture not to lie in the circle of Sterling's arms these many months. She knew he'd suffered as well, and she suspected neither of them would sleep tonight.

"You look beautiful, Frannie," Luke said.

She had no father to give her away, so he was doing the honors. It seemed oddly appropriate, even though he had been the first to ask for her hand in marriage. It was difficult to believe that the reason she'd given him for refusing was because she feared the loneliness of moving around in the world of the aristocracy.

"You look rather handsome yourself. A bit tired perhaps," she teased.

"I awake every time my son does, bless him, and he's not one for sleeping through the night."

"I suspect in a few years his nightly doings will continue to keep you awake."

"I fear you're correct there. Catherine warns me that he has the look of a scoundrel about him."

"Jack has told me that he's not going to let his daughter out of the house until she's forty." Emily, named after his mother, had been born in the late spring, on the cusp of summer, and within a few moments of her birth, she'd effectively wrapped her father around her tiny finger.

Luke laughed. "God, have you ever seen him so besotted? You'd think he thought he was the only man to ever have a daughter."

She refrained on commenting that Luke acted as though he thought he was the only man to ever have a son.

"He's letting all the girls at Dodger's go," Frannie said. "While he's always paid them well enough that they didn't need to earn coins on their back, he's decided the expectation was there. They're going to come to work at the orphanage, but he'll still pay them their wages."

"For a man who once cared for nothing except the next coin, he's certainly spending freely these days."

"He can well afford to. We can all afford to. We've had a good life, all in all."

"You'll hear no arguments from me there."

But as good as her life had been, she was antici-pating how much better, how much more enjoyable, it would be sharing it all with Sterling. Being with him every day and every night. Talking with him. Making love with him. Taking long walks, viewing the world through his eyes, learning how to help him see it through hers so when the time came, nothing would be diminished.

As they neared the church, she squeezed Luke's hand and took a deep breath. So many carriages in the street and people standing around on the lawn.

"The church must be filled already," Luke said.

The law didn't allow for private church ceremonies. Even those who weren't invited could attend if they wished. It seemed the wedding of a duke brought out a good many of the uninvited.

"You don't have to do this, Frannie," Luke said quietly. "We'll just drive on. You can get married in the country."

With tears in her eyes, she looked at him and smiled. "He'd invite the world if he could. It's his way of confirming that he has no doubts that I'm the wife he wants. He's a duke, Luke, and he has chosen me. I love him beyond all measure. I'd walk through hell for him." She took a deep breath. "What are a few hundred people when compared with that?"

He held her close and said quietly, "It's nothing at all."

*   *   *

Partially hidden behind an elm, Feagan grinned his wicked grin. The elite always drew a crowd. His fingers ached to slip into nearby pockets, but he wrapped them tightly around his walking stick, leaned forward, and damned his rheumy eyes. He didn't want to acknowledge that the dampness might have been brought on by the sight of Frannie confidently greeting people as she strolled beside Luke.

As Frannie got nearer to the church steps, he could see that at her throat she wore the pearls that had once belonged to the love of Feagan's life.

He glanced up briefly at the clear, cloudless sky. "Do ye see 'er, Mags? Do ye see our gel? Beautiful, absolutely beautiful. Going to be a bloody duchess." He shook his head at the wonder of that. "I promised ye I'd take care of 'er. Maybe I done all right by 'er, after all."

Once the couple disappeared into the church, Feagan tottered away, heading back to the rookeries. "Miss ye, Mags, m'dear, I surely do. I'm a-thinking it won't be much longer now afore I be seeing ye."

But until then . . . well, there was always a pocket somewhere begging to be picked.

Frannie stood at the bow of the ship as it sliced through the water, the wind whipping through her hair. Sterling was taking her to the South of

France for a few days. On a ship. She was on a ship on the water!

He'd unpinned her hair and it was flying wildly around her. Every now and then she'd grab it and hold it in place, then release it.

"Like it?" he asked, nuzzling her neck.

"It's marvelous."

Following the wedding ceremony they'd gone to Luke's, where a reception had been held. So many people had been there, including Lady Charlotte—although apparently Marcus Langdon was no longer calling on her.

The hardest moment had come when Jim had walked up to offer his best wishes. His green eyes had held a wistfulness.

"I wasn't the right one for you, Jim. She's out there somewhere. You'll find her."

But she could tell that he didn't believe her.

After the reception, Sterling had brought her to the ship.

"Wait until you see it tonight," he said. "We'll have a full moon and so many stars."

"I don't know how to swim."

"Hopefully, you won't have to. When we return home, I'll teach you how to swim."

They stayed on deck for an hour before they went to their cabin. It had been so many months since they'd been together that clothes were scattered over the floor as they worked quickly to divest each other of their garments. Then they fell onto the small bed in a tangle of limbs.

"We'll have much nicer accommodations in France," Sterling assured her as he nuzzled her neck.

"Doesn't matter. As long as you're there, it doesn't matter."

"You do know that as my wife I expect you to buy an inordinate amount of clothes."

"I've already ordered fifty dresses."

He nipped the side of her breast. "Not for the orphans. For you."

She cradled his face. "I never bought clothes before because there was no one I really wanted to impress. Rest assured, I have every intention of impressing you."

"Good. Although I suspect I shall always prefer you without clothes at all."

He kissed her thoroughly as their hands traveled over each other's body, relearning the shape and curves of what they'd once known. He had more scars now. She bent over and kissed the long scar on his side that she'd given him, then she kissed the puckered wound where he'd been shot. He kissed the scar on her forehead. But none of the changes they saw altered their feelings . . . or if they did, it was to deepen them. They'd survived. They'd always survive.

When he entered her, there was nothing to separate the heat of his flesh from hers.

"God, you feel so good," he murmured near her ear. "So hot, so slick, so wet. I've never done this before, you know."

She pulled back to look at him questioningly. He grinned. "You're my first with no covering and I must say, I like it very, very much. I fear, Duchess, that you are going to have many children."

Laughing, she wrapped her legs around him, tightened her body until he groaned in pleasure. Duchess. She'd never thought she'd love having the word applied to her. But even more, she loved the thought of having his children.

"I hope they all take after their father," she said.

"And I hope they all take after you."

"I can't wait, Sterling, I can't wait to give you a child."

"You'll have to wait—nine months at least."

"Only nine months. God, I'm so happy. I love you so much."

"I love you with all my heart."

He began to rock against her, the sensations building into glorious release.

Afterward, she held him tightly, relishing the moment.

"I love you, Frannie darling," he murmured.

She smiled. Even when her name changed . . . it didn't.

Epilogue

From the Journal of Frannie Mabry,
Duchess of Greystone

*My most precious memory is of Sterling,
with tears glistening in his beautiful blue
eyes, as he held our firstborn son within
moments of his arrival. Although it was not
fashionable for the husband to be so near
while his wife gave birth, Sterling insisted.
He didn't want to miss out on witnessing
any part of life while he still had the ability
to view its glory.*

*Sterling would also see our second son
and our only daughter come into the world.
He danced with her on the evening she had
her coming out and on the day she wed the
Duke of Lovingdon. While his vision had
narrowed considerably by the time our first
grandchild made his appearance, Sterling*

was still able to behold his scrunched-up face and laugh with abandon.

Our troubles were much less following the arrest of Bob Sykes. His trial did not go at all well for him. It was his misfortune that one of the primary witnesses speaking against him was not only a duke, but one who came from a long and influential lineage, one whose title was among the most powerful in Great Britain. The other witness was a well-respected inspector from Scotland Yard who had the uncanny ability to decipher murder with the fewest of clues.

Jim had often told me that I should avoid witnessing a hanging at all costs, but as hangings were still public in 1852, when Sykes danced in the wind, Sterling and I watched from a hired room that overlooked Newgate Gaol as justice was served. Perhaps it is petty of me, but I took great satisfaction in watching such a mean and nasty man blubbering and soiling himself before the noose was ever placed around his neck. I never attended another hanging. Jim was right. It was a ghastly thing to witness, but I slept more soundly at night knowing the likes of Bob Sykes would never again darken our lives or those of orphaned children.

Sterling and I took Nancy's son into our home and into our family. I never thought of Peter as having any relation to Sykes, and he never exhibited the meanness that had characterized his father. I told him many wonderful stories about his mother. He knew only that his father had met with an untimely and tragic end. Peter brought immense joy into all our lives, and we were grateful to have him.

Through the years, our family traveled the world. Sterling and I built two additional orphanages and a home for wayward mothers. Our charitable works were many and in them was woven Feagan's legacy of making a home for lost children. Whether or not he was truly my father remained a mystery, for while he denied it, I wasn't certain I quite believed him. His was a world of deceptions and dodges. But even if he was not my father according to law, he was according to my heart.

Jim—or Sir James as he was called after he was knighted—continued to hold a very special place in my affections. Once, when our paths crossed, he told me that the kindest thing I'd ever done was to not marry him. Perhaps because he was passionately in love with a woman who possessed the wisdom to adore him as he deserved.

When Sterling's eyesight did finally fail him completely, we were up in years, content to sit in our garden and reflect on what a wondrous and exciting life we'd led. He did not see my hair fade into silver. For him it was always a vibrant red. I watched him age gracefully and with dignity. He leaned on me much more than he did his walking stick, which was how it should be, because when I needed him most, he was always there for me. Each day I thought I could love him no more than I already did—and the following morning I was always proven wrong, for I awoke loving him just a little bit more.

I'd never wanted to be part of the aristocracy, but I couldn't deny that with him by my side, it was exactly where I belonged.

"Life is a journey, Frannie darling," Feagan had once told me. "Choose well those with whom you travel."

As always, I've followed Feagan's counsel.

Next month, don't miss these exciting new love stories only from Avon Books

Obsession Untamed by Pamela Palmer
Delaney Randall is snatched from her apartment one night by Tighe, a dangerous Feral Warrior—one of an elite band of immortals who can change shape at will. He needs Delaney's help to track a dark fiend, but soon becomes wild with an obsession for her that is as untamed as his heart.

Since the Surrender by Julie Anne Long
Captain Chase Eversea receives a mysterious message summoning him to a London rendezvous . . . where he encounters the memory of his most wicked indiscretion in the flesh: Rosalind March—the only woman he could never forget.

The Infamous Rogue by Alexandra Benedict
The daughter of a wealthy bandit, Sophia Dawson once lost herself in the arms of Black Hawk, the most infamous pirate ever to command the high seas. Now she is determined to put her sinful past behind her and marry a well-born nobleman, but her ex-lover has returned for revenge . . .

Beauty and the Duke by Melody Thomas
Ten years ago they were young lovers, sharing sinful touches and desperate ecstasy. But he was bound by his promise to wed another. Now they say he's cursed, that any woman who shares his bed will meet an untimely end. Should Christine be afraid of the devil duke and his ravenous desire?